> Jordan:
> Always been [nile?]
> makes me
> you and yo[u] [ars?]
> to come. I hope your life is full of
> happiness and success. Thanks for your
> support and hope you enjoy this novel.
> — Ky W
> Dec - 12 - 16

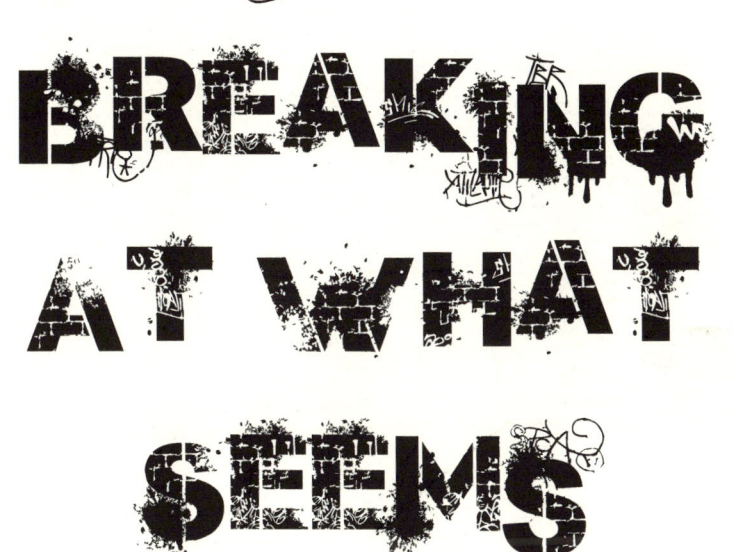

BREAKING AT WHAT SEEMS

By: Kyla M. Wassil

Breaking At What Seems   Kyla M. Wassil

Written by: Kyla M. Wassil

Breaking At What Seems   Kyla M. Wassil

ONE

As a child, we perceive life in a carefree manner. We approach obstacles without fear, and stand completely resilient. Our eagerness and readiness for adventure claims no relent, having known no bounds of limitation. When I was just a small boy, I perched upon the top of my mother's couch as if I were surveilling above my fellow descendants. From the bird's eye view, I'd remain watching while patiently waiting for a local resident to engage in illegal activity. Once given the chance, I'd immediately swoop down with the talons of a phoenix taking them out. Seemed legitimately heroic in the mind of an adolescent daring to take on the world all his own.

Only as I grew older did I finally begin to understand that heroes belonged behind the colored schemes of a comic book. College wasn't something I wanted to pursue, so instead I decided to make my childhood imagery as realistic as possible by joining the police academy right after high school.

Seven years into my career field I have seen and dealt with unimaginable situations. I have learned that death comes in all forms and fashions; it has neither a time frame nor expiration date. It's a frightening thought having known that in life; that death is all around us just waiting like a black hole to suck in its next victim. It only claims but one expectation, and that is when it comes for you there is no escape.

I have so many stories that are beyond an average person's belief, then again what the hell is an "average" person nowadays? I've been told it takes a special person with a strong mind to be a law enforcement officer, but to be an officer for the NYPD is on a total different level of expectance.

The academy was challenging, but not impossible. Yet, school wasn't what changed me as an individual. The job in itself completely shredded what capability I had to be a simple street walking civilian. Everywhere I go on or off the job, I am alert and well aware of my surroundings. Sadly, it comes with my title. I stand marked with three blue chevrons on each arm to signify that I am an Auxiliary Sergeant for the New York Police Department.

    My next step I strive for is to display the gleam from a set of butter bars that shall one day soon rest on my collar signifying that I am a Lieutenant. At this point I am a well-trained problem solver/peace keeper for the city of Manhattan. Midtown North Precinct adopted me just a year after I had graduated from the academy. I just so happened to be at the right place at the right time and according to my Chief, I handled the situation at hand better than any other young gun he had seen in all his years.

    Now, I have my very own patrol area in which I'm responsible for the perimeter of a rather long block than what other officers are used to having at one time. I am also responsible for one main quadrant located at Tompkins Square Park, yet my personal jurisdiction exceeds all the way out to 2nd Ave down to East Houston Street. Some may consider it torturous; I like to think of it as a grand privilege.

    Having a decent amount of experience under my belt gives a nice salary pay. Fortunately for me, I am still a young 25 year old male who is single. Needing a change of scenery away from mom and dad, I scanned nearby locations in Nomad and found myself gawking over the Milan condominium building. I now reside on the twelfth floor in room 1207. I have a comforted balcony that oversees the city and a large enough apartment giving plenty of space for a lonesome guy. At night, my eyes glaze upon the variations of bright lights and pedestrian movement. I'd be lying if I said I never become destitute from the lack of companionship. Of course, I spend a lot of time with my best friend, Max Harty who just so happens to be my partner on duty as well.

Max specializes as an unmarked investigator who has two years more experience on the force than I do. We both have endured a lot of maniacal and unjust principles in our time, but I believe that's what has brought us to be so close. The day I nearly lost my wits, I was on my knees covered in his blood from a gang shooting; I then realized that I had to save the man's life. No matter how much training you might have had or how much knowledge your brain carries about a specific subject, there's still not a damn thing that prepares you for something like that.

I remember it all like it was yesterday, Max and I had a night watch in the Upper East Side of Manhattan. Hungry by the stroke of midnight, Max suggested we'd stop by at a local food truck for a bratwurst he oh so favored. In doing so, we both noticed a group of darkly clothed individuals hanging around a selected territory marked by their gang. Once I noticed their colors hanging from their clothing, I warned Max to keep a close watch on their movement. The longer I watched, the more agitated the group had become with my offensive gaze. One noticed my uniform and yelled "*Pig Alert!*" I immediately dropped my food and drew my pistol, kneeling in a firing position. Shots were being fired left and right and it was too dark to distinguish who had the weapons and who did not. Max and I had to be precautionary to not hit an unarmed culprit. Max caught the gleam of a .45 beneath the street lights, pushing me over in response.

I remember busting my head off of the asphalt so hard the stars flickered in the sky. Through a blurred vision, I watched Max stand as a human shield before me and the echoing of several rounds being fired sent him down beside me. Within minutes after all live shots had ceased, nearby commotion from innocent spectators flurried about. As my nerves seemed to have nailed me to the ground for safety, I knew I had to check on my partner. I rolled Max over to view his wound, he took a bullet to his lower groin. Whoever shot him had had practice in order to know how to shoot below Max's vest. He was bleeding so badly the shock had him in an incoherent daze. I pressed one hand into his wound while requesting for immediate medical assistance over my radio. I was in such a panic it was almost like the dispatch was responding back in tongues. As Max lied motionless before me, slowly bleeding out; I felt my eyes burn. It wasn't because I was exhausted; it was because I found myself crying. There was no way in hell that I was going to sit there and watch him die.

The second he gasped for breath as his skin paled, I stuck my hands to his chest thrusting several compressions to keep his heart beating. Sometimes, I can hear my thoughts echo from the intensity I belted out for Max to stay with me. It seemed like a fucking lifetime before paramedics showed up to the scene. Once they arrived, they claimed it was because of me that Max had survived from such a vital bullet wound.

I never pride myself on the fact that I'm the very reason Max is still alive and well today. He on the other hand, brushes it off as if he were invincible, though I know he means well. That's just Max's personality. I know deep down in his heart he is forever grateful to me, which is why he refuses to work alongside any other.

In faculty of that night, we both decided to get our first tattoo with our motto 'Fidelis Ad Mortem' which is Latin for *faithful unto death*. He wears his on the forearm of his dominant hand. I chose to bear mine diagonally legible down my right ribcage. Wearing our artistic branding with unlimited pride, they are still constant reminders of why we chose the life we led.

We never ascertained a valid profile of who allegedly attempted to write Max off, even though the investigation was ongoing for quite some time. The only person who was taken into custody was a guy by the name of Demario Yaikus. He was suspected to be high in the ranks of his gang's hierarchy, yet refused to give up any names or information about that night. In exchange for attempted murder on a police officer, Demario was taken for collateral damage. Though we all would have much rather had the actual shooter himself to be incarcerated, having one less gang member roaming the streets was still a job well done for us. There is no sarcasm when it comes to why we are here, why we do what we do each day and continue to wake up and proudly put on our uniforms. 'Enforce the laws, preserve the peace, reduce fear, and provide a safe environment.'

Breaking At What Seems   Kyla M. Wassil

    Riding the elevator up to my new found home, I nearly fell asleep due to exhaustion from last night's watch. My recent hours were a strenuous graveyard shift from 5:30pm to 2am. Random as hell, but we have to go by the basis of what our command needs covered. Usually, our chart shifts month to month, so I am never set on regular scheduled hours. It took me two long years just to get weekends off. As a rookie straight out of the academy, you can just forget about it.

    I'll never forget how devastated my mother was when she found out I had to work Christmas and New Year's Eve two years in a row. Forgive my parent's; we are the typical northern Italian's who are very family-oriented and Catholic to the bone. Some days, I need a damn officer's jet pack which is like an Adderall and a pot of coffee. My mother frowns upon the fact that I have yet to bring home a mate. She is always hounding me, *"Kevin where is she? When are ya gonna bring a nice girl home for me and your father to meet? You should consider divorcing your job and settle down."* What my mother doesn't understand is that I have an undying passion for my expertise. Not to mention I hate admitting that I have horrible social skills towards the opposite sex. It's almost as if I've forgotten how to speak English when I do happen to make an attempt. It's not so much of the fact that I'm shy by any means; I just would end up becoming nervous and bore the poor girl to death with how to properly shoot a hand gun.

I had fallen face first into my bed for a few hours rest, to rejuvenate my mind and body until the morning sun crept through the silk curtains that hugged the frame of my bedroom window. I sat up, taking a minute to adjust to my new settings before I began my morning ritual of a hot shower and a cup of coffee. Seeing as how I enjoy my leisure time of being unaccompanied, I found myself lounged about on my balcony's fold out chair. I pulled the daily paper to my face, feeling the heat from the sun's rays emit through like a heated blanket. Not thinking anyone was around to listen to my monotonous narrating of an article that interested me, I fell naïve to the world around me. As I continually murmured to myself, a sudden interruption caught me off guard.

"Do you always talk to yourself?"

I glanced upward from my paper, nearly jumping from my skin. *"Jesus! I had no idea anyone was listening. And no—not usually."* I cracked a shameful smile.

For a moment, I do what I always do when encountering a stranger. I profiled her appearance, memorizing every distinct detail about her in ten seconds flat. Max calls it my 'ten second run-down'. The woman was by no means boastful as she cloaked her identity within a black pullover. The hood was pulled atop her head with her jet black, needle thin hair lying against each shoulder. She had pale skin, a short black skirt, fishnet leggings and combat boots. I watched the smoke sift through the air as she exhaled.

Even though she came off as a grunge new age version of Joan Jett, something about her struck my interest.

"My name's Savannah Rayn. It would be apparent that I happen to be your neighbor." **She giggled.**

"Kevin Strode. And yes, you're right. That would be quite apparent." **My eyes focused in on her expression.** "You like living here?"

She gave a side smirk as her eyes darted toward the buildings before us. "I did. I feel as though I've been stuck here forever, so it seems." **She exaggerated an exhaled.**

"Can't be all that bad? I mean, I can concur with the fact the city is hard to escape. But there is so much more to it than the poverty shielded by the uncharacterized intellect that yearns to reclaim its value of a high class aristocratic nation." **I smiled behind my coffee mug.**

Savannah nearly choked while laughing at my sarcastic remark. "You're totally full of shit! But you also made me laugh and I appreciate that. Honestly, I would love an escape. Just to spread my wings and fly, ya know?"

I felt myself envision the possibility of having the ability to fly as another smile formed on my face. "That would be something different all right. The only thing that would stop me would be my fear of heights."

Savannah's brows drew together. "Says the man who lives on the twelfth floor of a condominium that clearly enjoys his high up city view every chance he gets."

"Have you been spying on me?" **I laughed.**

"Well, when you become curious about an attractive new male neighbor who has yet to bring home a love interest, then yes I guess you could say I'm so called "stalking" your daily behavior."

We both laughed for a moment enjoying the comfort of a future outlet. That morning I sat outside for a few hours getting to know Savannah. For once, I didn't stammer or bore her with my work. I decided to push that subject off and converse about life itself. I knew Max would be exhilarated once I told him. Something about Savannah made me feel a sense of comfort, lacking the awkwardness that longed to ruin a new relationship. The second I got up to refill my coffee mug; I realized I had drunk the entire pot. Scratching at my five o'clock shadow, I became indecisive about whether or not if I wanted to make another.

Walking back out onto my balcony, I noticed Savannah had gone back inside. I shrugged it off knowing I'd see her again eventually. That afternoon Max and I met up at the Riverside Park for a ritual run. One of the most important strengths to have as a law enforcement officer is cardio. Living in a large city, you can't always haul after criminals in the cruiser. The only other option you have is your planters. Max and I generally enjoy running 5k marathons for charities or simply ran until fatigued. The longest we have ever run together was ten miles throughout the streets of Manhattan. Max carries a larger stature than I do, so on gym days he usually hits the weights for a longer

period. Then again, the guy stood over 6ft tall while my growth stopped at 5'9".

Generally, Max and I stop once we reach the small dog park just to watch the owners bond with their furry companions. At one point I gave intense thought and consideration in joining our K-9 unit, but the thought of sharing a lifelong partnership with a cop on four legs seemed inhumane. Especially, after witnessing some of the shit our precinct puts those dogs through. I was certain the happiest day of those pup's lives is the day they finally retire. I do however have utmost respect for what our unit does because, I shall not forget that thanks to those four legged animals, I and many other policemen have had our asses rescued.

Making our way down towards the bench area, I sat for a minor rest period. Max stood before me stretching his legs to reduce cramping.

"So, I met my neighbor this morning. Or should I say was startled by..."

Max puffed out a rugged breath attempting to slow his heart rate. *"Is she hot?"*

"I knew you were going to respond with something such as that. How are you to assume they are a "she"?"

"Well?" **He dropped his leg, placing his hands on his hips.**

"She's kind of punk/Goth looking. But when I saw her face, she is actually pretty."

Max pressed his lips together as I went about painting a mental picture for him to process.

"Did you give her your ten second run-down? Psh, I shouldn't even have to ask that. I know you did. I can't complain though, typically because you never talk to or about women. Even if you now seem potentially attracted to punk rock chicks, at least it's a fucking start." **He laughed.**

"You're such a dick sometimes." **I chuckled back.**

I watched with concern as Max applied pressure to the same spot that bullet hit him a few years back. He grimaced in pain as I mirrored his expression. *"Still hurts, huh?"*

"From time to time, yeah. It's just a battle wound though. I'll be all right."

Agreeing we both had our fill on exertion activity for the day, we headed back home in order to prepare for another long day tomorrow.

After a long shower, I remained in just my boxers and a pair of NYPD issued sweat pants stepping out onto my balcony for the night's fresh air. I placed my hands firmly against the railing, closing my eyes as I took in several deep inhales.

"Well, well if it isn't Mr. Arachnophobia... gasp... and he's half clothed on this night?"

"Christ! How many times are ya gonna do that? I swear I never hear your damn door open."

"*You'll get used to me bombarding your silent meditation sooner or later. Besides, you don't always hear what you're not trying to.*" **The moon illuminated her smile.**

I turned my attention to her sitting Indian styled on a foot prop as her eyes sized me up and down with supposed absent temptation.

"*I don't know, before too long you just might be one to induce a heart attack in the midst of your conveying.*"

"*Oh come on, Mr. Officer. You should always be willing and ready for the madness that awaits you…and your contoured chest and stomach muscles…*" **Her words veered off.**

I ran a hand through my wet hair as I smiled to myself. "*You're very observant.*"

"*Like I said, I "stalk" your behavior.*" **She bared an innocent smile.** "*Do you… um—enjoy enforcing the law and saving damsels in distress?*"

"*On most days I absolutely enjoy my job, yes. And not all of them are to be considered "damsels".*"

Savannah stood to her feet approaching the railing, dramatically leaning over. "*But if I were in distress, longing for a masculine officer to come to my rescue—you'd be my savior, correct?*"

I shook my head, laughing at her performance. "Yes…of course I'd come save you."

"And give me the very breath within you to bring me back to life?"

"Mhm. I'd have no other choice." **I laughed again.**

"Good, I just had to be sure on what and who I was dealing with. Most people freak out when police are around. I couldn't imagine a sane reaction after noting the fact one is your next door neighbor."

I straightened my posture, giving a comical authoritative impersonation. "Ma'am, I'm gonna have to ask you to keep the noise down, no loud house parties or I'll be forced to intervene and restore the peace. Thus far, I expect you to remain acquit and abide my warning."

Savannah belted out into laughter. "Very nice, good sir. I give my word that I shall heed your warning, abiding the laws of this vengeful city. God forbid you'd have to come kick my door in at any given time."

"Thank you. I guess I'd better head off to bed. I have a twelve hour patrol shift tomorrow. G'night."

"G'night, Serge." **Savannah called after me.**

I lied awake in my bed for a while until I felt my eyes begin to slowly shut. It was nice being able to talk to someone who didn't fear my position, but respected it while talking to me like a normal human being.

The following day…

Dispatch statics through my radio as I'm making my way down Avenue A.

"713…"

"713 here go head."

"10-62A on 640E.5th St. Location, NYC Housing Authority."

"10-4. I'm headed east bound on $4^{t.h.}$"

"Resident called on noise complaint. Caution is advised."

"507. I'm on it."

Arriving on scene, there were a group of teens hassling one another. A nearby neighbor called on behalf of a disturbance she feared was leading to retaliation of violence in relation to a gang disagreement. I went ahead and requested backup over dispatch before stepping out of my vehicle. I scanned the sight as two young guys were throwing slang towards one another, frightening residents that stood by. As another patrol car rolled up with his lights flashing, it caught everyone's attention.

"713 here, patrol 1017 just arrived on scene. No sign of 245. Initiating investigation now."

Both Officer Gibbs and I stepped out of our vehicles, quickly approaching the scene. I unclipped my firearm for precaution and as second nature it may have been; I never got comfortable with it.

"Excuse me, gentlemen. I received a call informing a disturbance upon possible aggressive tendencies. You boys mind telling me what the issue is?"

One kid with a torn collar refused to speak to either of us, so I directed my attention to the other who stood prominently aggressive.

"Look, either you can calm down and cooperate by answering my questions, or I can take you both into custody. Your choice."

"Look, officer. It all started because this fool thought it was okay to start running his damn mouth about shit that is none of his fucking business."

"Please, watch your language. I understand that you're upset. But try to explain in a more civil manner. What is it exactly has he "ran his mouth" about?"

The second suspect lowered his eyes from mine. "Over some shit…I mean stuff I don't feel is necessary to discuss with you or any other cop."

"Is that a remark insinuating drugs or gang affiliation? Look, I don't need all the details. I am only here to resolve the issue. You guys cannot result into violence, understand? We all have disagreements. We are all human, that's to be expected. All right? But when potential hazards are foreseen you need to understand you're not only placing yourselves in danger but you're also involving the innocence of those is around you. I cannot step foot off the premises until it is clear to both Officer Gibbs and I that you two are calm enough to be left alone. Do I need to advance in further control, or are you two going to discontinue your public dispute and keep the peace?"

They both stared at one another momentarily before suspect number one responded. *"I don't want to* *get arrested, or thrown in jail over something so ignorant. I do apologize for the "so called" disturbance."*

"If you both are in agreement, then I'll be happy to leave."

"We're good."

"Okay, now keep in mind that this is my patrol area amongst other officers. If we get another call about the both of you disturbing the peace or reengaging in violence, detainment will be the result by law. Understood?"

They both nodded in agreement, allowing me and Officer Gibbs to leave the scene. Luckily for us, no extensive report had to be filed and no one was thankfully taken into custody. Paperwork is the worst not to mention most tedious part about my job. As if fate was in their favor, those two boys must have reconciled the issue, causing no further agitation.

By the end of my shift, I was pretty worn out after handling a multitude of troublesome calls throughout specific neighborhoods. As soon as I entered my apartment, I kicked off my boots and headed straight for my balcony. My shirt was untucked with most of the buttons unfastened. I glanced over towards Savannah's balcony seeing her lounged out across the ledge. Instantly, I became concerned about her safety.

"You know, it probably isn't such a good idea for you to be rested upon the ledge like that."

Continuing to read her book she responded. *"A lot of things seem to lack the definition of "good", anyhow. I suppose it is not safe for me to be sitting up here, but I enjoy it and I am causing no harm to anyone around me."* **Savannah boldly claimed.**

"Other than myself? Probably not. I'm sorry, even when I'm off the job I'm still technically on it." **I grinned.**

Savannah pulled her eyes away from her book to meet mine. *"Well, I appreciate your caring."*

"What are you reading over there, anyway?"

She closed the book, sliding down to her feet. *"Some paranormal novel by J.R. Ward. It's rather good, actually."*

"You into that kinda stuff?" **I arched a brow.**

"Yes, along with murder mysteries."

"Like The Hardy Boys or Nancy Drew?"

Savannah chuckled along with me. *"I would suppose so if my reading level was stuck on a fourth grader's status. I seem to have all the time in the world, so I spend the majority of it reading when you're not here to keep me company."* **She admitted.**

"Well, any time that I'm home, I would enjoy nothing more than to keep my fellow neighbor entertained."

"Aren't you just the charmer? How collectively assertive you stand."

I was pleased by her sarcasm as I took a quick glance about the city lights. I could feel her eyes laying into me like daggers. *"You should uh…come over here sometime. Not that I don't enjoy our late night balcony retreats. I would sometimes prefer the company in a more personable zone, if you will."*

"That would be splendid. I would love to."

I held a smile bright enough to reach the solar systems satellites only to reflect enough power to light up the entire universe. *"Great."*

Breaking At What Seems   Kyla M. Wassil

Two

It wasn't very long until I found myself spending every free moment I had with Savannah, whether it had been on the balcony or her coming over just to visit.
    It was early Sunday morning and my alarm rang, waking me from a deep slumber. I was looking rather scraggly and there was no way in hell I could show up before father Delatonni for his service

appearing the way I did. I gave myself a quick shave before setting out for the Fifth Ave Barber Shop. I have been a regular of Vinni's since I was just a small boy. My father and I used to come here regularly when I was growing up, either he would take me or I'd come in with my grandfather before he'd take me to the park for some ice cream. I still miss him till this day. My mother tells me all the time that I am my grandfather's spitting image and that of my father's. I guess we have extremely strong genes with the olive skin, dark hair and deep set brown eyes. I was the supposed 'Italian lady killer', but the reality of that lacked thereof. Pushing through the glass door rang the bell's chime through the air. Vinni was seated in his station reading the paper through his bifocals.

"*Well if it isn't my favorite law enforcer. Come on over here, ya bastard.*"

"*I swear you sound like my pop you old mook.*" **I chuckled.**

"*What are we doing today, your usual?*"

"*Yeah, just give me a 1/4 guard on the back and sides, leaving a 1.5 on top.*"

"*You know that's gonna show that scary ass scar of yours.*"

"*Yes, Vinni.*" **I sighed.** "*I am quite aware of that. I've had this head my entire life.*"

"*And that's what's wrong with ya.*" **He laughed.**

"Just cut my damn hair before you croak from the annoyance of your self-satisfied sarcasm."

The duration of thirty minutes had flown by as my head felt lighter. Spinning me around with a hand held mirror to allow scrutiny, I ran my hand against the fresh prickle on the back of my head. I gently ran my fingers against the deep recess of the lightning bolt that halfway peeked from the top of my cranial, receding down the right side fading behind my ear. A slight frown tugged at the corners of my mouth as I brushed the loose hair particles from my chest and shoulders.

"What the hell is that face for? You look as if I just scalped you."

"No, no. it looks great, as always. I was just in a daze, I guess."

Vinni corked his jaw, marring an expression of disbelief with his hand rested upon his hip. I didn't feel like explaining what happened to be on my mind when knowing me for the majority of my life time he should already have known. I slapped a twenty dollar bill in his hand, giving a pleased smile.

Reentering the streets of Manhattan, I caught a cab to haul me up to Saint Patrick's Cathedral. Of course as I enter the doors bringing the altar into view, my mother announces my presence as if it had been years since she had last seen me. She does it every Sunday, honest to God.

"There's my handsome boy! Come over here and say hello to your father." **My mother requested with hype.**

"Mom, it's been four days since I've seen you and pop."

"Well, I wouldn't make it such a big deal if you'd learn to come around more often. I'm just thankful to the lord above that you're alive. Seeing as how you insist upon remaining apart of that terrifying job of yours."

"Oh Christ, Eva. Give it a rest. That poor boy has been a cop for years now."

"Lukas, watch your mouth. We are in the lord's house!" **My mother gasped.**

My father gave her a smug look in return as he pulled me into his embrace. Max and his fiancée, Elizabeth came in shortly after; taking a seat beside us. As Father Delatonni took the altar beginning his sermon, I tried my best on not falling asleep. I only disrupted my mother's grace having not taken my holy communion for the day since I failed to go to confession this week. My parents are huge Catholics and had me baptized within these walls because of it. I always went to Sunday school as a child and got to endure Catechism.

After celebrating my first holy communion, my father wasn't so strict about my life decisions but always warned me about what was right in God's eyes and what was not. My mother used to believe I was

destined to be a priest because after Sunday school she and my father would usually find me swinging on the playground, reciting my bible verses. Most everyone who attends my church has a warm smile and touches my forehead when they greet me, blessing me as if I stood a miracle of God's. I am a survivor of something fierce that once threatened to take my life as a young child. I wouldn't consider myself a miracle, maybe just coincidentally lucky. If I were to say that around my mother she'd have a damn near heart attack and redefine the definition of 'luck'. According to her and most Catholics, luck is a figment of denial, faith is the distinguished moral granted by our lord. It is because of him that we breathe and have the gift of life. I am not as headstrong as my mother when it comes to the bible, but I do believe in absolution not through confession, but through making the right choices in general. Maybe that is just the officer in me. My mother says I've been corrupted by voluntarily engaging in the pure evil that Lucifer disperses about our city. I am considerably ludicrous for having enjoyment in dancing in the flames of the devil's playground. All I can do is mind how my parents feel and address any issues no matter how pretentious they may seem.

    After our service as per usual, I had a nice family dinner back at my parents before headed back home to rest for another long shift. I grabbed a glass of water before walking out onto my balcony. To my surprise, Savannah was leaned against the railing as if she had been waiting for me.

    "I was beginning to worry about you."

"Is that so? I do apologize. However, I had service today and then ate dinner with my family, it's kind of a Sunday ritual."

"I see. It's nice to know you have higher beliefs."

"Got to believe in something, I guess?"

"How open-minded are you exactly, Kevin?"

I watched Savannah pull off her hoodie, dropping it into the chair behind her. She ran her black polished nails up and down the Chroma of her arms in slight allurement. I took a deep breath in through my nostrils as she ran a hand through her dark stringy hair, pushing it back and away from her face. Her eyes crystalized a deep blue, almost portraying a purple as the moon illuminated her gaze that cast upon my rugged figure. I swallowed so hard I felt my Adam's apple rise and drop back into place as her expression became disfigured. A prompt flick of my eyebrow had her eyes narrow as one hand met the pendant that clung to her necklace. I drug a hand down my unkempt face as curiosity had me begging for just a little more. Savannah took in her bottom lip with her top teeth, expressing want and dare to move forth with whatever game we had created.

"Why are you looking at me in that way?"

"The very same reason I seem to be captivated by yours in return. You wear a cross?"

"Is that hard to believe?" **Her brows furrowed.**

"No. I must admit, I am horrible when it comes to profiling a woman's personality. I'm only well-skilled when it comes to profiling criminal minds and actions before they are executed. But it has been instilled in me. I just didn't know…"

"That I believed in faith, too." **Savannah interjected.**

I nodded. "I guess you could say that? Shame on me for judging you off-hand, I meant no offense."

"Kevin, nothing you ever say or do has ever caused offense."

"Good to know, I'd be upset if I ever harmed you in any way." **My eyes locked in on her every move.**

Assertiveness had her face upturned into a large smile as she continued to fidget with her necklace out of nervousness.

"It's getting pretty late. As much as I'd love to continue staring at you while you gloat over possible sexual transgression between the two of us, I'd better head off to bed. Early to rise as usual."

"I'd say you kill me slowly, Kevin Strode. Then again, I would just be contradicting the truth behind that statement."

I wasn't sure on how to process what she said; then again Savannah had a rather different perception

on life, so I never asked questions regarding her peculiar attributes.

The following day…

"713 come in…"

"713 responding go head."

"Reported 502 on E. 11th headed west bound."

"10-5 for Med incase 23101 occurs. What's the vehicle description?"

"White, 1977 Chevy Nova model, license plate G as in George, K as in King, numbers 2334. Suggested speed is at 60mph and exceeding."

I flicked on my lights and sirens, flying down avenue A to reach the driver in time. Two other officers met up with me at the intersection of 1st avenue and 11th.

"I have the vehicle in view—he is swerving all over the road. Driver has yet to slow down or heed the sirens. Patrol car 1024 is vocalizing warning through his intercom."

"10-4. Officer Strode this is Sergeant Mack O'Riley. I'm making the nearest right hand turn to create a barricade at the end of 3rd."

"If he makes it beyond that point, I'm out of my jurisdiction."

Just as I finished my sentence, the driver decided to take a drastic turn and crash right into a parked car.

"Shit!" **I slammed on my brakes.** *"Send medical immediately. 10-45B, driver may have some serious injuries. He hit the opposing vehicle at a rapid speed."*

Medical arrived on scene almost as soon as I jumped out of my car to check on the driver. As I approached the vehicle, I started giving verbal commands. Even though I knew the impact probably knocked the driver unconscious, I still had to follow protocol.

"Sir… sir, if you can hear me please place both hands on the wheel and do not move! I repeat, place both hands on the wheel!"

Smoke rose from beneath the hood of his car, causing a fogged scene. As I neared the driver's side window, I saw the driver face first against the steering wheel; motionless. I grabbed my shoulder mic to report back to dispatch.

"Driver is unconscious, looks to have a head injury from the sight of blood on his face. No other victims were involved, luckily."

Once the emergency medical crew approached the scene, I stepped back letting them do their part as I returned to my vehicle to file an accident report for

both the driver and the owner of the damaged car. Today seemed to be national break the speed limit day. I honestly couldn't wait to get home. Most days, I love my job and others I'm just merely disappointed about the lack of intelligence my generation carried. I was overwhelmed with stress and the only slight release I had was the informative about the driver being alive and well but suffered some minor head injuries. I had no other outlet besides hitting the gym or running the park. Pathetic isn't it?

  As I reached the door to my apartment, I caught a man entering Savannah's place. I had never seen him before now in which my plan for inviting her over tonight was totally ruined. So instead, I took a long hot bath, soaking in my pity of the inexistence of my social life; drowning in the loss for affection.

  I lay awake in my bed letting the ceiling fan dry the access droplets the towel had missed while fidgeting with my police badge necklace solely used for undercover missions. I felt I should give myself unnecessary reminders of why I chose the lonely life I led. Without realizing it, I must have fallen asleep somewhere in the midst of mental destruction when I thought I heard someone in my house. As my eyes slowly opened, a silhouette of what appeared to be Savannah stood harmlessly at the foot of my bed. The moon cast a glow across the snow glistened flesh of her torso. She was clothed in a black silk robe that hung open shamelessly. I sat up, unaware if I were dreaming or not.

  "S—Savannah? How'd you get in here?"

"I felt the want you had. It's so powerful it drove me to stand before you."

As I sat up rubbing my eyes for a clearer view, Savannah dropped her robe to the floor. My own panting startled me as my gaze fell upon her petite body. I crawled to the edge of the bed pulling her against me without any hesitation or question as to why. The longing lust and wonder I held towards her unleashed until the morning sun seeped through the curtains. I cracked my eyes open, groaning with the objection of not wanting to wake up.

Looking beside me, Savannah was nowhere to be found. I searched frantically from side to side before getting out of bed. Examining myself in the mirror, I had no visual evidence of prior physical activity though my member stood firm this time of the morning. Yet, what I didn't understand was why my body felt fatigued but relaxed. I was certain that Savannah had left claw indentions and bite marks upon my neck and shoulders. The exotic thought sent pleasurable chills up my spine, intently hardening me further. My morning erection was enough to send my ass directly down to Saint Patrick's Cathedral for an overdue confession and so I did.

I slithered through the heavy wooden door, plunging onto the velvet seat within the dark corridors of the confessional; unannounced. I felt the uproar of frustration as I sat contritely maimed as the penitent.

"Bless me, Father, for I have sinned." **I sighed.**

"Bless you, go forth my son."

"Lord you know all things and you know that I love you. It has been nine days since my last confession."

"I noticed you did not receive your communion last Sunday. Now I am aware as to why. Proceed with your sacrament."

"I had a sexual dream last night, one unlike any other I've ever had before. I honestly thought it was real…I mean it surely felt real. But I know my want towards this woman might be out of desperation from not having a lover. I know I should not think of this woman is such a manner having not known her long."

"My son, as long as you can accept Jesus Christ and welcome his love then that is all the reassurance you need. Do you have intimate feelings towards this woman?"

"I haven't known her but maybe a month now. I do enjoy her company when we talk, but I have never taken possible intimacy into consideration. Father, I am a police officer for the NYPD. You know this. My job is usually my only interest in which that is all that consumes my time other than coming to service every Sunday and spending quality time with my family."

"Maybe you need to revise your outlet at hand. Or try explaining to this woman what feelings you have recently discovered. I cannot give council on premarital sexual relations nor speak of them to you as you very well know. All I can do is guide you towards Christ and what is right. You have been a Catholic all of your life—you know what is to be expected of you to reconcile your faith."

I bowed my head in frustration. *"Yes, Father. I am sorry for these and all the sins of my past, especially for the one I committed last night."*

"You shall embrace the love of Jesus Christ, for he is a part of you as you are of him. Say the Lord's Prayer each night before lying to rest until I see you on Sunday, along with seven Hail Mary's and all of your sins shall be forgiven. I bless you my son, in Jesus' name I pray, Amen."

"Amen."

I stepped out of the confessional displeased. I understand and respect my religion of choice. But for Christ's sake I am a young, well fit male who needs affection every now and again. I of course am not one to promenade around and take any offers from the street, but to know I have a potential mate living next door increased my oblige request, making resistance all the more impossible.

To ask for forgiveness with sincerity, yet still betraying the Catholic rites out of defiance very well puts me side by side with most other Catholic's. No substitution for lacking moral value was needed. It was just casual sex, not some heinous crime I'm used to seeing every day.

Ignoring the want for immoral self-gratification, I chose to wear myself out on my pull-up bar along with doing a few hundred push-ups. An abrupt knock on my door had me on my feet in less than a second. Looking

through the peephole no one appeared on the other side. I placed my hand on the doorknob, hesitant to turn it while I listened further. Once another knock followed, I pulled it open to see Savannah in a wife beater and cut-off shorts leaned against my door frame.

"What took ya so long?"

"Sorry, I was busy working out. Come in?"

"So that was what I heard? I thought you were beating someone up with all the masculine grunts and groans you were making." **She playfully shoved me.**

"Oh, I didn't know you could hear all of that." **I nervously grabbed the back of my neck.**

For a moment, I silently watched Savannah peruse the vicinity of my home while I sipped on a bottle of water.

"I like what you've done with the place."

"By that you mean all of my gluttony involving academic awards and such from my precinct."

"Well, it's what I imagined a guy's apartment would look like, just yours is much neater."

Savannah ran her hand over the bible that sat atop my end table while glancing up at my crucifix. A smiled tugged at the corners of her mouth once her eyes met mine.

"So, what brings you over?" **My voice broke.**

"You're a smart man, Kevin. I am almost certain you can guess why."

"To be quite honest, I had a dream about you last night. One in which was so vein I had to force myself to go to confession." **A crackly laugh escaped my throat.**

Savannah looked as if she didn't know whether she wanted to laugh or entertain the fact. "Then I guess that makes two."

"How do you figure?"

"The fact of wanting you just the same had me knelt down beside my bed asking the Lord for guidance. Yet, it befuddles me on how I relent to ignore the desire and long to pursue it."

"Come here." **My voice was low.** "Let me try something."

Savannah complied with my request, taking cautious steps until standing inches away from me. I placed my hands gently upon her cheeks, pushing her hair away from her eyes. Hers remained glued to my chest as I ran the pads of my thumbs down her jawline. Closing her eyes, Savannah fell submissive to my touch, overlapping my hands with hers. I moved in closer, pressing my lips against her forehead while breathing in her scent for the first time. Captivated to the soul, I fell merciful to her absentminded power to transmit such magnetic vibes, not only spiritually but physically as well.

Opening her eyes to sharpen her gaze sent a

shudder through my entire body. It felt like she was looking through me, possibly searching for something more than what met the eyes.

"This may come off as a ridiculous question, but have you not been active for a while?"

"Honestly," **I swallowed hard.** *"It has been a very long time. Why?"*

Savannah pressed her lips together dropping her eyes towards my pelvic region. I felt the heat formulate an apparent blush upon my cheeks as I cleared my throat, standing at a loss for words.

"Kevin, I didn't come over to entice you, nor break you from your Catholic bound realm. Should you voluntarily fall to temptation, I shant be displeased with disagreement as thou proceeds to conform in venial harmony with his dangerous dark angel—who seemingly preys upon his weakened flesh." **She winked.**

"Very biblically aspired you seem." **I felt myself smile.** *"I find great attraction in the words you speak. Though you're right, they come off in devilish tongues, I can't help but to want you against me in the way my mind envisioned the night before."*

"Oh, Sergeant Strode. I do believe you seek no other than unlawful behavior in your very own sanctuary on this night."

"Then so be it, may the lord forgive me for the sin I'm about to willingly commit." **I groaned.**

I pressed my lips against hers, pulling her onto my waist slowly making my way down the hall and into my bedroom. Lying Savannah gently upon my bed top, I proceeded to enjoy every second I had her within my embrace. Without feeling bad about my actions, I gave her all I had.

It wasn't until the next morning that I realized my dream was a definite understatement. The physical connection was much needed and unregretted by all means. Waking up to her lying on my chest was one of the greatest feelings I've felt thus far. I beamed with conceit, feeling like my egotism was returned to me. Running her fingers through my hair, I felt awkwardness once her index finger traced the line of my scar.

"That's a pretty intense battle scar you have there, Kevin. What happened?"

I took in a deep breath knowing this moment would eventually come to surface. *"Do you really want to know?"*

Savannah sat up, looking me square in the eyes. *"…Yes. I want to know all things about you."* **She paused.** *"But only if you're trusting enough to share."*

I exhaled once more. *"It all started when I was seven years old. It was a week day and that morning I had not been feeling so great but my mother forced me to go to school anyway. She told me if I were to continue feeling under the weather to have the nurse give her a call to come pick me up. Well, I was mildly nauseated during the*

Breaking At What Seems

Kyla M. Wassil

morning portion of my day, by lunch I tried eating and ended up with the embarrassment of throwing up all over myself and the lunch table. So, my mother comes to check me out realizing I had been running a rather high fever. Keeping me home, dosing me with Motrin every so often didn't seem to break my 102 degree fever. That night I continued vomiting, unable to hold down any bit of liquid so my parents hauled me off to the hospital. Need I mind you I was a healthy little boy. I was hardly ever sick, which is why my parents took it so seriously. Once we arrived at the hospital, they immediately retook my temperature and by this point it had spiked to 103.2 degrees, which is fatal to anyone. I became unresponsive nearly falling in and out of consciousness to refrain from seizing. I was rushed to a room where a doctor could examine me. I remember going through a large MRI machine and what they found horrified my parents. They discovered a large abscess rested in the temporal lobe within my right hemisphere. I was falling into a major relapse after given medication for treatment when the neurosurgeon decided the next step had to be a surgical removal. I was told they went in and drained the abscess itself then closed me back up. Thinking everything was fine… soon things took a turn for the worst. Instead of me healing, my health only worsened. I had language malfunctions that led to confusion which later caused me to become lethargic. The doctor decided to reopen my incision and found dead tissue from a viral bacterial infection that set in due to having surgery in the first place. Apparently post-surgery infections are common." **I shrugged.** "On the verge of death, my doctor was left to make a very conscience, moral decision in order to save my life. He took healthy brain tissue from a body that was readily available in the morgue at the time. Taking the preserved bodies' brain tissue to create a new temporal lobe, he cut out what was infected of mine replacing it with the donors. Eventually, it would mesh with mine functioning completely normal without causing any further disruption. The doctor claimed it was the first time in his career he'd ever had to do something so critical, but he refused to let me die. I thank God for his help each day I draw breath. The incision itself left me with close to twenty staples in my scalp for two weeks and in result, I have this awesome scar. I haven't seemed to undergo anymore crucial medical problems to that severity, so I guess I am pretty blessed."

Savannah sat in complete bewilderment, trying to process everything I told her.

"You definitely are a damn miracle, Kevin Strode. It takes a strong individual not just mentally, but physically as well to survive something so fatal. I am the one to be considered "blessed" just to be accompanied by your existence."

"I guess looking back at it in retrospect I wanted to give back the life that had been given to me through saving others in need around me. Not in the way of a medical doctor, but that of someone who protects you from harm and gives you a sense of security, if that makes sense?"

"Perfectly. I definitely give you admiration for such humbleness. You're truly inspiring."

Moving from scar examination to the ink that inscribed my skin, Savannah lightly traced the calligraphy styled motto that constantly reminded me as to why I chose my life's path. Her eyes flickered with warmth as she sat in deep thought.

"What are ya thinking about?"

"That no matter dead or alive, you will always carry heroism and integrity. I bet I will see you continue your mission long after your soul has parted with your body. You'll perch upon the highest building like a silent vigilante and grasp the feeling of reliving by conquering the deeds of a guardian angel. Lurking through the misted air in search of someone to save only to give them a reason to believe that fate does in fact exist."

All I could do was force the breath caught up in my throat out through my nostrils. If this is what it's like to have a female around, then obviously I have been missing out.

"Finally…someone who understands why the hell I do what I do each day, no matter the stress or physical fatigue it imposes on my body." **I pulled Savannah in for a tender kiss.**

"I guess I'd better head back to my apartment to freshen up for the day. I know you have work within the hour. I will see you tonight when you get off."

I felt myself frown as I got up to escort her to my front door. She gave me a long drawn out kiss on the neck then another to my lips before letting me go. I

knew I'd be anxious to see her again while on my shift but I had to retain my excitement in order to perform as expected on duty.

"Just received a 211A located at 2187 Frederick Douglass Blvd. Suspect is armed. Calling all units in the area to maintain control and safety."

"10-4 on that. Officer Strode responding, I'm on my way."

I hit my gas pedal flying down the street. Even though the call reached beyond my jurisdiction, I was granted permission through my Chief to precede all action to the scene. Four other units pulled up simultaneously creating a barricade around the area. Being advised from my precinct, I was privileged to control the scene and have rank above the others who joined me.

"Stand-by officers. I'm moving in to get a closer look at our suspect."

The officers did as I commanded using their car doors as barriers; positioned and ready to shoot. I drew my pistol nearing the front entrance of the store as my nerves increased with each step.

"Sir, I need you to walk out slowly with your hands in the air!"

I could only see a man dressed in khaki pants, an orange winter coat and a ski mask—aiming his gun at the cashier.

"I need everyone to be on guard if I can get him out without firing."

I stood with agitation drenched in fear as the suspect turned toward me, pointing his gun at my chest.

"Just give me the word Sergeant Strode, and we'll take him out."

"No, I want to have as less of a disturbance and decreased opportunity for violence as possible. Stand-by!"

The suspect put his hands slowly in the air while walking towards me.

"That's it, come on out. There's a lot more of us than there are of you. Walk out, slowly!"

As he walked outside, I demanded he drop his weapon and kick it towards my feet. Complying with my instruction, I commanded all officers to swarm in and arrest him. Just as I went to assist, another suspect flew out the back entrance with the cashier yelling that he was getting away."

"Shit, there is another suspect on foot fleeing the scene! I'm following him down the alleyway, now. He too is wearing a ski mask with dark clothing." **I informed dispatch.** "Hey... Hey! Stop right now! I am a police officer and I command you to stop and surrender! If you refuse to comply, I will shoot you!" **I panted.**

The man continued running, taking a sharp right turn jumping on top of a large dumpster to grab ahold of a fire escape.

"*Son of a bitch...*" **I gasped for air.** "*Damnit, I said stop! What makes you think I won't climb up after you, huh?*"

The fleeing suspect left me no choice. I climbed up behind him, grabbing his foot to pull him downward. Aiming his gun towards my chest, he fired off a round barely missing my head. I could feel the bullet breeze past my left ear leaving me with shellshock. A nervous sweat ran down my temple as my heart began to accelerate.

"*We heard a shot fired, Sergeant Strode are you all right? What is your position?*"

I ignored my radio, continuing to climb after the guy who was giving me a run for my fucking money. Kicking in a window to enter an abandoned apartment room sent shards of glass my way. A jagged edge cut into his leg, halting his movement as he screamed in pain.

"*Sir, stay put! I'm coming! I will seek medical attention for your wound. I need you to please stop moving. You will only worsen the cut and deepen it with friction.*"

The man tried prying his leg from the large piece of glass until I reached his location. Advancing to grab him by the back of the shirt, the suspect faced me in the failed attempt to shoot me once again. I grabbed both of

his wrists fighting for the gun until I was forced to snap the hand concealing his gun. His bones cracked and he screamed with mercy as he released the firearm. Regaining control, I spun the man around slapping on a pair of handcuffs to restrain his further effort to escape. Through panted breath, I informed all nearby officers that I had the man in custody. They rounded the corner helping us both climb back down safely but my nerves were on fire.

"Are you okay?"

"Yeah, I'm good. It's not the first time I've had to chase someone down." **I smiled.**

Mirandizing the suspect, one of my fellow officers threw him in the back of a patrol car hauling him down to the Bergen County Jail. I returned to my vehicle to begin writing my report. Afterwards, I drove back into town to reenter my patrol area. I found myself a vacant spot to park down by Tompkins Square. I was two hours shy from concluding my shift when exhaustion began to set in as I fought from nodding off while surveilling the area. Before I knew it, I *had* fallen asleep.

I'm casually posted up against a store downtown. Lighting a cigarette, watching locals pass up and down the sidewalks. I felt a deep hunger for a specific type to walk by and catch my attention. Becoming anxious, I puffed harder on my cigarette. I took a quick glance at my watch to see a blurred view of 9:45. It was getting late and most people were heading home for the night, yet I wasn't

Breaking At What Seems

Kyla M. Wassil

ready to leave. I could feel the aggression in my chest stretch to nearly cracking my ribcage. Dropping my finished stogie, I witness two young females crossing the street, walking in my direction. One was a brunette and the other was blonde. I have never taken more than one at a time, so excitement overwhelmed me. I guess my gaze was so intense it caught the attention of the two girls. They gave me a concerned smile walking by, laughing amongst each other while disappearing into a nearby alleyway. I knew this was my chance, so I took it without hesitation. I pulled out a handkerchief doused in chloroform, quickening my pace to reach them. I took the handkerchief in one hand bringing my arm around the blondes face, pressing it tightly to her nose and mouth. Before the brunette had the chance to scream, I tucked my left hand deep into the tress of her silky hair, smashing her head against the brick wall to knock her unconscious. Time flashed forward to scenes of horrific rape followed by a gruesome, torturous murder. I felt so alive watching them beg for mercy, crying over and over for me to stop and set them free. How they wouldn't tell anyone what I've done if I would just let them go. I knew from the get-go that there was no possibility for them to continue living. I had to get my fix and a two for one special had my mind fissuring at the sutures from extreme pleasure. Standing in the middle of nowhere, trees surrounded me. I was alone and I knew it. Security warmed my worried thoughts as I dug a deep hole, tossing the dismembered bodies down inside. I felt myself smile sardonically before leaving the site.

"713 come in."

The static of dispatch trying to reach me through my radio startled me back to abrupt consciousness.

"713 here go head." **I yawned.**

"Precinct 18 is unaware of your location."

I furrowed my brows realizing I had slept thirty minutes over my shift. In complete panic, I threw my patrol car into drive, heading back towards the station to get off duty.

"I apologize. I am fine. I was surveilling my patrol area and lost track of time. I'm headed that way now."

"10-4."

Arriving at my police precinct, Chief Mortkin was expressing concern as I rubbed the exhaustion from my eyes.

"Sergeant Strode, what happened? We were about to send the damn search team after you."

"I'm sorry, sir. I was exhausted from the call I had earlier in the night. It won't happen again."

"You're damn right it won't! Kevin, we cannot afford scares such as a missing officer. You know damn well we have to take that shit seriously in this city. Turn in your gun and go home to get some rest, ya hear?"

"Yes, Chief."

Breaking At What Seems
Kyla M. Wassil

  I stood almost faint in the hot shower trying to make sense of the nightmare I had. I have never had dreams pertaining to such violence. I know I have seen some of the worst things in my career, but this was different. Almost as if I had committed those murders in a previous life—it felt so real. I stared at my ceiling until my eyes refused to remain open any longer.

Breaking At What Seems   Kyla M. Wassil

THREE

I was bent over the fact I had overslept from a potential catnap I fell victim to while on duty. Having been my first offense, Chief wasn't so harsh on my punishment. Instead, he had me work a music festival we were having smack-dab in the middle of Central Park. Apparently some big names were to perform. Of course, the all mighty NYPD horse unit was to be seen bustling about the premises, while I amongst a few select others had to patrol on foot.

The horse unit generally gets under my skin, always so smug with ostentatious behavior like they own the damn place. To me, they were just a bunch of gluttonous, power hungry jockey pigs.

On the other hand, the whole music scene was something I figured would strike Savannah's interest. I grabbed a bottle of water taking a few swigs as I opened the door leading to my balcony. Savannah was lounged out trying to catch some sun.

"Hey you..."

Savannah sat up as if she was already aware of my presence. *"Good morning, Kevin."*

"Damnit, why is it I can never surprise you in the way you always seem to with me?"

"It's probably because it's hard to scare someone who lacks the emotion of fear."

"Never thought of it like that. Anyway, there's this festival happening down at Central Park and I am in charge of surveillance for the extent of twelve hours. It came to mind to propose an invitation, if you're interested?"

Savannah's eyes squinted while considering the idea. *"Sounds like a fun time. I believe I read about it in the paper not too long ago. I will attend on one condition."*

"And what might that be?" **I arched an eyebrow.**

"*You must promise that if I become drunk and disorderly, that you won't arrest me but instead detain me within the walls of your bedroom.*" **A devilish grin pulled her cheeks up.**

I puffed out a rugged breath to the unexpected circumstance. "*I can't say I disagree with that although, if you were to let's say "resist" my authority, I'd definitely have to take physical action.*"

"*Oh baby!*" **Savannah laughed.**

"*I'd better get uniformed up for the day. It starts at one. Hope to see your face somewhere in the crowd.*"

Sergeant Gibbs and I had the same shift and patrol area, so I hung around him for most of the day. Standing side by side with him made me look like I skipped several meals. His stout stature kept most spectators on alert when he was around; he's kind of hard to miss.

Soon, people from all over began setting out their fold up chairs and blankets to have a pleasing view of the concert. Vendors and food trucks were spread throughout the area selling merchandise and whatnot. Some vendors sold balloons and glow sticks to entertain the younger crowd attendants along with face painting stations and blow up bouncers.

The pandemonium echoed throughout the park as the first performer took the stage. After a few songs, a high pitch squeal came from behind me causing me to shriek. I quickly turned to see my mother dragging my father along while she carefully balancing a funnel cake.

"Awe, my sweet boy! Look at you all dressed in your uniform. You look so sharp. Tell him, Lukas, doesn't he look so professional?"

My father nodded with annoyance. "Yes son, you appear jaunty."

"So what brought you two down here to partake in all of this madness?"

"You could only guess, your damn mother drug my ass here. She is a big fan of that "Michael Bubble" guy."

"Buble!" **My mother corrected.**

"Oh Christ, same thing! Anyway, I guess we are hanging out to see him. How long are ya on duty for this thing?"

"Twelve straight hours." **I sighed.**

"My God, now that's madness. Well, if you get tired, post up on a nearby tree and take you a snooze, son. I'll be on watch for ya." **My father joked.**

My mother became anxious about a vendor selling tee shirts with the listing of performers in the festival. Grabbing my face, she gave me a large smack of the lips on both cheeks.

"You be safe now, Kevin. Some of these people are just awful. I'll grab you a shirt, too. Love you, sweetheart."

My father squeezed my shoulder giving a wink before following my mother. I just smiled to myself

while giving them a wave. Within the hour, Sergeant Gibbs and I began to feel hungry. Glancing through the crowd all day so far there was no sign of Savannah. I knew it'd be nearly impossible to find her with all of these people, but hope still lingered.

"Still on duty but engaging in a code-7."

"10-4. Just keep your eyes peeled."

After Sergeant Gibbs informed our command about lunch, we grabbed a Philly Cheesesteak from one of the food trucks. While in the middle of our meal, we watched another officer escorting a drunken female off to his patrol car. Sergeant Gibbs and I just looked at one another shaking our heads.

As the sun began to set, my extension of hope began to diminish. They announced a female indie rock vocalist was about to take the stage and the crowd had become louder than they've been all day. I made my way to a neighboring tree to lean up against while trying to rest the onset of pain that tingled in my lower back. As my eyes scanned over the dancing bodies they landed directly on the person I've longed most to see. Savannah was slowly motioning her body like a soul free hipster in her aura of serenity.

As if she felt my gaze, her eyes met mine as a large smile flashed upon her face. I gave a nod letting her know 'yes, I see you over there' as I returned the gesture of a warm smile. My heart fluttered while watching Savannah enjoy herself, like she had no care or worry in the world; just dancing in a field all alone, giving her true spirit a loving intervention.

Dealing with all the horrible and unthinkable things I do day by day, Savannah has shown me that there isn't always reprehensible deficiency behind a motive. Good is to always follow, even if you have no control of the outcome. We must enjoy what we're given before it's too late.

In slow motion, she walked in my direction baring the innocence of a deity. Respecting the fact I was on duty and could not engage in public displays of affection, she instead ran her hand down my face and arm, leaving a trail of tingles that sparked my nerves.

"Were you enjoying the view?"

"Absolutely," **I cleared my throat.** *"How could I not?"*

"Well, I happen to enjoy that woman's music. Her voice is soul shaken, almost to the point of revitalization."

"Wow, that's pretty deep. Glad you fancied her talent and ability to do so."

Savannah's eyes drilled into me. *"So, I've decided to behave myself. Even though you standing so dominant in uniform makes it incredibly difficult."*

"I like the idealism of being irresistible, but only to you."

"Look who now is trying to be the "enticer" of the two. I don't want to keep your attention, but I would love to come over once you get home. That is, if you're cogency is still up to par by the end of the night."

I clenched my jaw yearning to have her mouth against mine. *"Behave yourself, Ms. Rayn."*

She casually laughed, walking back into the crowd. I remained still, not moving my eyes until she was out of sight. From my peripheral, I could see Sergeant Gibbs approaching me.

"Aye, Strode. Who the hell were you just talking to?"

"Oh, her name's Savannah. She's my next door neighbor. Why?"

He shook his head. *"Just wondering, call me crazy but I should probably get my eyes checked."*

I just laughed assuming he was complimenting her apparent beauty.

By the end of our shift I was dead on my feet. Trying to conjure up a second wind just to handle Savannah seemed highly unlikely.

As I answered my front door, Savannah stood with her hands on her hips. *"I knew it. I knew you'd be too tired."*

I side smirked, sharing her disappointment. *"As long as I don't have to continue to stand, I'm quite sure I can manage."*

"That's the answer I wanted to hear. Top is my favorite, anyhow." **Savannah pressed her hands against my bare chest, shoving me through the doorway.**

"Why might that be?" **I studied her intentions.**

"Because, it's the only time I get to take control of you..."

Call me well out of the loop, or maybe even out of practice but I didn't seem to understand how Savannah could go for hours upon hours. She usually had me ten times past the exhaustion than police duty has ever claimed me. Collapsing to complete lassitude, I fell into a deep sleep.

Sitting in my car, I silently watched joggers pass by in a park. The fall leaves rustled against the grass and pavement as the chilled wind blew. I lit a cigarette, patiently waiting for my next victim. Most people who passed by were much older couples performing a fast walk or slow jog. I wanted their hearts already pounding, just to feel the satisfaction the moment I topped the acceleration just by relishing in my planned event. An attractive young male came running by with what appeared to be his wife. I didn't much have a thing for male victims, I usually left them alone. Not because I wasn't completely comfortable with my sexuality, but the fact of one to ever potentially overpower me would only force me into killing much faster than I wanted to. It all just seemed like a pure waste of time.
Women are a great fascination, they struggle and attempt to be twice as aggressive, but the hopeless fear their eyes held told me they've come to the realization that they're in a losing fight. I have a particular type, the hair

color is meaningless to me, but their body must be petite. I get overly excited about their extent of strenuous agility as they try to escape like a trapped rabbit in a cage.

    I looked for a woman who had been pushing herself to the max, so close to exhaustion that I could smell the sweat as it excreted from her pores. As sick as it sounds, I wanted to hunt her down and take control like a wounded doe because I, the proclaimed hunter, failed to shoot her and take her down with one shot. Watching someone suffer is an adrenaline rush, like I am the only one who can save them. I am the one who is allowing them to continue to draw breath, being shadowed with doubt makes the game all the more fun to play. Being in control is what I long for. Despite my male egotism, I adhere to my moral values and what pleases thy self immensely.

    Soon, a woman came running up on my left-hand side. She had on bright pink leggings and a multi-colored windbreaker. Her dirty blonde hair was pulled back in a scrunchie, with a matching black headband. She wore headphones that lead down to a cassette player that was attached at her hip. I mentally slowed her pace to gain a closer look. The way her ponytail swished from side to side, the uneven pattern of her breathing, the glisten of sweat rolling down her temple—I had to have her. Once my heart quickened, I knew she was the one.

    Ensuring that no one was in the area, I grabbed the baton that lied in my front seat before stepped out of my vehicle. The woman bent over for a moment to catch her breath, giving me time to position a hiding spot down in the location in which she was running.

I patiently stood between two large trees waiting for her to pass by. Holding my breath, she came running by. I gave a swift swing, clubbing her in the back of the head. Before she could hit the pavement, I let her collapse into my embrace as I carried her back to my car with haste. Remaining weary of any eyewitnesses, I popped my trunk dumping her body down inside. Binding her wrists and ankles with twine, I took a prideful glance at her unconscious body, eager to get her back to the barn.

Slamming her body onto the metal table, her eyes opened fully as fear and panic set in rather quickly. I became agitated and clasped my hand around her precious throat to cease the sound of her terrified shrill. By the time she took her final breath, I was stained with her blood. I ran my reddened fingers delicately along the sharp metal objects that refused to shine due to being covered in the vital principle of life, itself. Zipping up my pants, I felt my hands begin to tremble. The echoes of her screams bolted through my body like a live defibrillator set too high in voltage.

"Ahh, Jesus Christ!" **I sat up panting as sweat ran down my temples and chest.**

Savannah was no longer next to me; I guess she decided to sneak out again while I was asleep. I ran my hands through my hair aggressively, causing pain to my scar from digging so harshly. This has been the second dream I've had about murdering someone in cold blood. It would make more sense if I had been on sight for recent crime scenes involving manslaughter, but I haven't in over a month. I have never seen these victims in my entire life and I needed to figure out why and how my mind was making up such horrific successions of imagery. I called over the only person I knew who could help me that specialized in criminology; Max. Within the hour he was banging on my front door.

"Hey, I'm so glad you made it! Come in?"

"What's going on, exactly?"

I exhaled, shaking my head. *"I—I don't even know how to explain it or where to lead off at."*

"You expressed that you were having intense nightmares, start from there. What are you seeing exactly?"

"Murders. Innocent victims being sought out at various locations and me…Max, it's me who was committing the unlawfulness. I can never see myself because it's always in first persons view. It's scaring the shit out of me." **I panted.** *"I have only had two and with each dream, they become longer and more detailed."*

Max scratched at his chin in deep thought. *"How peculiar? Well, either you've been watching too many horror movies, or something else is bothering you psychologically. That is a bit out of my range of expertise, but I will do what I can. In the meantime, you should probably go see Father Delatonni and express these dreams to him. Maybe he can give you some spiritual guidance?"* **He suggested.**

I nodded in agreement. *"I guess I could try that."*

"Hey, it's your best bet right now. Have you just recently begun having them?"

"Uh—yeah. I probably had the first one several days ago. Why?"

"Well, there you go. It's not so bad. Kevin, it's to be expected when working the job you do. Hell, I've had some pretty traumatizing nightmares once before as well. Who knows? It could just be a phase, just trust in our Lord and he will guide you back towards a lighter zone of comfort."

I thanked him for the expert advice before escorting him out. For a long moment, I sat on my couch in a daze before deciding to go for a run to clear my head. I recognized the park's setup in my mind. The nature and its surrounding environment was that of Fort Tyron Park that was located in the upper region of New York. It's far from where I currently resided, but I remember visiting it a time or two when I was younger. As vague as my childhood memory was, it seemed as if I couldn't really remember much from that time period while thinking about it. Taking Max's advice, I got dressed and caught a cab to Saint Patrick's Cathedral.

Father Delatonni was practicing a reading at the lectern when I entered. As the doors closed behind me, I dabbed my fingers in holy water blessing my entry as I walked down the aisles of pews. His eyes met me, spreading his arms wide for a welcoming hug in response.

"Kevin, my son. The heavens must be in tune with me lately. I had a feeling you were in some sort of need. What can I assist you with today? A confession maybe?"

"Hello, Father. Uh, not exactly... well, maybe? I'm not really sure to be quite honest." **I frowned.**

"Well, whatever is troubling you, I'm sure we can find a way back to peace by following the Lord's light. This is a holy sanctuary, you can tell or ask anything of me and I shall do my best in guiding you in the right direction." **His voice was humble.**

"I guess I'd like to try through confession."

"Excellent. Let me prepare and I will meet you inside."

I opened the door of the confessional, taking a deep breath as I found comfort within the confined space. Father Delatonni was soon to enter as he opened the sliding window.

"Bless me, Father, for I have sinned."

"I bless you, go forth my son."

"It has been five days since my last confession. For starters, I have engaged in sexual desires with the woman I previously introduced to you in my last confession. Though we are not in a bound relationship, I still find myself shamelessly attracted to her. I have also been suffering nightmares lately. Only having two, they are beginning to frighten me, Father."

"What are the happenings within your conflicted dreams?"

"I have seen myself murder three young women, through clobber and unyielding perilous intent. Yet, I have never seen these individuals before in my life. Father, they felt so realistic."

"It's simple—just follow the rites of the Lord. As you except Jesus Christ as your savior, he of all knows how to keep you safe. Your mind may be battling some demons that have yet to come to surface. Subsequently, you may figure out the reason why. Until then, pray about it. These women may resemble fears you have and committing heinous murder may be your way of preventing something that is worse to come. Although, I cannot predict the future, I do believe things affect us even in the security of our own mind while we lay to rest. Keeping a strong mentality can hinder spiritual possession."

"Yes, Father."

"As for your other relations with this woman of yours, I believe you truly mean well and have absolute faith in your religion. I assign you to recite the Lord's Prayer when you are most feeling stress and temptation. Ten Hail Mary's, twice a day until Sunday's service. Christ will be there to guide you back towards the lighthouse for it is our shared sanctuary. In Jesus' name I pray, Amen."

"Amen."

I stepped out of the confessional shoving my hands deep into my pockets out of frustration. Once I

entered a cab, I asked the driver to please turn off the radio to allow me to hear my own thoughts clearly. I mentally asked for pardon in regards of my rudeness. I wasn't in the best of moods and by my body language; it made it all the more apparent to Savannah. She felt as if she were a bother to me and left me to be alone for the evening. That only caused further frustration as I fell into bed by my lonesome.

Breaking At What Seems   Kyla M. Wassil

FOUR

I *stood over the trembling body in silent*

observance. Tracing my fingertips from her belt line all the way up through her abdomen, I rested a vicious palm on her sternum. I watched her deep inhale lift my hand as it fell again, catching the quiver of her lips as she troubled to speak. The rustling of the chains that bound her to the table were like a sinister symphony to my ears. My victim lied helplessly beneath me while I remained in the abyss of carnage thoughts. Her eyes begged for release, wanting to escape her fate of being slain by a psychopath. My hands appeared dirty and scarred, a temporal memory of past attempts involving disobeying hostages who disagreed with my way of playing. Cries began to formulate within her throat, before they could exceed in frequency, I clasped my hand tightly around her esophagus; feeling my jaw tighten. Glancing over at the display of utensils a tremble trailed its way down my spine, causing my left eye to twitch. I knew my level of excitement was reaching an unrestrained stage.

"713..."

The sound of my radio threw me into consciousness. It took a moment for me to realize where I was.

"713 here go head..."

"273A location 206 E 4th St. Public citizen claims to have seen child roaming around the area. Caucasian, age possibly 4-5 years, sex is male, last seen wearing a blue tee-shirt and khaki shorts: dark hair, no shoes."

"10-4. I'm heading that way now. Is the child currently outside?"

"Unaware. Witness claimed it was about 30 minutes ago. He did not call until he offered the child help. The child ran off, but is still suspected to be in the same area."

"Pulling up to the location now."

I flicked my lights on, hopping out of my patrol car to begin investigating. The red building appeared dilapidated enough to be detrimental to anyone who lived inside. A few residents were standing outside smoking while talking amongst one another. I grabbed my flashlight peering inside the fogged windows to see if I could spot any movement. A gentleman of African descent broke my attention.

"Excuse me, Officer. Are you lookin' for that lil' boy?"

I turned my attention towards the man, giving an absentminded glare. *"As a matter of fact, I am. Are you the one who called about the neglected child?"*

"Uh huh. That was me. Am I in trouble now?"

"No sir. I just need to ask you a few questions."

The man brushed his cigarette in the recess of the brick wall, ensuring the cherry was put out by running the end across his pallet. Stomach bile rose in my throat as I struggled to keep an uncharacterized expression.

"Sure, what can I do to help ya?"

"I was told you had last seen this young boy about thirty minutes ago. Correct?"

"Yeah."

"Where did he look to be heading? Do you know?"

"I think he was looking for his mom or dad. I've seen him running around here before. Always appearing dirty and malnourished. I've seen his folks before, but they never say much."

I grabbed my pad and pen from my left breast pocket, scribbling down important facts the man was giving. "Is this child always hanging around here unsupervised?"

"Sometimes, yeah. I keep an eye on him when he's out playing, usually."

"Okay, what direction was he heading when you last saw him?"

The man lifted his arm, pointing behind me. "That way."

I glanced over my shoulder following his gesture. "Thank you, sir. If you happen to see him again before I do, please call the police station if I am not in the area. My name's Sergeant Kevin Strode, badge number 713. In case they ask which officer you spoke with."

I informed my unit over my shoulder radio the information the man gave me about the child. I felt an unfamiliar strand of anger sear inside of me as I continued looking for the missing boy. Rounding the back of the building, I saw a small child dressed in a blue shirt and khaki shorts, rested upon the pavement with his knees hugged into his chest. I placed my flashlight back into my belt, cautiously approaching the feared child.

"Hey…there. I am a police officer and I'm here to help you. Can you tell me where your mom and dad are?"

The child's eyes met mine with enlargement. Before I could kneel down before him, he took off running towards the back of the building. I took off right behind him watching him dive through an open window. I gave a look to my left and right before peering inside of the room. Climbing through the window, I drew my pistol looking around. The room was a mess, the bed was all stained and it was unbearably hot inside. The ceiling fans attempt to circulate dusty air lacked the vigorous effort. The bedroom door was cracked down the center as if someone broke through it at one point. I was focused on what was beyond the door until a light sound came from the bedroom closet. My eyes looked in its direction, luring me slowly as the sound of panting came from the other side.

"Are you in there? It's okay, you're safe with me. I'm not going to hurt you. I'm here to help you—I'm a good guy" **I whispered.**

Pulling the door back, I saw the little boy cowering in the far corner. When another sound came from the living room the little boy gasped before covering his mouth. I placed an index finger to my lips, hushing the child while I investigated further.

"Shh…stay there. I'll be right back."

I peered both ways down the hallway before entering the living room. A woman was passed out on the couch with an empty syringe lying on the glass coffee table. My chest heaved so hard it pressed tightly against my bullet proof vest, causing me to have a rugged exhale.

"Hello…is anyone else here? I'm from the NYPD and need you to come out and show yourself—whoever you are…"

I listened for a moment when rustling came from the kitchen. My head cocked towards the noise as my gun followed the direction. *"Who is in there? I am a police office and I am armed! I need for you to come out to where I can see you with your hands up… now!"* My voice tightened.

The woman on the couch moaned as she struggled to wake up. Treading footsteps neared my direction with haste and before I could guard myself a man jumped me from behind, holding a butcher's knife to my throat.

"What the fuck are you doing in my house?"

I swallowed hard feeling the blade slice into my neck.

"Drop your weapon or I'll slit your goddamn throat!"

I raised my hands, reciting my officer's creed in my head as I lowered my gun. *"Sir, I am only here to* help. I saw your son outside by himself and wanted to ensure he was safe inside of his home."

"So you thought it was okay to just break into someone's home? We have rights too, you fucking pig! I should call the police and have them arrest your ass for trespassing and entering illegally without a fucking warrant!"

"I am the police, damnit!"

"I don't give a fuck who you are! You broke into my home and it is my right to kill an invader, especially when I feel my life is endangered. You know your fucking amendments don't you, officer?"

By this point, I assumed the man was high on some very strong street drugs and what he was doing was uncontrollable. Now was when I had to engage force in order to save my own life. Feeling the blade pressed tighter into my neck, warm blood trickled downward causing my heart to pound. I was not going to be held hostage or even have my life taken by some drug addict who was high out of his mind. The sudden urge to become violent struck me as I grabbed his wrist with me left hand, jabbing my right elbow into his ribcage. He let out a grunt of pain as I immediately took him by the throat, charging him straight into the wall. Still holding the knife; the man's pupils were pinpointed inside of a reddened gloss.

"Sir, I need you to let go of the knife!"

As the man stood in contend trying to breath, particles of saliva flew from his mouth landing on my face. My eyes widened as I threw him down onto the ground with all my might. In the process, the man dropped the knife placing a dent into the wall with his head.

"Get down! Stay where you are and put your hands behind your back, now!" **I placed a knee on his lower back pulling his hands together to slap on handcuffs.** *"You just assaulted an officer, attempted to kill him and not to mention neglected your son in which you do not deserve! If I get a disease from your saliva I will ensure your stay in prison is far beyond your imagination, now stand to your fucking feet, ya son of a bitch!"*

Notifying dispatch to send back up, I proceeded to Mirandize the man while waiting for another unit to come take the child and the mother from the scene. Child Protective Services took the child and sent the mother to the emergency room to reach sobriety. As for the father, he was arrested and taken directly to the Correctional Service Department.

Sitting on the back of the ambulance as EMS dressed the cut on my neck, I watched CPS carry the little boy to their company car. He peered over the lady's shoulder waving goodbye to me. My mouth slightly opened as I gave a smile returning his gesture. I swear I died a little right then.

I looked upward towards the sky giving the Lord mental appreciation. Released from duty early due to

my injury, I got to go home to rest for the remainder of the day.

Sitting on my balcony, I zoned out trying to forget the madness that occurred earlier on. Sipping on a bottle of Gin, Savannah caught my attention.

"That's the first time I've seen you drink like that. Is everything all right?"

I rolled my head over in her direction with a dark smile. *"Why don't you come over here and I'll be happy to explain how my day went."*

Instead of another session behind closed doors, both Savannah and I remained on my balcony hoping no one was creeping on our outdoor display through curtains and hidden telescopes. Halfway through the bottle of Gin, I didn't really care about my actions and of course, Savannah entertained the rare occasion. As her lips crashed into mine a flicker within my cerebral cortex shocked my entire nervous system, sending memory clips through my brain. The harder she kissed me, the more I saw. The mental fragments appeared more like old photographs of childhood memories mixed with crime scenes. I tried to ignore what I saw as Savannah's kiss sent passionate desperation through my body, leaving me to want more. Digging her nails into either side of my face had my hands pressed into her hips; keeping us tightly knit. Letting my mind wander, I began to see more than what I intended to. I felt fear rise within as I attempted to pull away from Savannah, but she refused to let me.

"Wait…stop…stop…stop for a second, please?"

"Why, what's the matter?" **She panted.**

I looked into her eyes as an aroused smile tugged at the corners of her mouth.

"I—I don't know, I just keep seeing weird shit and it's making me feel strange."

"Kevin, you're fine. You've also been drinking a heavy load this evening. I'm not even close to being finished with you, so if you don't mind I'd like to continue what we started."

I sagged back against the lounge chair letting her take control of me.

The following morning…

A tapping sensation atop my chest awoke me as my eyes opened to the bright sun beaming through my irises. I brought a pigeon into view who was seemingly staring back at me with its head cocked.

"Jesus!" **I sat up shooing it away.**

Knocking over an empty Gin bottle in the process had my head spinning as I tried to suppress the hammering within the walls of my skull. Squinting from the harsh solar rays, I looked around for Savannah. Once again, she was nowhere to be found.

"Always leaving me, I swear."

  I threw my feet over the side of the chair to meet the floor below. Regaining balance before falling through the sliding glass door, I drew in a deep inhale to lower my frustration of a very apparent hangover. Leaned over my counter, watching coffee drip into the pot brought back memories from last night. I scratched at my morning scruff while remaining in an unstrained focus. Running my hands through my hair, I tried to gather just what it was that Savannah did to me each time we were together. I'm to the point I nearly crave her presence at all times and become ill-tempered when she isn't around.

  A sudden tap on my door broke my attention. Turning my head in its direction, I suddenly became upset that whoever it was on the other side broke my extensive train of thought. Cracking the door slightly, I spotted Max on the other side.

"You gonna let me in, or just stand there looking stupefied?"

"Sorry. Come on in, Maximillian." **I smiled.**

"Christ, you look unrested and reek of booze. Have a long night I assume?"

"Considering the fact I passed out on my deck half naked and about had a damn heart attack thanks to a fucking pigeon rested on my chest, yeah I'd say so."

"What exactly were you doing last night?" **Max chuckled.**

"*Drinking to forget yesterday and some other shit...*"

Max tilted my face to examine the cut on my throat. "*Shit, that bastard got you pretty good. Rumor has it he was pretty high off of meth and some other things.*"

"*Figured.*" **I took a sip of my coffee.** "*What of the mother and child?*"

"*They are placing the mother in rehab for six weeks, minimum. As for the boy, well he is in foster care for now. Also, on a more personal note... your blood work came back negative of any signs rendering anything transmitted.*"

"*What a damn shame. Sometimes, I find it hard to fathom how people live and the actions they take in order to destroy themselves along with those around them. And good, I'm glad. I've never felt more disrespected until that very moment.*" **I shook my head zoning out as Max spoke.**

"*I can agree with that, someone once spit in my face...I ended up decking him in front of my female supervisor who in return wrote me up, forcing me to take anger management. So, don't feel bad. Anyway, have you been seeing anyone lately?*"

My brows drew together to his sudden curiosity. "*Why?*"

"Being an investigator, I tend to notice more than most and well this isn't something that takes special skill to see." **His eyes lowered to the floor.**

The gleam of an open condom wrapper sat beneath my lounge chair.

"Awe, hell." **I pinched the bridge of my nose.** *"Yes I have, so what?"*

"Well, I'm glad you're using protection." **He laughed.** *"Who is she?"*

I looked over towards her balcony, frowning in her absence. *"My neighbor..."*

"Ah... interesting. Glad neither one of you has to travel far for some affection. In all seriousness though, I'm happy that you are at least having contact with someone else for once."

"What are you here for anyway? Besides prying in on my personal life...that is."

"It's Thursday? We go running at the park?"

"Shit... let me get dressed right fast."

I was more stimulated than usual as I absentmindedly gawked at each woman who passed me and Max on the track. The longer they continued to run past, the more uncontrolled I became. I have never felt this type of need and didn't understand what was happening inside. A young blonde with her hair pulled back into a ponytail was approaching us. I gave her the

ten second run down as she flashed a smile directed at me before she disappeared behind me. Max caught it as we both turned our heads back simultaneously to get one last glance. Looking back at one another, we gave a smile of approval and continued on.

That evening, a steady rain fell from the overcast sky above. Instilling a gloomy mood set, I parked beneath the trees down at Tompkins Square; falling into relaxation. A couple ran by with their golden retriever trotting happily alongside. I tuned out random radio conversations that didn't pertain to me as I watched for more people. Just when I thought boredom was setting in, that same blonde from earlier came into view.

"What the hell?" **I flung my car door open, feeling the rain soak into my uniform. I wanted to grab her attention before she ran out of sight.** *"Hey!"* **I yelled.**

She turned her head in my direction stopping in mid-run. Pulling out one of her earbuds, she furrowed her brows in response. *"Uh, yes?"*

I felt jittery as I neared her. *"The rain is getting pretty heavy and lightening is in the area. Just thought I'd warn ya."*

"Well, I appreciate it…Officer?"

"Strode, but you can call me Kevin." **I grinned.**

She looked at me for a moment before responding. As she positioned herself within close

proximity, my mindset perturbed. *"Didn't I see you earlier running with some other guy?"*

"Yes, that's a friend of mine."

She smiled looking at my uniform, giving her bottom lip a quick bite. *"Well, how awesome it must feel to be a part of the NYPD?"*

"Ehh, it has it perks." **I gave a shrug.**

The longer we stood gazing at one another in the rain the more I wanted to tear her to pieces. I had no logical explanation as to why I wanted her so badly, or could distinguish the *way* I actually wanted her.

"I'd better get out of this rain and so should you before you ruin your uniform."

"It has seen much worse than the serenity of precipitation. Can I offer you a lift to your vehicle, maybe?"

She pressed her lips together with uncertainty. *"I guess so. I parked all the way on the other side."*

"Hop on in!"

She sat still, shivering from being completely soaked. I turned the AC off watching droplets of water run down her face. All I could think about was how I wanted her. My mind unraveled intense fantasies as I pulled up to her vehicle.

"Thank you so much."

"Anytime. What's your name?"

"Mandy." **She smiled before closing the door.**

I memorized her vehicle before driving off. A sharp pain set in my neck causing a pounding headache. I didn't know why I wanted her in the way that I did, especially right off the bat.

After my shift had ended I decided to sit on my balcony watching the rain continue to fall. Savannah sat in my peripheral reading while toking on a cigarette.

"You know, I wish you'd stop disappearing in the way that you do." **I sat forward, glancing in her direction.**

"Is this where you ask why I haven't called, where I've been and remind me of the simple curtesy of leaving you a note?"

"Ouch... no? I just hate it when I open my eyes and you're no longer with me."

Savannah closed her book, placing it down beside her. *"I guess I don't like getting attached. Most guys would agree upon that, anyway."*

"If you haven't noticed, I'm not like most guys? I don't mind it if you were to stay. Just stop running off like that. Yes, I'll admit it does worry me."

"Awe, look at you being a concerned officer. You're too cute."

I shook my head laughing at her sarcasm.
"Officer or not, I would still worry. Seriously though, I won't mind."

"Well, I guess I'll remember that for next time. I wouldn't want you finding someone else…"

My face became serious in response to her comment. Whatever random thought or feeling I had earlier towards that Mandy girl had to be put to rest.

Breaking At What Seems   Kyla M. Wassil

FIVE

Standing in the middle of the poultry aisle at the Fairway Market, bitterness scratched beneath my skins surface. I wasn't one to enjoy shopping, but considering my circumstance of being a bachelor left me no other choice. My eyes danced over each cut of meat as my stomach rumbled with hunger. I swear, if I food shop on an empty stomach, I wind up buying more than necessary and if I were to go on a full stomach, I hardly buy anything at all. I guess it's a psychological issue I suffer, but I'm quite sure I am not the only one who feels that way.

Deciding on some sirloins, I placed them into my basket continuing to the next aisle. Looking over the canned foods, I grabbed a few containing corn, peas, and carrots. Noticing someone in my peripheral, I turned my head in their direction. If the world wasn't small enough, it was Mandy. My blood surged through my veins with the power of 1000 watts. Staring momentarily, Mandy felt my gaze as she looked in my direction.

A quizzical smile played on her lips. *"Well, if it isn't Officer Strode?"*

"What a small world, right" **I casually grinned.** *"How are you?"*

"Ugh, pretty good. Trying to get this shopping done before my parents come into town."

"Where about are they coming from?"

"Michigan. How have you been, Kevin?"

"That's a nice drive. About the same. Trying not to let my job stress me out."

I reached over to grab a can of baked beans as Mandy pulled out her cell phone. *"I'm not sure if this is okay or not, but if you want you can give me your number* and I'd be happy to come hang out with you sometime? That is, when you're off duty." **She giggled.**

I nervously grabbed the back of my neck as I slowly reached out to take her phone. Entering my digits, I watched Mandy's smile enlarge. *"There you go, and even if I'm on duty and you need something or perhaps you're in trouble, just give me a ring."*

Mandy looked at the screen then back at me. *"Sergeant Kevin Strode, you are officially saved."*

"Excellent. I guess I'd better finish up here and let you continue as well. It was so good to see you again."

"You as well. I'm going running later at Tompkins if you want to meet up?"

"Uh, yeah. I can probably do that. Just shoot me a text and I'll let you know for sure."

Mandy gave one last smile while waving goodbye before disappearing around the corner. I grabbed the last few items on my list and proceeded to checkout.

After stocking up my refrigerator and pantry, I pulled out a bottle of water, taking a minute to rest. It was still early in the day and I had nothing to do on my day off. My apartment felt kind of empty being just me and I didn't want to pay an outstanding pet deposit just to have a furry companion. Instead, I went out to grab a taxi to take me to the Fauna pet shop located by Central Park.

Entering the store, the clerk behind the counter immediately greeted me by offering assistance.

"Good afternoon, sir. Is there anything you are looking for in particular?"

"Just browsing right now but thanks."

"If you have any questions, don't hesitate in asking."

I pressed my lips together with a nod as I casually walked down the aisle of rodents. Peering inside the hamster cages, the little balls of fur were nestled up together, sleeping. Didn't seem like much of pet to satisfy my entertainment and they didn't smell too great, either. I looked over the cages containing rats and small feeder mice realizing a rodent wasn't what I wanted. Just seeing all of their toys and food variations had me at a loss. Something small and rather simple in taking care of was what I needed.

Rounding the corner to where the birds were located, a white Cockatiel rested on its perch caught my eye. I stood in front of its cage making clicking sounds with my tongue. The bird's eyes opened, cocking its head to the side making sounds of its own. Placing my finger through the metal bars, the bird's feathers ruffled. In an instant, the bird flew against the cage nipping the tip of my index finger.

"Son of a bitch!" I jumped back nearly knocking bird seed off the shelving behind me.

Blood trickled down my finger, dripping onto the linoleum below. I gave the bird a smug look as I placed my wounded finger inside my mouth. Metallic rolled across my taste buds as I attempted to stop the bleeding. In that moment, I stood in an obscure stance feeling agitation unlike any other rise in my chest.

    A woman feeding the fish drew away my attention from wanting to dismember the feathered Nazi. I stood next to her as my eyes flickered into each tank. The fluorescent lighting captivated my interest as I watched the neon fish swim around aimlessly. The woman noticed my existence while continuing to feed the little critters. Her Spanish accent was off-putting as she spoke to me in broken English.

    "Hola, you looking for new fish?"

    "I think so? I don't want a lot. Maybe just one or two."

    "Oh okay…I see, I see. They are easy to take care of. You know, not so much of a how you say…hassle?" **She smiled.**

    Brightly colored fish confined in solitude had me looking harder than I probably should have. I picked one up in its tiny water container examining its makeup. It was a beautiful magenta color with black strands in its tailfin.

    "Awe, you poor thing. You're all by your lonesome. I guess that makes two of us."

    "I'm sorry, did you say something?" **The woman asked.**

"No, I mean yeah I was referring to this little guy. What is it?"

"Oh, that's a Beta. They no good together. They will attack and fight to the death!" **She exaggerated.**

I stood with my mouth agape, pretty positive that my facial expression was horribly stupefied. *"I take it that is why they are separated?"*

"Si, si. That may be good for you to have one. Easy to take care of. Just need food, water, etcetera." **Her tongue rolled.**

"I think I'll take him then." **I smiled, looking into the container.**

"Oh great, Señor! Follow me. I take you to get a bowl for your new amigo." **She replied zanily.**

The woman explained to me on how to take care of him and handed me a canister of fish food especially made for Beta's. She seemed more excited about the damn thing than I was.

The ride home for him wasn't the best; each bump we hit sent vibratory ripples through his container. I was lucky the little guy made it to my apartment alive and well.

I poured myself a glass of Gin on the rocks while watching the fish adjust to his new environment. I thought long and hard for a name to give him when Gerry randomly came to mind. I couldn't tell you why, but I was dead set on it.

To break my concentration of watching Gerry

swim in pointless circles, my phone vibrated across the counter. It was a text from an unsaved number. I could only open it with a sadistic smile after visually obtaining the informative of it being Mandy. I pressed my lips together looking out of the sliding glass door having Savannah on my mind. What could a friendly run possibly disturb anyway? Despite the fact of me wanting to viciously attack her each time I've been around her, I still have yet to come to a conclusion as to why I was so fascinated by her. It wasn't the fact of Savannah not fulfilling my needs as a guy; it was that I seemed to have wanted something different. Maybe something more from Mandy than what Savannah was offering up front that I was still trying to configure.

    I threw on an old Yankees baseball tee and ran out to catch a cab. Sneering with devious anxiousness, I was pulled from my thoughts as another man bumped into me in the hallway. I gritted my teeth burning with anger as the man stood in apological innocence. I shook my head brushing it off, but before I could continue on my way, I happened to glance over my shoulder to see the man entering Savannah's apartment—again. I drew in a deep inhale so tight I could feel my sternum compress. Leaving my nostrils to flare, I jerked the shoulder he ran into and quickened my pace towards the elevator doors.

    Arriving at the park, I scanned the layout in search of Mandy. My eyes suddenly stopped on the beautiful breath refrainer herself, perfectly bent over a bench stretching her thigh muscles. I felt my pulse tick in my neck as I lacked salivation on my dried pallet.

Taking my time to near her just to relish in a pleasurable view; the closer I became, the harder it was to control my inner intensions. I balled my fists feeling my knuckles crack as Mandy stood up embracing me with a hug. My heart thrashed against my ribs feeling her body against mine. I gently placed my hands on the small of her back resting my unkempt face against the smooth of hers. Giving her a tight squeeze, Mandy released a short breath into my ear, accidentally causing my hormones to rage.

"So glad you could make it."

I almost didn't know how to respond after the feeling she just gave me. *"Y-yeah, I needed to release some built up tension."*

"Ready when you are." **She smiled.**

Little did she know I was ready for more than just a casual fucking run through the wilderness; hell, I wanted to become a part of it. We started off slow, jogging side by side talking back and forth. I guess this was a good way to pose socially acceptable.

"So, what do you do for a living?"

"I work for the New York Magazine company."

"No shit? That's pretty awesome."

Mandy shook her head laughing. *"Yeah, maybe someday I could publish an article based off of the amazing, very charismatic NYPD Sergeant, Kevin Strode."*

"Don't give me so much credit. I'm not that big of a deal."

Mandy grabbed my arm looking taken aback by my remark. *"Are you kidding me? You save and protect people, do you not?"*

"Well...yeah?"

"All right then, not just anyone can handle that shit or was meant to do it for that matter. I highly commend your courageousness."

I felt my cheeks sizzle in diffidence. *"It is one hell of a career. Thank you for your compliment."*

Mandy picked up the pace leaving us to sprint for the next half mile then faded into a steady run until we completed a full four miles.

Picking a place in the soft luscious grass, we stopped to stretch. Placing her hand on my shoulder for stability, Mandy pulled her right leg back to begin. Withdrawn from my actions, I placed a hand upon her hip meeting her eyes.

"Do you want to know how easy it is for me to take control of you as you stand like that?"

"Okay, Mr. Officer. Show me."

I placed my left foot behind her right, positioning my right arm horizontally across her chest gripping the back of her arm. With one swift motion, I pushed my weight into her watching her lose balance.

Digging her nails into my shoulder as I gently laid her down onto her back set off a deeper desire. Our faces only centimeters apart, I fancied the way she was panting beneath me. Looking upward through the trees before me, I caught a glimpse of what I thought was Savannah standing between them. I let out a rugged breath instantly pulling away from Mandy.

"Kevin, are you okay?"

"Huh?" **I looked again but saw nothing.** *"Yeah, I just thought I saw someone standing over there."*

I reached my hand out to help Mandy stand as she dusted off her backside.

"Wouldn't want a member of the NYPD getting cited for indecent exposure." **She laughed.**

I let out a subtle laugh trying to lighten up. The sun was almost through setting, leaving a blue tint to our surroundings.

"I'd better get back home, I have to work tomorrow."

"Where's your car? I'll walk you to it."

"Shouldn't I be the one doing that?"

"Oh please, I can take care of myself. Jeez—even off the job, you're on it."

"Can't help it?" **I shrugged.** *"Besides, I took a taxi here."*

"*Don't you have a car?*"

"*A police car, yeah. But I only get to keep it momentarily.*" **I smiled innocently.**

Mandy placed her hands on her hips. "*Why don't I just take you home? Saves you some cash.*"

"*Can't argue with that? I appreciate it.*"

Mandy began walking towards her car. "*Hey, I'm just returning the favor.*"

Sitting inside her car, I felt my sweat stick to the leather interior. My eyes caught her firm grip on the gear shifter as she threw it in reverse. Messing with the stick shift made my breathing shallow. I licked my top lip inviting the saltiness onto my taste buds. Falling into a daze, the gleam of perspiration layered on her chest had my nerves tingling. Never caring to pull my eyes away, Mandy caught my intent stare as we rolled up to a red light.

"*What is it?*"

I swallowed hard. "*Oh, uh—nothing?*"

"*You weirdo. It's okay, I honestly don't mind the absentminded gawk you portrayed.*"

I laughed nervously keeping my eyes outside the window for the remainder of the ride home. She's right, maybe I am a little on the strange side. For Christ's sake, I just purchased a fucking fish to fill the empty

void of my apartment. Pulling up to the Milan, I motioned for her to stop.

"Well, this is me. Thank you again for the ride."

"Anytime. When can I see you again?" **She was quick to follow up.**

"You have my number. We'll come up with something. Drive safe."

"Bye, Kevin." **She smiled.**

 I shut her car door glancing all the way up the front view of the building. Entering the elevator the sudden reminder of that clumsy asshole from earlier deteriorated my mood. I found myself pacing back and forth in my living room like a caged lion.
Ripping my shirt off, I jumped onto my pull-up bar doing as many reps as I could until fatigue set in. Fighting to give one last pull, I failed due to overpowering exhaustion as my weight dropped straight to the floor. I wanted to confront Savannah about this mysterious gentleman who kept visiting her, yet I felt it was none of my business. I had to keep in mind that she doesn't like getting 'attached'. Then again, I didn't want to be second best and the thought of sharing a female with someone else tore at my gut. Maybe I just didn't understand how relationships worked nowadays, considering it has been years since I've been involved with anyone. I still didn't agree with having more than one sex partner and if that's how she wanted to play, then I guess I will just hold out on her

next time she comes over to get her fix. I stared through my sliding glass door once more before yanking the curtains shut for the night. The feeling of jealousy was something I wasn't used to. It's been years since I have felt anything susceptibly close to it.

Seated on a barstool, smoke clouded the dim room as rock music blared through the jukebox. I was fixated on a group of girls playing a game of pool near the back. Motioning the bartender for another shot, I downed it as it tore through my esophagus. The hanging lamp above the pool table cast a perfect lighting on this particular female's midriff. I pressed my tongue against the inside of my cheek, tasting the residue of Vodka. My muscles tightened as she bent over to take her shot. My eyes ran down each curve of her body causing me to become excited. I knew I wanted her, but this time I wanted to take it easy with her. I wanted to feel her inside and out. Certain to make it happen, I knew I had to try a different approach. No sneaking around and hiding in a dark alley to attack them unnoticeably. I wanted to gain a limitation of trust and comfort, that way she had a slight idea as to what I wanted on this night. Feeling my gaze, her eyes met mine as she gave an inviting smile. In order to maintain control, I asked for two more shots. Downing one, I took the other over to her. She and her friends were giggling amongst each other as I approached. Silently offering her the shot, she gladly accepted placing the glass to her lips to immediately down it. I didn't say much only to keep my identity concealed. Throughout the night,

Breaking At What Seems   Kyla M. Wassil

I fed her and her friends round after round until they were completely unstable to operate a vehicle to get home safely. Flirting with me, running her hands repeatedly up and down my chest showed me she was more than interested in letting me have her. I paid the cab driver to take her friend's home while choosing to take her with me. She laughed and slurred a conversation along the way, but I was too busy focusing on getting to our destination. Pulling her door open, she fell into my arms struggling to stand upright. I assisted her into the dark barn I considered my home. Before getting completely into the door she was already all up in my fucking mouth. I hated when bitches became belligerently sloppy after a night of drinking. Guiding her to a double mattress in the far corner, I shoved her down onto her back. Pressing my body tightly against hers, I reached above grabbing the rope that rested on a ledge to bind her hands together. She seemed to entertain my idea of masochism as her teeth sank into my neck. Not liking the aggression coming from her end of the spectrum, I back handed her across the face watching blood trickle down to her neck. Completely incoherent, I ripped off her belt, yanking her jeans down to the floor. I spit onto the tips of my fingers to lubricate myself before penetrating deep inside of her. Fear didn't set into her eyes until I rammed into her past the point of pleasure. She begged for me to slow my pace, she even cried for me to stop but I wanted her to shut the fuck up so I could enjoy myself. I didn't do this often, so I wanted to savor every second of it. Beginning to cry, I took a frustrated hand to her throat to silence her peevishness. Hearing her gasp for air had me go harder

Breaking At What Seems

Kyla M. Wassil

and harder until I reached my peak. Releasing onto her stomach, I slid my other hand beneath her head grasping a handful of tangled hair. Leaning into her ear, I sinisterly whispered "You shouldn't trust just anyone." She began what I expected most which was flailing about trying to get me off of her. God, did I love it when they became affray. I unbound her hands letting her slam her hands into my chest while she cried. I figured I could use a little entertainment after getting off. My devilish smile only upset her all the more. The bitch called me a 'perverted psycho' so in return, I snatched her up by the hair, dragging her to my table. Placing her limbs into restraints, her screams rang in my ears. "Why must you be so fucking loud?" She twisted and turned every which way trying to break free but we both knew it was no use. She screamed so harshly her vocals began to crackle as laryngitis set in. 'What a stupid bitch' I thought. I was unsatisfied with the fact of having to silence her sooner than I wanted. Taking ahold of a scalpel that lied in a metal tray had my hands trembling. Bringing it into her view she begged for me to spare her life. But what for? So the whore could run off and tell the goddamn authorities? Of course she threw the line 'I promise I won't tell anyone'. Yeah well tough shit. In her wildest dreams would I find my inner constraint and set her free while my fucking semen was plastered all over her abdomen. I think not! "What a fucking shame, you couldn't shut your fucking mouth and let me enjoy myself." I pressed my lips together. A trace of shivers rattled through her being as I pressed the scalpel's blade into her throat. One *quick slice and the bitch quelled further noise as I stood spattered in warm blood.*

The sound of my alarm had me gasping for air as I lied still, staring at my ceiling fan. Covered in sweat, my heart pounded in my chest. My mindset remained dark as my demeanor portrayed someone other than myself. I stood shadowed by menacing intensions, watching the city below me.

"What's with the rough posture this morning?"

My eyes pulled towards Savannah leaned over the railing, expressing concern. *"Just one of those days, I guess? Where have you been?"*

"I could ask you the same."

Her avoidance in response had my pulse ticking beneath the surface. *"I was giving you space, since you claim no interest in something serious."* **I scoffed.**

"I never said that, Kevin. I just don't want you getting attached to me is all?"

I threw my head back with a sardonic laugh. *"What the fuck do you mean me? How do I know the feeling isn't mutual?"*

"You wouldn't understand." **She shook her head.**

I returned the gesture at her lack of faith. *"Try me…"*

"Honestly, I don't know. I just feel like I am supposed to be around you for a reason."

"Then why always disappear afterwards?"

"Because, it's almost as if I'm searching for something."

"I'm not quite sure I'm following." **My eyes darted.**

"I haven't yet figured that part out yet."

I huffed, looking out into the city once more. Tucking my shirt in, I became frustrated while adjusting my belt. *"Well, when you finally decide what it is you're in search of then please enlighten me. I gotta go before I'm fucking late."*

Just like that I left thinking maybe she'd except a taste of her own medicine. Of course remorse set in after I had time to think about it. I tried to not let it cloud my mind while I was on duty. Driving down 1st avenue, dispatch came over the radio.

"713, we have a 273D. It's urgent!"

"713 here. 10-20, please?"

"327 E 8th Street. Neighbor claims husband is drunk and disorderly. Incident reported upon disturbance of peace. Relent screaming and yelling has the anonymous caller convinced led to altercation."

"I'm on it!"

"*Officer Gibbs here, I'm heading down Avenue C now. Sergeant Strode, I will meet you there.*"

"*10-4.*"

I sounded my sirens and flicked on my lights, speeding down the street to get there. Having an unsettled attitude already was not going to be a good outcome for this call. Pulling up to the scene, Officer Gibbs and I entered the building together. Following the echoes of disagreement led us straight to the suspect's front door. I balled a fist giving the door a firm double knock.

"*NYPD. Open up!*"

Officer Gibbs and I waited for a response. The deadbolt unlocked as the door cracked open with a woman in tears appearing on the other side.

"*Ma'am, is everything okay? We got a call recalling a disturbance coming from your home.*"

The woman attempted to maintain her composure out of fear. "*No Officers, there is no problem here.*" **I watched her lips quiver.**

"*Ma'am we are here to help you. Nothing is going to happen with me and my partner standing here. Can you please open the door and let us inside?*"

A muffled voice came from the background. "*I don't think that's such a good idea. Like I told you, there is no problem here.*"

I huffed with disbelief. *"Ma'am if you don't let us in, we will come in by force. It's your choice. We can do this the easy way or the hard way. I'm trying to do my job and you're making it very difficult."*

"Keyshia, if you let those motherfuckers in you'll be one sorry bitch!" **She attempted to shut the door until the toe of my boot wedged in between.**

Officer Gibbs and I looked at one another before making a decision.

"Please just leave, he isn't lying about what he said."

"Either you unlock the chain and let us in or I'm kicking your door in!"

Within that moment, Officer Gibbs and I watched her head get slammed into the door hearing her body slam to the floor.

"Stand back! We're coming in!" **I drew my pistol while raising my foot, kicking the door open.**

On the other side, a gentleman stood in aggravated rage, pointing a pistol at my head. *"The bitch may be knocked out, but you two will be far beyond that if you come any closer."* **He warned.**

"Sir, just please calm down. Put the gun down now or we will shoot you!"

He defiantly pulled back the pistol's hammer showing no mercy. The only thing we could do was take

him over by force before both of us were to be shot on site.

"Did you not fucking hear Officer Gibbs? He said put the Goddamn gun down or we will shoot you!" **I cocked my pistol back, ready to fire.**

"Drop the gun and put your hands up, now!" **Officer Gibbs reinforced.**

"You will be promised several life sentences if you kill an officer. Keep that in mind."

The man swallowed hard, clenching his jaw before putting his hands up. Officer Gibbs and I ran in slamming him to the floor, taking the pistol from his possession. I flipped him over slamming his head into the hardwood.

"You son of a bitch, you better pray the judge is in a good mood the day of your sentencing!" **I hissed.**

I jerked him up to his feet, walking him down to my patrol car while Officer Gibbs called the EMS to come take care of the unconscious female. As I walked him out, I read him his rights before shoving him into the backseat.

"Suspect is in custody. I'm on my way to the station now."

Pulling up to the front door of my precinct, two officers awaited outside to assist in escorting the man inside for processing. I handed him over and jumped

back into my car to finish my shift. Longing for some peace and quiet, I drove back down to Tompkins Square leaning my seat back to rest my nerves. Even though every day is a different story, the shit I see and deal with I can never seem to get used to. Closing my eyes, I listened to the conversations over my radio. This time I was smart to set an alarm on my cell phone just in case I happened to doze off, again. Plugging it into my auxiliary outlet, I put on some 90's rock falling into a state of meditation. The sound of hands slamming onto the hood of my patrol car awoke me. Standing before me with a daring smile was Mandy. I drew my brows together glancing at the clock on my dash that read 2:15am. Opening my car door, I smoothly stepped out to talk with her.

"Might I ask why the hell you're in the park at two in the morning?"

"I get bored sometimes, so I come here to free my mind a little." **She glanced around before focusing her gaze directly on me.** *"I don't just come here for the purpose of running, Kevin."*

"I see. I have an hour until my shift is up. I've had one hell of a night."

"I can imagine so." **Mandy drew in a deep inhale, staring through the trees.** *"This city never sleeps therefore I believe there is always some mayhem taking place."*

I placed my foot on the curb, grabbing ahold of my belt as Mandy sat against the hood of my car. I felt myself staring harder than I normally did as my eyes ran up and down her physique.

"Do you have trouble sleeping?"

Mandy's eyes flickered towards mine. *"Maybe...do you have trouble sleeping, sometimes?"*

"Here lately, I have been."

Her posture became serious as her expression gained interest. *"And why is that?"*

"Honestly, I think it's due to my job. But these past few weeks, I'm not so sure anymore. I've been suffering these awful nightmares." **My forehead wrinkled.**

"Do you think it has anything to do with things you've seen in the past?"

I looked up into the night sky as if the stars were going to reveal an answer. *"It's not so much of what I have seen once before, nor has anything in relation to PTSD. I am seeing things as if I were actually doing them."*

"Like memories?"

"Yes! Exactly what it feels like."

Mandy stood from the car, closing her space in on me. I took a step back swallowing the lump that instantly formed in my throat. *"Maybe you need a release, Kevin..."*

"How do you mean?"

"I see the way you look at me. Your eyes are serious, yet I notice a more in depth need...perhaps a want? To encounter lustrous suppositions your soul craves."

I took a hand to my stubble, giving it an uncertain scratch; sheltering my disposition. Mandy positioned herself back onto the hood of the car watching my body language. That sudden urge she always brought to surface chose to reveal itself. I dropped my hands approaching her in a dominant manner.

"Have you ever been with a cop?"

Mandy's gaze sharpened. "No..."

A devilish grin tugged at the corners of my mouth beneath a twitching brow of challenge. "Do you want to be?"

I slammed my hands on the hood with her in trapped in between. She took in a nervous breath before consciously clenching her legs around my waist. Intensely pulling my face to hers, our mouths crashed as we frantically tugged at each other's beltlines. The sound of my alarm had my eyes fly open realizing that I in fact had dozed off—once again.

"Well, fuck..."

Breaking At What Seems   Kyla M. Wassil

six

Entering the doors of Saint Patrick's

Cathedral, Father Delatonni motioned for me to come see him directly. I gestured to my mother that I'd return within the moment. Dragging my shined up shoes against the red velvet runway, my head only raised once I reached the steps of the altar.

"Kevin, how are you my son?"

"Hello, Father Delatonni. I'm breathing, to say the least."

"I've been having certain feelings about you lately. The lord even granted me with a dream to help you. You appear to stand troubled. As is you're fighting something fierce deep within, correct?"

"Yeah, how'd you know?" **I raised my shoulders in discomfort.**

"I am a speaker for the son, Jesus Christ. The lord reaches me in different ways. I blessed a vile of Holy water for you. Sprinkle it throughout your home while reciting the Lord's Prayer. Your home is your sanctuary in which you should always feel safe there. I have also noticed a difference in your attitude in the way that you carry yourself. You only come to confession but once a week now, when I used to see you as often as three times, even if you just wanted to chit-chat." **He pressed his lips together awaiting my response.**

"I guess my mind has been elsewhere, lately. I know I have been slacking on paying my dues to Christ. Maybe I just feel lost at the moment?" **My eyes veered off looking at my mother; her eyes filled with concern.**

"I know at times things may seem hard to believe, but you don't always have to see things to have belief. Knowing your faith in God is exceptionally strong will you then feel his love in return. The ability to feel emotions despite choosing to see what the mind wants the heart to

sense is enough to change anyone's opinion. The lord has a different way of showing us our chosen path, even through the most of difficult trials you face, keep in mind they are durable. Even if occurring events pose impossible to defeat—pray about it. He's there and he does listen to you. I don't want to see you in this way. I want to help heal your mind and soul as best I can."

"Thank you, Father. I appreciate the look out. I will uh, see you at confession next week? I give you my word."

Father Delatonni folded his hands before him, nodding in response. As I sat down beside my mother and father our service then began. Afterwards, I went over to my parents for a well overdue home cooked meal. At the dinner table, I pulled out the vile of Holy water staring through the liquid as if I wanted it to evaporate. I ended up dropping it on the floor from my mother startling me.

"So, what did Father Delatonni speak with you about today?"

"Eva, that's his business." **My father interjected.**

"Oh hush, Lukas! I wasn't talking to you."

"Dad, its fine. Anyway, he was just asking me how I've been lately."

"Well, he must be concerned for some apparent reason. Are you all right, Kevin?"

I leaned over to pick up the vile, shoving it into the pocket of my slacks. *"Yeah, ma. I'm fine."*

"He told me you haven't been going to confession as much as he wants you to."

I zoned out staring into my plate as I absentmindedly forked at my peas. *"What's that? Oh yeah, no I haven't. Work has been taking up majority of my time."*

"Kevin, there is always time for the lord. By the way, I went through the attic the other day with your father, ya know trying to get rid of some junk? I came across some photo albums I figured you would want to have a look at."

"Sounds like a plan."

After eating dinner, I sat on the couch beside my mother while my father rested in his recliner to watch a Yankees game. Pulling out the family photos was always a fun time, except for today. Flipping through the pages I recognized some, but others I found myself having a difficult time remembering the times in which they took place. I stopped on a photo of a bunch of children gathered at a table with who I feigned to be me in the middle; blowing out my birthday candles. Turning to the next page, I stopped on a photo of a kid in a swimming pool centering a duck shaped flotation device.

"Kevin, what's the matter?"

"Who is that?"

"Kevin, are you serious? Show your father and ask him."

I faced the album for my father to view and his face marred dunce in return. *"Kevin, what the hell? That's you, ya goof!"*

"I had some blonde hair as a baby, then."

"It wasn't until your father started taking you to that darn loon of a barber he insists on continuing to see." **My mother rolled her eyes.** *"I was so upset the day you came home with your head shaved in a high and tight."*

"Oh please, it was good for him. It was our father, son time. Right Kevin?"

I laughed at my parent's meaningless banter while glancing over some other photos. As I came across ones of me growing older, I recognized the locations but not the people who were in them. There were several photos of me and another blonde headed boy. The only person I could think of was it being a cousin.

"Hey ma, this kid who's in these photos is distant family, right?"

"Lord Kevin, what do ya have amnesia all the sudden?"

"I was just making sure. It's been awhile since you've shown me these photo albums."

"You sure you're all right, Kevin?" **My father asked.**

Breaking At What Seems — Kyla M. Wassil

My mood suddenly became irritable as I shut the album, handing it off to my mother. *"I'm fine."* My eyes met the television and we said nothing further.

Arriving back at my apartment, I saw Savannah's secret lover leaving her place. Rolling my eyes, I swung my door open giving it an unnecessary slam shut. Grabbing a glass of Gin, I stepped out onto my balcony. Leaning over the railing, I watched cars zoom along the darkened street. I didn't know why I was letting this shit eat me alive so badly, so I went back out into the hall gathering the courage to knock on her door. My pace slowed the closer I became. Finally reaching it, I pressed a hand against the frame taking in a deep breath. Deciding not to make a fool of myself, I rested my forehead against the door suddenly seeing horrible glitches. I felt myself twitch into a mode of seizing as images of Savannah being tortured in the worst way scintillated in my head. I lost my balance, falling into the wall behind me unaware of what had just happened. Shaking my head to regain coherence, I strutted back into my apartment feeling my heart pound in my chest.

Downing the remaining liquid in my glass, I slammed it onto the counter shattering it all over the place. Reflective shards stuck into my palm as blood surfaced through the tiny cuts. I dropped to the floor gripping the sides of my head, rocking back and forth in search of tranquility. I didn't like the things that I saw and I hated the way I dreamt during the night. I felt as though I was losing my fucking mind, but why? My mind circled with the inflicting thoughts as I became dizzy. In the midst of my self-intervention a tap on the door pulled me from my delusions.

"Are you just going to continue being mad at me for no reason, Kevin?" **Savannah asked, shoving through me.**

"I don't know what the hell I am feeling lately! You said you didn't want me to become attached, so I'm doing my best to not. What else do you fucking want?"

"You're not the same as you were when we first met," **Her eyes pierced me.** *"Something has changed in you."*

"First my damn priest and now you…" **I laughed sarcastically.**

Savannah grabbed my bottle of Gin, taking a huge gulp. *"You really want to know what I crave?"* **My eyes were attracted to the pulse within her jaw.**

"Yes!" **I sighed, plopping down onto my couch.**

Savannah walked over to me with haste climbing onto my lap. Grabbing me by the face, she looked me square in the eyes. *"I want to see something."* **Pressing her lips against mine, Savannah dug her nails into my cheeks.**

The harder she kissed me the more I saw flash before my eyes. Memories of murdering countless women by raping and torturing them, along with scenes of staking out just to stalk the innocence of my next

victim played in my head like an old film. I tried yanking away to stop what I was seeing but Savannah was persistent. I have never committed such baleful behavior in my entire life, but what I saw in my mind was too realistic to ignore; complete blasphemy. Savannah pulled back wiping her mouth as we both sat panting to catch our breath.

"Holy shit. You saw those things, too?" **She closed her eyes, placing a kiss upon my forehead before joining ours together.**

"Savannah, what the hell is going on…how is it possible that you just saw the exact same thing I did? Did you make me see those things, somehow?"

"I'm not really certain. I think I need some time to be alone…to think and reconcile."

"You're going to leave me to figure out this mess, alone?"

"Once I find a realistic answer, I will come to you straight away! But right now, I need to be in solitude. Do yourself a favor and pray about it. I advise you to find comfort in the meantime. For me, please?"

As Savannah stood to leave, I got up to follow. *"Wait! Where will you go?"* **I asked frantically.**

"Somewhere only I know. You will see me soon. I promise."

Leaving me to make sense of the impossible, I grabbed the bottle from the counter top taking a long pull while gazing into Gerry's bowl. *"Well… looks like it's just you and me, bud."*

Drinking myself into complete inebriation, I grabbed my phone sending Mandy a text to come over. Nearly passing out, a knock on my door brought me back to consciousness. I fell off the couch, stumbling my way to see who it was. Opening the door to see Mandy's face etched with the same thoughts as my own had her instantly crashing into me. With the absence of a normal greeting and lack of conversation, Mandy and I let our emotions do all the talking. Kissing down her neck feeling the warmth of her flesh against mine internally combusted my libido. I hoisted her up onto my waist taking her straight to my bedroom. This was the release I had been longing for, I felt as if I were reborn as I fell into her touch. It wasn't until the mornings first light peeking over the horizon did we fall numb to exhaustion. It seemed as if I wasn't the only one who needed tonight. Mandy never asked any questions, she just agreed and now there she was, lying naked beside me tracing my chest and abdomen with her nails in complete silence. The sensation eased my tension, placing me in a deep sleep.

"Kevin… Kevin, wake up!"

"Hmm?" **I groaned.**

Cracking my eyes only wanting to shield them from the bright sun light, I yawned while sitting up to stretch. Mandy was seated next to me wrapped in the sheets. A smile stretched across my face knowing last night actually happened.

"How'd you sleep?"

"Better than ever, actually. For once, I didn't have a nightmare."

Mandy ran a hand through my hair then down my face, giving a warm smile. *"Me too."*

"I apologize if I said some vulgar things to you last night, I was way beyond sobriety."

"You didn't say anything I didn't like. To be honest, I was waiting for the moment to receive your intellect invitation."

"Ha, is that so? What made you think I eventually would?"

"Your eyes… generally, you can tell a lot about a person within the first fifteen minutes of meeting them. No one has ever really looked at me with such intensity on a first impression basis. Besides, I was just as curious about you as you were of me…"

I scratched the bottom of my nose watching her climb on top of me. Noticing my scar, Mandy ran her fingers across it but never asked what it was from. Maybe she assumed it was from the job or on terms of a

sore subject. I kind of appreciated the fact she didn't ask why or how I got it. Making my sight from her lips down to her chest, I opened the sheets exceeding further down to the bare skin of her stomach; resting my eyes on a scar raised just above her right hip. Running my thumb over it, I furrowed my brows feeling its texture. Before I could ask about it, Mandy read my expression.

"I had my appendix removed when I was seven. I had a severe infection and was rushed into emergency surgery."

My eyes widened with concern. *"No kidding, I had emergency surgery too, when I was just seven years of age."*

Mandy let out a laugh. *"I figured that's where your scar came from."*

"How do you justify it not being caused from my line of duty?"

"I can just tell by how it's set into your head."

I pressed my lips together, nodding. *"You're very smart, I'll give you that."*

"Whatever." **She laughed, lightly smacking my chest.**

"I'm being serious." **I grabbed her waist rolling over on top of her.**

Taking a moment to stare into her crystalized eyes, I licked my lips slowly closing in on her mouth.

Magnetized by the touch, Mandy took both hands to either side of my face in a concentrated manner. Falling into her kiss, I wanted to lose myself. I pulled back, sliding off the bed to go start a shower before I fell prisoner to the comfort.

After taking a morning piss to soften my erection, I slid open the glass door stepping into the hot water. Moments later, I heard the bathroom door close. Looking in its direction, Mandy stood before the mirror throwing her hair up. I wiped the excess water from my face as it streamed down to have a clear view of her bare leg entering the shower. Hidden behind promiscuous tendencies, her gaze remained acute upon my glistened stature as I stood beneath the showerhead.

"I wanted a morning dose of the Sergeant before he reported for duty." **She grinned.**

My hands took her in by the face as my heart fluttered feeling her wet body pressed against mine. Becoming aggressively turned on, I slammed Mandy into the corner of the shower lifting her up onto my waist. A burning sensation was sent up my genitals from her tightness as I pushed further, letting her nails dig into my back. I struggled certain moments with the thought of Savannah lingering in the back of my mind. I was just finding the comfort followed by her suggestion. Mandy was absolutely gorgeous, probably the drink of water most men would die for just to have a taste. There was just something about Savannah that I couldn't put my finger on. I have noticed I consume darker attributes when around her, but it's the type I seemed to enjoy. As if she brings out another side of me I didn't know existed, yet she saw nothing wrong with it.

    Tearing the cords from my internal control panel, I felt myself ram harder into Mandy as she moaned loudly into my ear. As her sighs reached a higher frequency, they burned my nerves with turmoil. Tearing marks into my back, I slightly blacked out reaching my release while Mandy panted over my shoulder. We stood there in reticence, letting water run down our bodies before getting out. I watched the tiny streams trail down her torso as she stood with her head tilted against the tile and her hand pressed into my chest to settle her breathing. A wet kissed was placed to her chest for a long moment as Mandy ran her fingers through my hair.

    I clothed myself in the navy fibers of my armor, adjusting each object that clung to my belt. Walking into my kitchen, Mandy was finishing cleaning up the broken glass from the night before. I looked down at my hand to healing wounds, mentally shaking it off.

    "Yeah, I was gonna get that…"

    "Kevin, it's all right. I fed your little friend, too." **She beamed.**

    "That's Gerry. Figured he'd keep me company since I'm always here, alone."

    Mandy's eyes filled with sympathy. *"You're so adorable."*

Breaking At What Seems

Kyla M. Wassil

    I grabbed my cap from its hanger on the wall exiting the apartment after Mandy. Standing by her car, she leaped into my arms for one last hug.

"Be safe out there. I'll see you soon."

    I watched her drive off before getting into my patrol car. Cruising down 1st Avenue an unnerving awareness settled in my stomach. Locals were posted up against the walls of surrounding buildings, drinking coffee while lost in friendly communication.

    As I rolled up to a red light, a female baring mocha skin stepped into the crosswalk bopping to the beats supplied through her headphones. The sun's rays brightened her white Cami that comforted the top of her high waisted jean shorts and my chest bowed inward in pause. Meeting the front of my patrol car, her head turned in my direction as she flashed a smile followed by a wave. The girl couldn't have been a day over twenty.

    My hands gripped the steering wheel in response to the boring sharp pain that was sent through the right side of my head. I couldn't take my eyes off of her no matter how hard I tried. As her footing made contact with the sidewalk on the opposing side of the street, she gave one last look my way before continuing on. The car behind me incessantly honked their horn disturbing my daze. I glanced in my rearview to an impatient driver behind me waving for me to notice the light had turned green. I flicked my lights on, shoving my door open. The man's eyes narrowed as I tapped on his window.

"Can I help you, officer?"

Breaking At What Seems

Kyla M. Wassil

"Let me see your license and registration..."

The man's brows drew together as he sat hesitant. *"I've done nothing wrong?"*

"Don't make this difficult." **My voice tightened.**

As the man reached into his glove box, I directed traffic to go around the scene. His hands shook as he displayed his information. Noticing an empty Jameson bottle in his cup holder altered my intent as my attitude changed.

"Why don't you step out of the vehicle for me, please?"

"I don't see what the hell I've done wrong..." **The man became defensive.**

"Turn around and place your hands on the vehicle!"

I ran my hands up and down each leg frisking the man for public display. This wasn't something I wanted to deal with first thing in the morning.

"Have you been drinking this morning, sir?"

"What? N-no... why?"

"Then, you mind explaining to me why you have an empty bottle in your car?" **I yanked him by the shoulder forcing him to face me.**

"I don't have to tell you a damn thing..."

"Ha, okay wait right here." **I walked off to my patrol car to grab a Breathalyzer test.**

The man shoved his hands into his pockets holding a scorn on his face.

"Officer Strode here, I'm calling to report a possible 502. I'm preparing a Breathalyzer test then I'll be on my way to the range."

"Officer Gibbs here, 10-4."

I walked back over to the man who got the luck of the draw in pissing me off this morning. *"Open your mouth and blow until I say stop."*

"Man, this is fucking ridiculous! I don't even see how it's legal for you to stop me when I was behind you!"

"Either you can blow into this device or I can just cuff you right here for resisting an officer's orders." **I smiled.**

He looked around for a second before lowering his bottom jaw.

"Good, now fucking blow…"

His blood alcohol level was .03; just below legal calculation of being legally intoxicated.

"Well, you're lucky today. How long have you been drinking?"

"I drank that bottle last night."

Breaking At What Seems — Kyla M. Wassil

"*Maybe you shouldn't carry the evidence with you, it's illegal to drink and drive as well as carrying an open container of any kind.*"

"*I'm completely aware of the law, officer.*" **He sneered.**

"*Listen, don't get fucking smart with me! I deal with a multitude of jackasses like you on a daily basis. You keep up the back talk and I'll throw your ass in the back of my patrol car right now!*" **I pressed my forearm into his throat with warning.**

"*It's hard to believe you guys get away with such brutality...*" **His jaw clenched.**

I drew in a rough inhale through my nostrils as heat escaped the back of my collar. "*Give me the fucking bottle and you can leave.*"

"*As you wish...*"

As he reached out to hand me the empty whiskey bottle, I barely reached mine back watching him released his grip leaving the bottle to shatter all over the asphalt below.

"*Well now look at that, I'm going to have no choice but to cite you for littering on public property.*" **I shook my head walking back to my vehicle to write up a ticket.**

The man became irate as he read over his citation. "*$250? How the hell am I to pay this?*"

"You have up to thirty days to pay your fine. You violated New York's law 16-118. Littering is prohibited and this is your first offense that has been legally accounted for. If you need an extension, please contact the court house for further legal counsel. It was a pleasure serving you to keep our community safe. Oh… and if I were you, I'd revise your definition on what "cop brutality" actually means." **I gave a wink, walking back to my patrol car.**

Meeting up with Officer Gibbs to recertify our weapons permit, I couldn't have been more anxious to squeeze off my built up tension. Chief Mortkin was awaiting me inside the gun range along with the rest of our unit.

"Sorry, Chief. Had some jackass hold me up this morning."

"It's fine, I was well informed of your little debacle. In your absence, we discussed the simple gun safety rules. You want to give one of your perfect demonstrations the class can use as representation?"

I shrugged taking the pair of earphones from his hand, sliding them on along with a pair of safety goggles. I couldn't bare the disappointment his face would present if I had declined. I'm one of our precinct's top shooters and have won awards in marksmanship for my skilled aim since the beginning of my career. I adjusted my shoulders pointing my gun towards my target with a concentrated breath. Zooming in mentally on the head of my papered enemy, I squeezed the trigger until my clip was empty. Once I

was finished—the head no longer existed. I smiled to myself before loading an M4A1, firing away like some psycho deranged assassin.

After a long day at the range, Max invited me out for some drinks down at the Rue B. The Yankees were playing the Phillies tonight so it was a big deal to Max that we watched it together. I was in another one of my depressingly morbid moods so my consumption of alcohol was greater than usual. It started with two to three beers before I switched over to the whiskey.

"Kevin, you're going to be completely smashed. Haven't you heard the old saying "beer before liquor makes ya sicker"?" **Max frowned.**

"I can handle my own, Maxi. I am a grown man and I will take a cab home."

"Why don't I just drive you?"

"Nah, I should be fine. I may even just walk home."

"We will see how you're acting when the time comes."

I patted Max's shoulder with reassurance as I took a long sip from my glass. Walking the streets of Manhattan alone at night probably wasn't the best of ideas, but I figured it'd give me room to breathe and think while trapped within the caving remoteness of my brain. By the end of the fifth inning I was already feeling nothing less than cozy and mind altered. Max was so spirited that I dreaded to thwart his die hard

love for Jeter and the pinstriped heavy swingers of New York. Having enough excitement for one evening, I pulled out my wallet to satisfy my tab before standing to leave.

"Aye, Kev what the hell are ya doing?"

"I think I'm gonna call it a night." **I smiled at the bartender.**

"What...why? The game isn't even finished yet? There's still two more innings."

"I drank way too much, Maxi." **I felt the alcohol brewing a storm within my stomach with each subtle burp that escaped my mouth.**

"I fucking warned ya ,you jackass! Now we're gonna lose 'cause you're a quitter."

"Max, seriously? Don't pull that bad juju shit on me. You'll be just fine."

Max threw his hands up in defeat. *"Awe, come on, Kevin? I could so murder you right now."*

***Murder*...why yes—m urder. My brain sizzled at the thought of revolting murderous intentions.**

"I'll text you to let you know I made it home okay. Christ, pray about it."

"Oh yeah, some Catholic you are." **He mocked me.**

Breaking At What Seems

Kyla M. Wassil

  Pushing through the glass door to enter the streets of the city had my eyes lurking for trouble. Slurred speech with fuzzy vision matched that of a common drunken vagrant I was used to arresting for violation of keeping the peace. If I presumably stagger about like I just so happened to be doing, any nearby authorities would surely ask questions. I honestly could have given a fuck less on who thought poorly about my judgment in leaving the bar so intoxicated.

Hidden within the shadows that cast so extravagantly from the buildings, I traced the bricks with my index finger to prevent a possible stumble along the way. The bright city lights blurred together like a kaleidoscope of blips floating around me. The sound of late night traffic comforted me as I walked the strenuous two mile distance back to my apartment building.

Making my way through the doors of the lobby, I managed to maintain my composure for the eyes of Milan's concierge. My actions were in accordance to Savannah leaving me in the way she did. It frustrated me beyond reason that no matter how much of a fight I could have put up, Savannah's mind would still have stood impervious.

As the elevator pulled me to my floor, I slid down the reflective silver unable to keep the confined transportation box from spinning into a disastrous whirlwind. As the bell dinged to inform I have reached my floor, the doors slid open. I fell forward onto my hands and knees giving my best attempt in crawling to my front door. Falling inside my dimmed housing, I staggered toward my couch trying to kick off my shoes to get comfortable.

     Lying back against the leather texture, my eyes met the ceiling fan above causing me to stare off into space. Mandy left me several text messages all evening but I never felt like replying. Being alone probably wasn't the best thing for me at the moment, but all I wanted to do was see Savannah. Going another day without the very thing I wanted, I closed my eyes falling into a deep slumber.

     For several nights in a row I remained imprisoned not only in my mind, but within the walls of my so called 'home'; or what I considered it to be. I wasn't completely content from the other night. All I wanted was a bitch who wouldn't scream; it reminded me of my pathetic mother each time my father were to strike her vulnerable, shivering body drenched in fear. Being so small, I never understood why he treated mother that way and to witness the pleasing sarcasm in his eyes drew my curiosity to the surface of a born sore that festered for years. I couldn't just run out into an alley stabbing each agreeable potential that passed my way. I wanted someone to allow the appropriate time it would take to please myself upon ending their undeserving vitality. I had a principle of blood spattered lust that longed to flourish in the right way. I was going to get it one way or another and beneath the full moons lighting, my inner beast was ready to relish in wrongdoing as my horrific howls soared through the air in silent warning.

Breaking At What Seems

Kyla M. Wassil

I threw my hood on, lighting a cigarette to keep busy on my walk down the busy street. The only place that seemed to strike interest was a local strip club. Entering unnoticed, I seated myself at a table alone where I watched each dancer as I tried to pick the perfect catch. One who wore black leather covered in tattoos had the saliva waiting to drip from my thirsty jaw. The way she perfected a slow motion twirl down the pole made my nerve endings electrify. Noticing my gaze, the woman approached me after her performance on stage. Her eyes filled with need; I, in return, slid over my pack of cigarettes. Accepting my offer with a pleased smile, I joined in toking along with her.

Casually talking, she offered to give me a private dance. I knew it would be a test of my patience and self-control on whether I had the strength to hold out or not; and that was a struggle all its own.

The way her body motioned to the music as the red lighting blazed the glistened sweat on her back had me dangerously alert. By the end of the night, we both knew she was willingly ready to come home with me. I had an exquisite charm with the creature of woman, bringing them into my world was simple. But to keep them there was a different invitation.

Respecting my space, she stood in silence waiting for me to make a move. I motioned for her to lie down upon my bed and so she did.

Slowly dropping her leather coat to the floor, she lied back curling her finger enticingly. A sinister grin pulled at the corners of my mouth as I watched her sensual teasing play out. This time, I wanted to see what she was

Breaking At What Seems — Kyla M. Wassil

about, so I sat next to her giving her access to roam freely about my skin. My fingers twitched at the sensation of her sharp nails that drug down my cheek. Rearing back, the unexpected threw my inner volcano into eruption. Her hand met my face as she climbed onto my lap pressing into my throat, chocking me. My eyes wide with awareness, I let her continue as it excited me.

Unzipping my jeans, she slid me deep inside of her moist tissue riding the shit out of me like an untamed maniac. Getting lost in the moment, I had to remind myself on who here was in control.

Bringing my force of nature back life, I became aggressive by slamming her down onto the floor. At first, the act of coercion was consensual until my choking only gained instead of lessened in strength. Her nails dug into my forearms as if she knew I was out of my mind in that moment. Releasing for a moment, she gritted her teeth calling me a fucking bastard only embracing the violence I bestowed.

I wanted someone a little less accepting, not some bitch that was just as crazy and disturbed as I was. Shoving me onto my back, the woman stuck me in her mouth viciously inhaling every inch. A snarl had my nostril pulled up as her teeth sank in. I reached down beneath me in search of an old hunting knife I kept hidden between my mattresses, specifically for moments like this.

My dick wasn't what I wanted to fucking choke the whore with. I took a fist full of her hair, slamming her down several times before taking the knife directly to the back of her neck. Feeling it pierce through her throat, I wriggled the blade as she bled out onto my floor.

Depraved as I was, I motioned her head up and down a few more times finally enjoying the oral attention she sucked at to begin with. The sound of her final breath was like music to my ears, only a symphony the devil could acquire.

    I twitched, sitting forward on my couch regaining my surroundings. It was three in the fucking morning and I still felt drunker than ever. I grabbed my phone finally deciding to reply to Mandy's text message. I figured she would grow tired of my whiskey assisted text messaging, but instead she diverted them. Never to ask any questions, Mandy and I found ourselves tangled up within my sheets raging with the mighty imperative of tempest urgencies faltered by illicit coveting.

Breaking At What Seems   Kyla M. Wassil

SEVEN

The circulating chill from the ceiling fan twitched my uncovered leg, causing me to groan uncomfortably as my eyes opened. I watched the blades rotate too fast for me to grasp one in specific. Looking to my left was an angel silently resting in a peaceful state of mind. Her representation of serenity was the stripes to my plaid as I suffered mental strife for nights on end these past few weeks.

    I slipped out of bed as quietly as possible, resting my bare feet onto the hardwood floor. I sat Gerry on the glass coffee table observing his tedious life while a pot of coffee brewed in the distance of my kitchen. My gaze sharpened as his eyes met my reflection and for a moment we seemed to have a stare off until I sprinkled flakes of food into the placid water.

    Nipping at the food like a tyrant engaging in frenzy, I placed my hands on either side of his bowl peering down into the opening. Gerry came to the surface inhaling pieces of fish food a tiny fragment at a time until there was nothing left.

    The coolness of the glass rested in my palms caused an uninvited glitch within my right temporal lobe. My eyes squeezed shut as my muscles tightened in reaction to conflicted imagery that promised to shatter my skull if I dared to ignore the warning. More pictorial memories flashed through my head consisting of battered and beaten women whom I felt were familiar but couldn't bring a name to each profile.

    My teeth clenched so hard I could hear them grit inside my mouth as my fingertips lacked circulation due to extensive pressure against the glass. A whisper nearly lost upon wind drew my attention towards the doors of my balcony. Taking in a deep breath, I stood to my feet standing motionless as I waited for the voice to lure me further.

    "Savannah?" **I whispered.**

Sliding the door open with caution, I poked my head out feeling the welcoming sun emit its warmth across my unkempt face. Taking a vice grip to the railing, my head slowly turned in the direction of Savannah's balcony. The wind carried tumult agitation as my name broke through the air like a bullet piercing remnants of the dead.

There she stood, leaned over the balcony baring a cigarette between those luscious lips set in a devious smile. My eyes deepened as smoke exhaled through her nostrils.

"Who are we today Kevin, Dr. Jekyll or Mr. Hyde?" **She giggled.**

As tormenting as it's been without her company, I ignored the fact of how depressed she'd made me while on a secret voyage. *"Glad you've finally decided to show your face again."*

"Has someone missed me?"

"More than you can imagine. Where the fuck have you been?" **I was angered.**

"Oh you know, here and there while lurking upon roof tops, straying away from city lights casting a spotlight on Manhattan's inhabitants. Where have you been?"

"Out of mind to put it mildly while worried about your whereabouts."

"Like a typical cop would." **She cut her eyes, taking another drag.** *"I see you've taken consideration to my suggestion where comfort is concerned."*

"What is a guy to do?" **I sucked my teeth, hardening my posture.**

"Well, it must be captivating due to the vibrational echoes my wall endured all night until the early hours of this morning. Are we catching feelings? Or just imagining me through her..." **Savannah's eyes darkened.**

My posture threw all but caution to the wind as my skin boiled in offensive deplore. *"Maybe if you hadn't left me in the way you always do, I wouldn't have turned to the nearest affection. Like you have room to talk."* **My jaw ticked.**

Savannah looked taken aback as she disintegrated her finished cigarette with the tips of her fingers. *"What the hell are you referring to, Kevin?"*

"That fucking jackass I've seen on multiple occasions leaving from or heading to your apartment... and if he runs into me again, I will slit his fucking throat where he stands!"

"Wow," **Her eyes widened.** *"Someone has reached a volatile level of jealousy and aggression. That is so unlike you, it's kind of sexy."*

I laughed in reluctance to her compliment. *"She is a perfect outlet. I reached the release that I've longed for quite some time."*

Savannah rolled in her bottom lip as her eyes met the floor. *"Glad she has been of help to you, Kevin."*

"Am I sensing jealousy on the opposing end?"

"Don't allow the uproar of your ego to devour the impossible." **She rolled her eyes.**

Before I could respond, Savannah's eyes enlarged with awareness as she looked past me. *"Your company awaits the unresisting attention you're destined to provide."*

I turned my head to see Mandy dressed in a tank top and lace bottoms, offering me a cup of coffee. *"Hey you silent escape artist, who were you talking to?"*

Thank you and my neighbor…" **My voice broke as Savannah vanished from sight.**

"Hmm… well I guess your neighbor went back inside?"

I closed my eyes embracing the softness of Mandy's lips against my shoulder blade. She reached a hand under my arm to grip my chest, pulling me further into her. I glanced over my shoulder admiring the innocence she carried so well.

"How'd you sleep?"

"Great, until I awoke with you no longer lying beside me." **She frowned.**

I faced her, cupping her jaw in my palm. *"I assure you I haven't gone too far, sweetie. I just enjoy being on my balcony."* **I gave one last look towards Savannah's way before guiding Mandy and myself back inside.**

"What's Gerry doing on the table?"

"Strange enough, I decided to watch his behavior this morning."

"Well, all right then." **She smiled.**

I downed the remaining contents in my mug before getting ready for work. Mandy stood in the mirror applying makeup as I observed from afar while buttoning my shirt. Feeling militant as I held an unwavering glare, I had to have her against me. Nearly approaching her with exaggerate stride, I placed a hand on her hip with the other gripping her breast. Mandy bent forward to my unexpected gesture releasing a sigh.

"Kevin..."

"Shh..." **I took her tube of mascara, placing it back down onto the counter.**

Watching her in the mirror, I lowered my hand to the front of her dress pants feeling her hand overlapping as she fell into my touch. The moisture layered my fingertips as I went further until I reached my desired location. Mandy gasped, taking a hand to the back of my head.

"Oh, Kevin… that feels amazing." **She whispered.**

I gripped the back of her hair in a familiar way as evil preyed on my actions. I wanted to push past the limitations of what most people would allow. As Mandy reached back grabbing the front of my pants, I, in return took mine to her throat pulling her harder against me. I growled in frustration after hearing her ringtone sounding in the distance of my bedroom.

"You should probably get that."

Mandy sighed aggressively while adjusting herself on the way to retrieve her phone. It was someone from her job which had her grabbing her things in a hurry. *"We're not finished here."* **She said pressing her lips into mine before taking off.**

I stood there looking at my reflection in the mirror not seeing who I wanted to see. What appeared in reflection was a satanic creature that lacked obedience, tearing at the surface longing for its release. Whatever I was fighting deep within had to be taken up with Father Delatonni. I was unrecognizable to myself, and before too long, I may be to others around me as well.

Breaking At What Seems   Kyla M. Wassil

EIGHT

Driving along the streets of my patrol route, I was self-absorbed and consumed by my own dismal of inept thoughts that circulated throughout my electro-chemical reservoir. The more these envisions thrived, the more I was shaken in a future failure of temperance. Long, tanned legs dressed in navy blue shorts and a grey cardigan entered a coffee shop on my right hand side. The dryness of my mouth lacking the secretion of moisture had me parked outside, following moments behind.

A few other customers were in line before me, but I could still see who I wanted to from afar. The way she ran her fingers through her black hair, pushing it away from her face had me tugging at my belt. I licked my lips watching her pull the coffee cup to her tiny mouth, taking a cautious sip. Moving over to the station with straws and whatnot, she began to pour sugar in gently stirring it. My eyes pierced the steam that levitated above the dark liquid's surface. Placing the stir stick in her mouth I longed to fill, she licked off the sweet remains plastering me in desideratum.

"What can I get for you, sir?"

Bringing my attention forward to the cashier, her face scorned with impatience. I couldn't tell you how long my attention was drawn to this woman at the additive station, but from the awkward stares I received from those around me caused a longer pause for response.

"Shit, whatever she's drinking..."

"A Mocha Frappuccino?" The cashier pressed her lips together.

By her agitation, I returned the gesture by clenching my jaw. *"Yeah, if that's what the name of it is."* I arched an eyebrow.

A gentleman behind me snickered at my smartass remark. Returning my view to the woman I was intently gawking at, I spotted her seated alone at a table by the window; reading from her Tablet.

Taking a firm grip on my cup, I tried my best to control the impulse of wanting to knock the cashier the fuck out for being so rude.

Nearing the woman, she felt my presence as her golden eyes reached mine. My, how magnificent she appeared. Damn near flawless mocha skin, eyebrows perfectly arched and teeth so white I longed to sink into my skin. I knew it was the same girl that had stuck my attention days ago—and now she was inches away.

"What are ya reading there?"

Her head immediately turned in my direction. *"Oh, um a novel by E.L. James..."* **She answered nervously.**

"Really? I'm not much of a reader, but I admire a pretty young woman who can lose herself within the pages of contemporary romance. I also didn't mean to startle you."

Her smile widened as she became more relaxed. *"For a man who seemingly so doesn't read, you sure know a little something about genres."*

"I have a lot of useless facts in my head." **I admittedly shrugged.**

My eyes were suddenly drawn to the hand she ran up and down the inside of her thigh. Swallowing hard, I nearly lost myself right there as she gazed at my uniform.

"Are you still on duty?"

"Just started my shift actually, I'll be on until later tonight. Why?"

The girl pulled her Tablet to her chest, grabbing ahold of her coffee cup as she stood to her feet. "I don't have class until noon and I've always wanted to do a ride along with an officer."

"Is that so? What are you in school for?"

"Criminology and suggestive law study."

"Makes sense." **I scratched my chin.** "If you follow me to my precinct we can run a back ground check and you can ride with me for a bit if you really want to?"

"I'd love to, Officer Strode." **She winked.**

"Please, address me as Kevin."

I took in a deep breath as my eyes guided my body out the door behind her. Could it be that all this time it was in fact this simple to get some tail just by being in uniform? The five minutes it took to arrive at Midtown North couldn't have seemed so prolonged.
 The results took fifteen minutes to come back; in the meantime, I had her fill out tedious paperwork. Staring at her I.D. the name Jene Scavenski imprinted in my brain. Chief Mortkin allowed her access to ride with me and it didn't take long for her to jump into the front seat of my patrol car.
 We rode through the veins of the city, remaining

within my jurisdiction. She'd ask subtle questions within shortness of breath being filled with excitement. The truth is I didn't know a damn thing about this woman. Even though I was supposed to practice enforcement for the law and keep everyone around me safe. I could be putting myself in potential danger by becoming this risqué. I just couldn't fucking help myself with the way the light caught the perfected body seated next to me. I've never seen anyone grasp a Venusian persona such as her. If my inflicted personality would just abide by the limitation of mental restraints, I wouldn't be in this predicament to begin with. Just because she bears a clean record does not mean she wasn't prone to causing destruction in the future, or perhaps has never been caught doing something unlawful.

    To my surprise, today was unusually quiet over the dispatch, so I parked beneath a shady tree down at Tompkins Square. The thoughts rolling through my mind entered extreme turbulence once Jene reached over running her fingers across my brass insignias.

    An intrigued smirk tugged at the corners of her mouth as her eyes reached mine. My jaw clenched to the sensation of her nails tracing the back of my neck as she closed in on the side of my face with a whisper.

    "Have you ever thought to break the rules, Kevin?"

    "What are you implying?" **My voice crackled.**

    I have never been one to bend the rules while on duty, but here lately I haven't given much thought to giving a damn about my actions. I knew the streets and alleyways of Manhattan like the back of my hand. I knew exactly what she wanted and I was more than willing to give it to her.

    I reached up to turn off my police camera, undoing my seatbelt as Jene slid her hand between my legs. Looking around cautiously my soul completely cremated underneath my skin as she slid off her shorts crawling onto my lap. Grinding hard against my suffocating erection, Jene unzipped my pants pulling out my length to view it.

> *"I want you fuck me and while doing so keep in mind just how dangerous this is for the both of us..."*

    She sighed pushing me completely inside of her. My body tensed up to her tight, moist tissue engulfing my size until our pelvises pressed flush against one another. I gripped her hips letting her ride to her satisfaction until the devil rose within me.

    Taking both of her hands behind her, I held them tightly together to keep her from touching me further. Panting as an orgasm formed in my gut, I pressed my face into her chest as she threw her head back moaning aggressively. Becoming dark minded, I sank my teeth into her neck as she slammed into me harder.

> *"Ugh. Oh-my-God, Kevin!"* **She growled.**

    I liked being in control and having the power to do whatever my blackened heart desired. For whatever reason my mind has altered these past few weeks, I have never felt more alive. Almost as if I found another side of me, though it was possessively tormenting and demonic; I couldn't get enough of its infinite mortality.

My eyes narrowed as her body convulsed, releasing warm liquid around me as she fell against me drawing my head to her chest. Breathing deep, I realized I contained myself only to relish in a greater pleasure once I saw Mandy again. What a crude bastard I was?

"Calling all units in the area! We have a 187 case. Other suspects are subject to being witnessed on site."

"Shit..." **I groaned, pushing Jene back into the passenger seat.**

"What the hell is a 187?"

I frantically zipped my pants barely missing the skin of my dick, throwing the car into reverse. I flicked on my lights and sirens, hauling ass down the street.

"This is 713 responding, what's the location? I'm heading East bound from Tompkins Square Park, now."

"541 East 13th Street."

"This is Investigator Maxwell Harty, responding to dispatch. I am on the way with the crime scene unit. Officer Strode, I will meet you momentarily."

"10-4."

Jene quickly slid on her shorts, yanking her seatbelt secured. *"What's going on?"*

Appearing panicked, I did my best to calm her nerves. *"There's been a homicide reported towards the Upper East Side."*

"How exciting..." **Her voice broke.**

Pulling up to the building another mindset consumed my mentality. Jumping out of the car, Jene stuck right behind me. I drew my pistol creeping around the side of the building locating an entry way. Kicking through a door, planting hasty feet upon the glazed floor below, I felt Jene tuck into my side; trembling. Looking from left to right hearing movement coming from the floor above had me jerk my motion as I began to run.

A loud thud had Jene and I tearing up the stairwell to reach our destination. Pausing movement, I stood silent to listen further. My heart was beating through my chest as Jene's panting echoed in my ear. I turned to cup her mouth with reassurance.

"Jene, calm down. I won't let anything happen to you, I give you my word." **I whispered.**

She nodded as the dilation of her pupils reflected my appearance. Further commotion came from the apartment as a scream soon followed. Piercing my ear, I suddenly busted through the door ready for whatever was on the other side.

"NYPD, come out with your hands up, now!" **I yelled.**

Breaking At What Seems

Kyla M. Wassil

Shots were fired from the end of the hallway that barely missed my head.

"Holy shit!" **I ducked, pulling Jene down with me.** *"More officers are on the way, come out you bastard! I am armed and will fucking shoot you, damnit!"*

An eerie silence took its toll on my irrationality, disturbing what was required of me as a law enforcement officer. Slowly making my way towards the hallway, a trail of blood leading to the kitchen caught my attention. As my neck stretched for a further view, all I could see were legs leading out from a stiff body.

Looking over my shoulder, Jene was hugging herself baring a pale face as her lips quivered. I motioned for her to stay put as I entered the kitchen. The body became a noted victim lying in a pool of their own blood, suffering horrific stab wounds to the chest, face and abdomen.

I knelt down to check for a pulse when the ruckus of a closet door busted open. Simultaneously, Max and Officer Gibbs entered the house, running to my position. Max's face was horrified as he looked at the victim's body when a man came running at us with an axe, chopping away at the air as I tried shoving him off. He missed my head and shoulder, chopping into the kitchen table. Each wield of the axe became more intense as he longed to end my life.

"Max! Go make sure Jene is okay!"

"No, I'm not leaving you!"

"There are more people in this fucking house, damnit! They are armed, go find them!"

Max took his uncertain leave, searching for the others alongside Officer Gibbs. Knowing he could have shot this man for assaulting me, he let me have this fight.

Gritting my teeth, I gathered my inner strength to grab his hand—breaking his wrist to release the weapon. Turning over to reach for my pistol that flew from my hand, I felt weight drop onto my back as a wooden chair shattered around me.

The man kicked me in the ribs several times before stepping on my hand I used to reach. Rage filled my body as his hand took ahold of my pistol and for once I didn't fear for my life. I instead embraced the danger looking the bastard in his soulless eyes.

Jene appeared behind him busting his head open with a wooden leg from the broken chair. His eyes rolled into the back of his head as he fell to his knees. Jene stood over him with tears, covered in sweat as I immediately rolled over to retrieve my pistol.

I could hear Officer Gibbs and Max in the background screaming at another suspect. I placed cuffs on the man Jene had knocked out, meeting everyone back in the living area. The man they placed in cuffs was scraggly, wearing a beard brushed with grey. His clothes were worn and his skin was dirty.

"You dare to kill a fucking Officer, you piece of shit?"

I took ahold of his collar, throwing him from Max's grip. He landed on the floor completely helpless as I struck the man over and over again in the face until the veins in my fist busted beneath my skin's surface.

"Jesus Christ, Kevin, that's enough!" **Max yelled, pulling me off.**

Officer Gibbs ran over picking the man up to escort him outside while the Crime Scene Unit barged through the door. I heaved aggressively as I wiped the blood from my nose, sharpening my gaze upon Max.

"Jene, come on. Let's get ya outta here."

Max yanked me aside, tightening his grip on my collar. *"Kevin, you can't be displaying such madness! Especially in front of a fucking ride along. Christ, you can lose your job for such violence against a suspect—you know this! What the hell has gotten into you, lately?"*

"Nothing? The son of a bitch almost killed both Jene and I! Wouldn't you have beaten the shit out of him if you walked on site to see your best friend dead?"

"Kevin, that isn't the case here." **Max clenched his jaw.**

"Bullshit! I'm taking her home."

"I'm just looking out for you, Kevin. Go home and cool off, please?"

I brushed off his remark escorting Jene back to my patrol car. For a moment, no words were exchanged upon not knowing what to say.

"Well, I missed my class today." **Jene sighed.**

"I deeply apologize for what happened. My days are unpredictable. I figured you fully understood the risk you were taking when signing those papers."

Jene reached over grabbing my hand. *"Don't apologize. It was all well worth the venture."*

"By the way, I didn't get the chance to thank you for saving my life back there. That was very virtuous of you." **I smiled.** *"You're going to make an outstanding investigator if you choose to do so."*

Her hand reached up rubbing my cheek. *"I'll definitely think about you while tangled up in my own fantasies."*

My eyes enlarged as I struggled to swallow with the reminder of not getting off earlier. Mandy was certainly in for a surprise in the coming days.
I took Jene back to the station to sign a release form before dropping her off at the Berkeley College.

"Have a good day and be safe." **I threw on the charm.**

Opening the passenger side door, Jene grabbed her tablet, leaning over to peck my cheek. *"No, you be* *safe, Officer Strode."* **She winked before heading off into the building.**

I sat stroking my chin absentmindedly wishing it were something else lying in the desperation to be handled. I was well overdue for my visitation to Father Delatonni, though I was shamed by the things I had to relay.

Breaking At What Seems   Kyla M. Wassil

NINE

Standing near the Ferris wheel, I am captivated by the variation of flickering lights. My eyes remained fixated upon the laughing passengers riding in each gondola. Shadows of passing citizens fell upon me as I stood solitarily in worn overalls brushed with dirt particles. The only companion I claimed was that of the solo red balloon that clung to my right wrist. Hearing joyful laughter off in the distance drew my attention as I turned to witness children of my age playing a carnival game. My eyes darted on the tiny goldfish confined in small plastic bags full of water. Nearing the game, the carnie persuaded me to play with his overbearing toothless Joe persona. The object was to get a plastic ball into a glass bowl, seemed easy enough. But it wasn't, in fact the fucking game was ridiculously hard considering ping pong balls bounce once coming in contact with glass. Defiance rose in me as the carnie laughed at my failed attempt, but I wanted a fucking fish and for this jackass to shut the hell up. So my next move was to throw the entire bucket of balls upward hoping by chance one of the bastards landed in a bowl. Balls pinged and scattered all about as my gaze became acute while I held my breath. By luck, two balls landed into a bowl and a smirk pulled at my mouth as I darted my eyes towards the carnie, awaiting my prize. He handed me two bags containing lonely goldfish, I couldn't have felt more pride as I strutted my way home with two new companions.

  Suddenly, I am sitting in a room surrounded by fish tanks of all sizes containing different species of fish. For hours, I'd find myself sitting in the center of the room gazing upon the fish as they swam around longing for a change of scenery, maybe even a possible escape. But they couldn't leave me; no one who I brought into my world was ever allowed to leave until I granted permission. Taking leave from my vice grip always ended

Breaking At What Seems

Kyla M. Wassil

in a shower of blood as I stood boisterous over the mess I made.

Rising from a deep slumber, I hung my feet over the edge of my bed. A knot in my chest had me rather disturbed with inner turmoil. Making my way into my bathroom the lightening burned my eyes as I captured my reflection in the mirror before me.

Running my hands against the dark grain on my face, I took ahold of my razor. Splashing some water onto my skin to comfort a less jagged shave wasn't my best idea. Rounding the razor against the underside of my jawline sent a burning sensation through my nervous system as blood trickled down my neck.

"Ah, shit!" I instantly threw my razor against the sink.

Standing peeved as I took a towel to my wound, I heard a knock at my door. Releasing a rugged breath, I went to see who it was. Without using the peephole, I instead swung the door open to no one on the opposing side. Looking from left to right then back again, the hallway stood vacant.

Slamming the door, I returned to finish torturing myself with an attempt to clean up my face. I dressed myself for comfort to enjoy a day off, trying to control my anger. Dropping flakes of food into Gerry's bowl, I leaned against the counter watching him feed while my coffee finished brewing. Grabbing a cup, I walked out onto my balcony to embrace the morning air.

"A Jets jersey and jeans? Wow, never seen you in attire such as that."

My head jerked towards the sound of Savannah's giggling. *"It's game day. Besides, I'm off so I'd rather wear anything other than brass and Navy."*

"Temper, temper. Did you not sleep well last night?" **She lit a cigarette.**

Smoke traveled through the air making its way into my nostrils uninvited. Smelling the secondhand drew me to wanting one myself. *"You mind throwing me one of those?"*

Savannah's expression became stupefied as she held up her pack. *"Kevin fucking Strode just asked for a cigarette? Holy shit, I need a recap!"* **She tossed the pack over to me, shaking her head.**

"I've never smoked one, but for some reason I want one."

I pulled out a stick inspecting it before placing it under my nose for a sniff. The smell of fresh tobacco triggered visions in my mind of times I've held one in my hand. Yet, as far as I could remember, I have never smoked one until this very moment.

"Here's a lighter."

I caught the pink plastic once it came into reach, gripping it within my palm. Placing the cigarette between my lips, I flicked the lighter igniting the tiny

flame. Chemicals and smoke filled my throat and lungs, singeing my bronchioles. I released a violent cough hearing Savannah crumble in hysteria as I bent over the railing trying to catch a clear breath.

"Jesus fuck! How do you smoke these things?" **I gasped.**

"Not like that." **She laughed even harder.**

"Ah, ha. Fuck you." **I then smiled.**

"Hey, you're the one who wanted to attempt it. You are a grown ass man, I am not gonna tell ya you can't. Though, I will say you probably shouldn't."

"Well, I wasn't raised to waste, so like the grateful bastard I am, I shall finish it."

Savannah belted out into more laughter, nearly choking. *"Surely you will. You're fucking crazy, Kevin."*

I clenched my jaw to her remark wondering if her words spoke truth. Am I fucking crazy? Have I lost my way to who I am or who I'm supposed to be? The vibration of my phone buzzing in my pocket interrupted our conversation as Mandy's name lit up my screen. A surge of sexual energy rushed through my veins knowing she was minutes away from entering my chambers.

"By the sudden change in your posture, I'd assume that your mistress is on her way."

"Damn, aren't you good at reading people?"

"No, just you…" **She defiantly flicked her cigarette butt off the railing.**

"You're lucky I'm not on duty or I totally would have just cited you for that."

"Ooh… how terrifying?" **She jeered with an eye roll.**

I could sense a bit of jealousy radiating from Savannah as she stood with her arms crossed. She may have been my social weakness but Mandy was my physical weakness and if I didn't get this urge out, I may end up putting a hit out for the innocence of someone else.

"I guess I'd better go wait on her. I will see ya later."

Savannah pressed her lips together with a nod in response. I sighed uncertain to leave her until a knock on my door had my pace quicken in its direction. Opening it to a flawless beauty, I was ready to devour down to the bones that stood before me. My pulse amplified as my nerves ticked beneath my skins surface once her hand met my face.

"Oh dear, Kev, did you cut yourself shaving?"

"Yeah, but I've experienced worse infliction to my body. Get your fucking ass in here and cut the chit-chat." **I groaned.**

Breaking At What Seems

Kyla M. Wassil

      Watching Mandy enter my kitchen opening a bottle of wine, I mindlessly tuned her out while my eyes redirected on the heaving cleavage that bored its view predominantly above her tank top. Sweat formed on my temple as her hands gripped the neck of the wine bottle; biting her bottom lip in the midst of a simple struggle to conquer the cork.

      The pop of its release torqued my fascination as she pulled it to her mouth licking the maroon liquid. The reminder of smoking not too long ago had me ignore the bulge beneath my jeans as I excused myself to brush my teeth.

      Trying to contain myself around her was like a heroin addict quitting cold turkey. I stood gargling mouthwash to drown the nicotine remains with menthol as my cheeks burned. To kill time, I ran the pad of my thumb against the slit my razor made earlier this morning, flinching to its sensitivity. Irritably releasing the contents from my mouth, I gripped the sink drawing in a deep inhale. Why I stood so touchy on this day was beyond my knowing.

      Reentering my living room, Mandy sat on my couch sipping on a glass of wine. For once, I was sober and I wanted to enjoy every second I was to be inside of her. The impatience tore at the seams as my breathing became shallow.

      Her lips met the rim of the glass, tilting her head back allowing the liquid to glide smoothly into her mouth. I let out a sudden sigh as her eyes met mine with wonder.

"Kevin, you're nearly panting over there. What's the matter?"

"Excuse my repugnant remark, but goddamn do I want to fuck that pretty little mouth of yours."

Mandy's eyes enlarged as she sat her glass gently upon the coffee table, running her tongue across her top lip provokingly.

"Do you, Kevin? How badly do you crave filling my mouth unto your satisfaction?"

"I want you to take all of me in. I want you so badly to take its vitality deep within your throat until I reach my release."

Mandy grasped my belt, lifting my jersey just above my navel to view my v-cut. Pressing her lips softly against my skin, Mandy extracted her tongue running a trail within my hip's recess, leading down to the edge of my jeans. Her warm breath solidified my erection as I undid my belt. My rigidness suffocated to the point of hurting from the harsh pressure my jeans suppressed.

Mandy's eyes met mine, narrowed but unwavering as her tongue ran alongside my length. I reached my hand behind her head gripping a fist full of hair.

"Take me all the way in, baby."

Mandy's sigh sent chills up my spine as she engulfed me entirely. I became aggressive from the

excelling pleasure as my knees threatened to give out. Slamming her head into me, Mandy dug her nails into my ass sucking at me harder. I didn't want to come yet, but I felt it deep in my gut as my breathing pattern became difficult.

"Look me in my eyes as I come onto that soft pallet that's hidden in the depths of those lovely lips."

Mandy's eyes reached mine as her suction locked onto me bringing on an orgasm instantly. Pushing her head back, I watched my release pump onto her tongue as she twirled circles around the head of my erection.

Yanking her to her feet, I threw her onto my waist, slamming her down onto the couch. Ripping off her jeans, I longed to relish in the taste of her on my tongue. The shine of her excitement had my face buried deep between her thighs.

Placing her legs over my shoulders, Mandy screamed and moaned while clawing into my scalp. I didn't stop until I felt her legs shaking; swollen and engorged, I was ready to push myself inside of her.

Wrapping her legs tightly around my waist, Mandy guided me in slowly. Adjusting to my size, I watched myself disappear inside her dripping vortex. Wanted to push beyond my limitations, I shoved into her completely as her eyes dilated looking into mine. Gritting her teeth, she yanked my shirt over my head dragging her nails down my ribcage.

Excepting my invitation for rough intercourse, Mandy planted her hands into my pecs, shoving me hard onto the floor. Knocking over the wine glass, I heard it shatter as liquid poured onto my chest. Mandy tore off her tank top riding me with the extremity of a tidal wave.

Secreting her hands in wine, she ran them all over my chest before inserting a few fingers into my mouth. Sucking at them only made her become fiercer. The disappointment of being handled didn't settle so well with me. Anguish unleashed as I rose up forcing Mandy to take hold of my counter top.

Gripping the back of her head, I shoved myself inside, ramming into her over and over again until she couldn't breathe. Reaching my hand to her throat, I felt my skin scorch with excitement.

"K—Kevin...Ah..." She struggled to speak.

"I advise you to fucking still yourself, because you're not going anywhere."

Mandy managed to escape my grip taking a strong grip to my throat in return, walking me towards the couch once again. Tripping over the coffee table, I fell onto my back feeling tiny glass shards pierce into my back. Mandy stood over me with a devilish smirk.

"How does it feel to lay helplessly, Kevin?"

I curled up a nostril, seething as my back continued to burn.

"Either come down here and finish fucking me, or you can go fuck yourself!" I growled.

Breaking At What Seems — Kyla M. Wassil

"Why don't you go fuck yourself, Kevin?"

"Because, I'd rather be inside of you!" **I reached up pulled her down on top of me.**

Mandy continued grinding into me until we both met our orgasm between aggressive pants. Falling to my side, neither of us moved until able.

The breeze chilled my chest as my eyes opened to me being alone on the glass sprinkled hardwood. I sat up with a groan as a headache set in adding pain to the cuts in the flesh of my back.

"Mandy?"

No response came in return, but the door to my balcony swaying in the wind caught my attention. I stood dusting the fibers from my back, adjusting my briefs on my way to investigate.

"Mandy…if this is some kind of game you're trying to play, I am not up for it today." **My voice tightened.**

There was no sight of her on the balcony which placed worry in my chest. I glanced over the railing to see the lively activity below.

"I saw her leave earlier this morning."

I looked to see Savannah baring a careless expression.

"Did you?" **I paused only to revisit her tantrum the day before.** *"Might I ask what the hell had you so bent yesterday?"*

Savannah exaggerated her exhale, cutting her eyes. *"It wouldn't matter anyhow."*

"How the fuck do you know that? Just tell me what's going on with you... with us? I think I have a right to know."

"Despite the fact I can never be with you, I can't explain. I don't even know if I can."

I shook my head with anger. *"You're jealous of Mandy, yet you pushed me to be with her in the first goddamn place? You left me for days and now you claim an unannounced entitlement on giving a fuck?"*

Savannah looked taken aback from my crude statement. *"It isn't that simple, Kevin!"*

"It would be if you'd just fucking tell me what's going on with you!"

Looking down twiddling her fingers, Savannah refused to answer. I released a sigh to calm my harsh tone. *"Savannah... please?"*

Her eyes rose to meet mine. *"She's on her way now."*

I turned my head looking back inside my apartment with confusion only to return my view to

Savannah being gone. *"H-how do you...what the fuck? Savannah? Ugh, goddamn it!"*

  I rushed inside my apartment slamming the balcony door behind me. An uproar within my chest burst into destroying my entire living room. Yet, everything I placed my hands on caused me to fall into a slight seizure, twitching my eyes to see countless bodies being ripped apart, destroyed and controlled beyond their will.

  Tormenting screams and cries for help echoed through my skull as thunder outside cracked with lightening across the overcast sky. My hand gripped the glass coffee table as I flipped it shattering it to pieces, throwing my fist into the air fighting a non-existent threat.

  The only person I was fighting was me. Exhausted mentally and physically, I fell to my knees pressing my fists into the sides of my head praying to will the torturous images and thoughts away.

  "Who am I? My God, please make it stop!" I cried. *"Please..."*

  The pinging of rain drops falling from an unforgiving saint above came pouring down onto the city. I pulled myself together throwing on a pair of pants and a shirt, grabbing a jacket to flee my apartment before I had gone postal.

  Signaling a taxi, I hopped in telling him to take me directly to Saint Patrick's. Running up to the door with haste, disappointment only crashed my hopes when they refused to open. Father Delatonni was inside commencing a private baptismal ceremony.

I sighed with defeat taking a seat on the bottom step, feeling the rain soak me to the bone. Looking up to the sky with disgust only had the rain come down even harder.

I couldn't tell you how long I sat outside, but I refused to leave until I saw Father Delatonni. Only wanting to reach serenity in my thoughts, I rested my head atop my knees as warm tears rolled down my face. Almost entering a state of sleep, the crack of the door opening had me sitting upright. A family came out opening their umbrellas as Father Delatonni escorted them out while thanking them for coming.

"Kevin? What on earth are you doing out here in this weather? You're going to get sick!"

"Father, it's so good to see you. Please, I desperately need your help!"

"Come in, my son. How long have you been waiting outside?"

"I don't know, maybe an hour or two?" I shrugged.

Father Delatonni shook his head, leading me to the church's kitchen. We sat at a table as he prepared a cup of hot tea.

"Here, drink this. It shall warm you. Tell me what's going on. I haven't seen you much lately."

Breaking At What Seems   Kyla M. Wassil

"Remember when you claimed to have witnessed something in me, perhaps something dark I may have soon come to battle? Well, it is becoming much worse."

"What exactly is happening?"

"I—I see things that I cannot control. I keep having these dreams, but they're not so much as dreams. They are more like fond memories I have stored deep inside that are coming to surface."

"What do these memories possess?"

"Mortem…horrifying victims I have never seen, Father. I am the one who is hurting them. I never see myself face to face in my dream as it all appears in first person. It's beginning to tear me apart."

Father Delatonni's face marked with worry as he listened closely. *"Is there a specific time you see these horrible things other than when you're at rest?"*

I shook my head only to think for a moment.

"What of this other woman you claim to have been seeing from time to time?"

"Savannah?" **I looked at my reflection in the cup of tea as it pulsed with ripples.**

The thought of always becoming angry while around Savannah donned on me as I pieced together my own problem. But how can that be? I thought of the day she kissed me and we suddenly shared the same cogitation.

"*Do you want me to come by and bless your home? You can even do it yourself by using a candle and the vile of holy water I gave you. It may be more effective if I use the Theophany water, blessing it as I walk through your home.*"

"*Are you suggesting paranormal activity has taken place within my home?*"

"*I'm not quite certain on that. But to ease your conscience, I'd advise the blessing of your sanctuary to feel safe. I'm no doctor, Kevin. I can only offer spiritual guidance in my attempt to help heal your inner suffering, for whatever may be harming your vessel that's inflicting hazard on your soul.*"

"*If you do go through with blessing my home, and this continues…*"

"*Then I suggest you seek professional help through medical attention.*"

I nodded in response, drinking the rest of my tea. "*Thank you, Father. I will try to commence the blessing of my home, myself.*"

"*Before you go, I have something for you.*"

He stood to walk towards the cupboard. Inside were bottles of water, rice, candles and other things I couldn't identify.

"Here is a pin resembling a guardian angel, for it shall keep you safe. Wear it whenever you feel is necessary. Also, here is a small bag of salt."

"Salt?" **I raised an eyebrow.**

"Yes, it symbolizes purity, fidelity, loyalty and most importantly, durability. Place it around your windows and doorways. It forms a barrier of permanence that no evil shall pass through. Let me know how things turn out for you. I'm worried about you, as is your mother and father. Pay them a visit to give them some peace of mind."

I buried the salt deep into my jacket pocket, leaving the pin rested on my collar where Father had originally placed it.

Grabbing the nearest cab, I sat shivering in damp clothing on the way back to my apartment. Entering my home, I noticed my living room was cleaned up. It appeared barren due to the loss of my coffee table and lamp I violently destroyed earlier.

On the counter rested next to Gerry was another fish bowl, floating inside was a turquoise Beta. Mandy had left a note beside it.

Kevin,

I figured Gerry would like to see another reflection despite his own. Not entirely sure what hurricane entered your home but I cleaned up the devastation. I care for you so much already, whatever you may be battling just know that I am here for you. -Mandy.

Pulling the new addition in closely for a look, I sensed a presence coming from the darkness of my bedroom. Mandy slowly entered the lighting, approaching me with caution. No expression wore on her face except tepidness by default.

"How'd you get in here?"

"Your door was unlocked when I arrived."

My eyes welcomed her gesture as she reached out to touch my face. Falling into the feel of her fingertips, I overlapped her hand with mine.

"Thank you, for cleaning up my disaster and for my new little friend." **I smiled.**

"You're quite welcome."

"Why did you leave me without a notice this morning?"

"Why are your clothes soaked?" **She pressed her lips together.**

Realizing the commencement of irritability rising in my eyes, Mandy answered quickly. *"I was still a little upset for your actions yesterday..."*

"My actions?" **My brows drew together.**

"You were rather forceful with me," **Her eyes searched mine.** *"It frightened me a bit. Kevin, I'm down for whatever. But I'm not one to be pushed into*

disrespectful slander when it comes to handling me during sex. Sorry to disappoint."

I opened my mouth to speak only to close it again. I ran a hand through my hair trying to find the words to say. *"It isn't disappointing, I am sorry for the way I acted. To be honest, I don't even know what came over me? I haven't been myself here lately. The reason my clothes appear damp is because I went to see my priest for some guidance."*

Mandy's eyes filled with concern as she turned me to face her. *"Kevin, whatever is bothering you, I am here to listen."*

"It isn't that I can't express it to you, I just don't know what it is to even begin."

Her eyes glanced over to the fish bowls as her cheeks reddened. I pulled her in by the waist, gently running a hand through her hair.

"I appreciate anything and everything you do. It will never go unnoticed. I wish I could tell you what it is I'm facing, but it's so ominously depicted by the spawn of evil—I just can't seem to figure it out."

Mandy delineated my jaw structure, running the pad of her thumb across my lips. *"Like I said, I'm here…no matter the cost. Just please don't turn me away."*

I tipped her chin to gaze into oceanic glossy eyes, pressing my lips against hers. Luring our bodies to

Breaking At What Seems
Kyla M. Wassil

the shower, our lips never dared to part as Mandy fell into accepting the disgruntled titan of my nature.

Breaking At What Seems   Kyla M. Wassil

TEN

***D**elicate as my mind may seem, it splits at the seams like a ship that's clutched within the Kraken's grasp. I'm no devil, though I pride myself unruly and detriment as I pose to others around me in such a way. I cannot control my urges, just like the trees cannot control* *each break away of leaves as the wind blows a gust so fury. Yet, I can control my strength as if one tiny, premature bud were to fall into my palm; leaving my eyes to gain upon its distinct beauty in which makes it different from all the rest. The purity of its pressure resembles that of the slightest force of gravity landing upon a land mine. Do I dare rescue one carrying a mind just as inquisitive? Or let them drown in the overrated trench of absolution? I never considered having a so called 'hit list', though I have a few in mind that I have yet to take the fuck out from this world. Who am I to play God you might ask? I claim to be no such thing, I am far worse than the all mighty ascendency that realms in secrecy above.*

    I lay awake, staring into the ceiling above. The thought of moving overwhelmed me, for I wish I entered paralysis. It took every bit of motivation within just to move from place to place today. Despite not feeling myself for weeks now, I have become comfortable in the flesh that clothed my bones.

    I stood for several long minutes just watching my fishes swim aimlessly around their tiny bowls. Keeping them a safe distance prevented stress and the cost of their lives. I stared at my new fish, trying to decipher a proper name. I laughed to myself when Ferguson came to mind, so I kept it as so.

    Exiting my front door, my eyes glanced down towards Savannah's when a faint shadow looked to have passed right through the wall. I stood in a momentary shudder, wanting to believe my eyes were only deceiving me. They darted towards the floor before taking one last look of reassurance; yet there was nothing there. I missed her; I became exceptionally aggressive while around her but I longed for the feeling. I liked the way it took over my thought process and how masculine it made me seem as I mentally choked the horrific thoughts Savannah would bring to light. I craved the barbaric passion that has recently been engraved into my being in the similar way her nails dug into my skin. Leaving me to remain bleeding, and burning.

    I wanted to feel it again; I *needed* to feel it again. I made it a must to have her over once I came home to the point I could barely focus on what I was doing on duty. My day was long, but it was certainly quiet until a car flew around the corner, nearly smashing into my front end.

    I could feel my eyes darken as the knot in my chest had the gas pedal pressed firmly into the floorboard. I flicked on my lights and sirens, hauling ass after this lunatic. Chasing him for nearly five minutes on a hot pursuit, the bastard finally lets up and pulled over. I reported to dispatch of a potential DUI on sight before exiting my patrol car.

    Pulling my gun from its holster, I swiftly approach the car. With a forceful bang, I slam the grip against his window ordering for him to step out. Misunderstanding me, the jackass decided to roll his window down with a blank look underlined with stupidity.

> *"I said step out of your vehicle, now!"*

Becoming impatient, I secured my gun before ripping his door wide open. He immediately put his hands up, sheltering his face. I huffed with disgust as turmoil boiled beneath my skin.

"Fucking Christ, get the fuck out for the third goddamn time! What's the matter with ya?"

I took both hands to his jacket, physically removing him from the car. I could barely understand a word beyond his drunken muttering. Turning his back to me, I slammed him against the car spreading his legs while retrieving my cuffs.

"You understand why I pulled you over, correct?"

"I—I uh, no…no I do not, officer."

"All right wise ass. How about you are well over the legal limit for intoxication while operating a vehicle? Your car reeks like a damn brewery. Do you understand now?"

"Man, I had like two drinks about an hour ago. This is some bullshit!"

"Since you want to lie to me, now I'm going to take legal action."

"Are you fucking serious?"

The intoxicated driver became overly aggressive as he tried yanking away from my restraint. I became irate, slamming him into the car once more as my voice rose.

Breaking At What Seems

Kyla M. Wassil

"*You have the right to remain silent. Anything you say can and will be used in the court of law. You have the right to talk to a lawyer and have him present with you while you are being questioned. If you cannot afford a lawyer, one will be appointed to represent you before any questioning if you wish. You can decide at any time to exercise these rights and not answer any questions or make any statements. Do you understand each of these rights that I have explained to you?*"

"*Man, fuck you! How's that for an understanding?*"

I shoved him over to my patrol car, throwing him into the back seat. A smile tugged at my mouth as he attempted to kick me with both feet. I flew in after him, pressing my palm into his throat.

"*Listen here, you smug bastard*" **I gritted my teeth.** "*I deal with a lot of ignorant fucks like you every day! I have no problem fighting you on the streets, I promise you will lose. Sit down and shut your fucking mouth or things will only get worse from here! Understood?*"

I raised my eyebrows waiting for another sarcastic remark to exit his mouth, but he said nothing further. He continued to stare out the window on the way to the station. Lucky for me, he was my last bit of entertainment for the evening.

On my way out, I asked a fellow officer to bum a cigarette while I awaited a taxi. Zoning out, watching the flow of the city around me a sudden disaster broke

my attention. I suddenly felt a hand smack across mine in which bared the cancer stick.

"What in the fuck is that? Are...are you smoking? Christ, Kevin, what the hell! Since when did you pick up a bad habit such as that?"

I clenched my jaw, bending down to pick it up. *"For your information, I've recently picked up a lot of strange habits. Don't be such a dick about it!"*

"Kevin, you run...like all the time. These things are just going to slow you down and kill you! What possessed you to even start?"

I shredded the wasted tobacco onto the pavement while glaring back at Max. His unwavering gaze had my nerves sizzling for I knew he awaited a more appropriate response.

"Look, I don't know? I haven't been feeling myself here lately. Smoking seemed to alleviate some of the stress since drinking only brought on violent outbursts in the result of destroying half of my apartment." **I sighed.**

"But smoking? Come on Kevin...if need be I'd rather take you out to find some college tail and guard the dorm while you fuck her brains out. Even meet you half way on a bottle of whiskey."

"I get it, Max! Christ, you're acting like my damn mother. I put it out. I'm finished, all right? Can you please loosen my balls before you castrate me?"

"I just care about ya. I'd rather see you go down from our line of duty, not willingly by manufactured chemicals and rat poison."

I forcefully ran my tongue across the front of my teeth praising the lord as the next taxi rolled up.

"That was beyond dramatic. I'll see ya tomorrow, Max."

"Yeah, be safe. And stop fucking smoking!" **He called after me.**

I shook my head at his nagging, slamming the taxi door shut. I had one thing on my mind and it was Savannah. Though, instead something else occurred that completely disrupting my plans. Opening my door displayed the unexpected.

Mandy was perched up on my couch, dressed in lace with a half empty bottle of wine resting on the floor. My upper lip twitched as I tried to find words to engage a proper greeting. Taking in her half barren body that lied submissive upon my couch had a burning ache torching within my gut.

"I want you to walk to me...slowly." **Her words broke.**

I swallowed aggressively, as the weight of my fluttered ego carried my heavy footing across the hardwood. She was in a dangerous mood yet, would it be so great that it pushed me beyond my own constrain?

As I stood only inches away, her eyes crawled

their way from my feet to my obscure expression. She traced her bottom lip persuasively with her tongue, causing me to nearly tremble.

"Kneel..." **She demanded.**

My gaze sharpened as I slowly lowered to me knees. Attempting to rest my hands upon the smooth of her things, Mandy was quick to halt my movement. I was taken aback by her rejection to my desirable intentions.

"Uh-uh... remove your hands."

"Where do you prefer them?" **My teeth clacked together.**

Reaching down fearlessly, Mandy took a hold of my handcuffs, bringing them into my view. Motioning for me to hold out my hands, I did as she commanded. With each click the cuffs made, the harder my erection ossified beneath my pants.

Leaving me to remain helpless and out of my own control, Mandy advanced to untucking my shirt. The gradual tug sent a pleasurable sensation across my briefs as our eyes locked with every movement she made.

Undoing each individual button irked my nerves as she ran her nails down my chest, leaving red stripes across my pecs. My exhale came out in a broken manner as she sat back into the couch cushion, spreading her legs.

Wetting the tips of her index and middle finger,

Mandy exceeding them down into her panties; slowly circulating them just to tease the wild beast chained before her. Falling into relaxation, her eyes closed ever so gently as soft symphonic moans escaped her precious mouth.

My breathing hardened into panting as my mindset became displaced due to her opposition. Having to regain control before climaxing, Mandy stopped while fixating her eyes deep within my own. My fingers were whitened at the tips from severe pressure applied as they gripped the edge of the couch.

Mandy slid her laced bottoms down to the floor, spreading herself open to show the shine of her flesh. I let out a rugged breath, failing to catch the one after it. Balling my fists, I couldn't take the pain in my groin much longer as I tried snapping the cuffs in half just to get to her. Leaning into my ear, Mandy placed the softness of her cheek flush with mine.

"Do you want to be inside me, Kevin?" **She whispered.**

"God, yes!" **I groaned.**

Grabbing the front of my belt, running her hand across the rigidness beneath caused a sigh to emerge. Raising an arrogant eyebrow, I felt myself slightly smile. Lowering my zipper, I felt my length stretch to the surface, free from further discomfort. Having me in one hand, Mandy scooted to the edge of the cushion placing my tip at her entrance.

I dropped my head back, ignoring the throbbing sensation as she wetted the head of my erection.

Wrapping her legs around my waist, I felt her thighs give my torso a tight squeeze as I entered her fully. Gasping aggressively, Mandy took her nails to the back of my scalp, digging them in as I plunged deeper.

"You can touch me, baby."

I spread my fingers wide, gripping them into her hips to hold her tightly against me. Unsnapping her bra, the smooth warmth of her breast pressed against the tight flesh of my chest had my intentions unravel.

Wanting me further inside, Mandy held my head into her chest crying from indescribable pleasure. I felt the temperature simmering into the threads that sheltered my back as sweat dripped down my spine. Kissing down my neck, meeting my lips with intense destruction, Mandy shoved my shirt down to the crook of my arms releasing the trapped heat.

Dragging my coarse facial hair against her collar bone with every thrust had Mandy slamming into me harder. Sweat soon reached my fingertips from her back as we both gleamed under the lighting.

"I want more of you..." I growled, hoisting her higher up as I stood to my feet.

I shoved her against the wall slamming into her until my knees weakened. I could feel the burn from the cuts recently carved into each wrist from excessive resistance.

"Get the keys from my beltline and undo these...now!" I demanded.

Breaking At What Seems — Kyla M. Wassil

"Fuck you, Kevin..."

My breath fell from my mouth as I made it to the edge of my bed. Kicking off my shoes and pants, I threw Mandy onto the mattress. Bending over to retrieve the keys, I felt a tight hold clasp around my throat, preventing me from breathing. Mandy latched onto my back, choking me until I fell backwards onto the bed.

I maneuvered my way higher up until my head reached a pillow. Mandy rolled over dangling the keys in the room's dim lighting provided by the window. Crawling on top of me, she shoved me back into her tight tissue as I longed for release.

"If you want freedom, you must work for it."

I drew in a deep inhale through my nostrils, digging my thumbs and forefingers into her hips, pounding into her adamantly. Mandy grew weak from being on top and with a smile of certainty; she undid my cuffs, tossing them to the floor. I lied for a moment panting...watching for her next move but she was waiting on me, instead. I rolled her over feeling her limbs magnetize around me while I drove in as far as I could. Going beyond the point of too many orgasms had us both collapsing to the bed, finding peace behind closed eyes.

For years, this bastard had been on my tail about where I disappear off to all the time and why I refused to live in town like a normal person. Well, it was simple...I

Breaking At What Seems
Kyla M. Wassil

for one am not normal and secondly, I like my fucking privacy. Because he was relative by blood, my cousin thought he had a hand in my decision making. I have plotted my moment of victory overtaking his pathetic life on multiple occasions. I'm sick of him always following me around, asking me questions about this, that, and the other. I feel it's because I have dirt on him that could damage him significantly.

Once I had caught him fucking a distant cousin behind an old barn we used to hang out at as kids. Kicking over a fucking metal milk pale, he turned and met my eyes. As I attempted to run off he caught my ass in the field, slamming me down to the dirt knocking the breath from me. The cold blade he pressed into my throat only excited me more. He told me that if I were to ever tell, he'd slit my fucking throat while I was asleep. Well, that never did come to pass since I became better at hiding my whereabouts. I didn't give a shit about what he did; I just wanted the fucker to leave me alone. After witnessing that ordeal is when he became possessive over where I was going on a daily basis, thinking I was trying to get away just to rat him out. Clearly, I wasn't. I wanted to be left in solitude, in my barn with the only companions I needed; my fish. At least my pets never argued with me, asked questions or talked back in any form or fashion.

Sitting in the middle of my dusty floor, I turned the lights out allowing myself to gain a clear mind. There's a place he likes to go down town to get drunk off his ass every Thursday night. I stole that same blade he threatened me with one night after he fell into an alleyway passing out. I was told to ensure he made it

Breaking At What Seems — Kyla M. Wassil

home safely, but I, of course didn't. Why would I? I didn't give a fuck about his punk ass to begin with. Once I saw the handle beneath the street light, I snatched it from his belt before disappearing into the night. I had been waiting for years to kill him. Not just for threatening me, but always bullying me growing up, throwing me around and beating me up for no apparent reason just because he was disgusted with himself. Well, now was my chance to execute my vengeance for his relentless ridicule.

I stood across the street watching his interaction inside the bar while I smoked nearly an entire pack of cigarettes. It wasn't until the moon met its highest peak that the bastard decided to come stumbling out into public with his sloth ass. I'd follow him into the alleyway in which he used as a short cut to get home before his wife knew of his late disappearance. Flicking the blade open as it gleamed beneath the streetlight, I'd let him hear me only to turn and realize who was following at a dangerous distance. With no words, slam him against the brick wall, slicing into his abdomen, pulling the blade up to his sternum. Before disembowelment killed him, I'd shove my hand up inside his chest cavity, taking ahold of his beating heart. The devil's son shall grin as his victim's eyes glazed over. Grasping the vulnerable organ, his fatal exit shall be marked with the perpetual image of my face as I squeeze until the explosion drenched me in warm crimson. Covered in his blood, as he slowly falls below; I'd take one final look at the knife of valor before wedging it between his fucking eyes. Even if he were my last victim, I'd be forever grateful.

Breaking At What Seems

Kyla M. Wassil

Without a sudden twitch, my eyes flew open only to land on the comely silhouette rested beside me. A pool of sweat rested in the dip of my breast bone as my heartbeat sent disrupting vibrations through the liquid by the quake of my breathing. My lungs burned in my chest as I entered a violent cough attack. The bitter mucus that rose into my mouth caused me to gag as I slipped into the bathroom.

Pressing my hands against the cool porcelain, I took a moment to catch my breath. The bathroom door slowly cracked with Mandy coming straight through. Running her fingertips gently across my back calmed my nerves.

Voluntarily starting a warm shower, Mandy only used her eyes as an invitation. It had to be at least five in the fucking morning, but I didn't mind. I knew she had to be to work by seven and it usually took her two hours to get ready. Women.

After waking up hours before my alarm, I drug my ass into the kitchen to start a pot of coffee. Ferguson and Gerry looked a bit lonely, so I mindlessly slid their bowls until they touched. I was curious as to how they would react by being so close together. At first, nothing changed. So I turned their bowls until they were flush with one another.

Soon, they noticed the other and immediately expanded their fins as their swimming became more aggressive. They appeared to be in attack mode, yet the only thing that separated them was a thick membrane of glass. Lost in my own world, Mandy's nibble to my ear startled me.

"Good morning, handsome."

"Morning. How'd you sleep?"

"How do you think?" **She arched an eyebrow.**

I just smiled, making my way into the kitchen area to grab a mug. The sight of Mandy's tight ass perked up in her boy shorts had me biting my lip as I went out onto the balcony. I hadn't seen Savannah in a few days and I became worried.

She wasn't outside like usual and I felt my heart frown as I took a seat listening to the morning air. I found myself continuously glancing over towards her domain's direction, hoping that maybe she would eventually show up. She never did.

Staring down into my empty mug, I took myself back inside where Mandy was sliding on a pair of red high heels.

"Mmm, how about I go to work with you and you wrap those legs around me. I won't stop until everything falls completely off of your desktop."

"Hmm...I'll have to put that on my "to do" list."

"I hope you have a good day, though."

"You too. I will see you later."

She pressed her soft lips against mine, running her fingers down my overgrown five o'clock shadow. I

stood in the doorway seeing her out as the man I despised most passed her with a paint bucket soon entering Savannah's apartment.

By the time my view returned to its supposed direction, Mandy had already disappeared around the corner. I made sure no one else was around before I crept down to Savannah's door. Placing my hands against the barricade sent a hot flash through my entire body when I heard a male voice in my head that wasn't my own.

"What a pretty little thing you are, the filthy thoughts in my mind are ones I've only dreamt of sharing with you until this very moment."

I gripped either side of my head, practically tearing my hair from the root. I couldn't handle what was going inside of me. I just wanted to see her, to know she was okay. Maybe it was the police officer in me, or perhaps just the fucking human being I felt I was slowly losing. I have no empathy, I have no remorse when it comes to the violent desires I have recently obtained.

I suddenly felt dizzy as I stumbled my way back into my apartment. I didn't have to be at work until two and I sure as hell wasn't going to make it in feeling the way that I did. Face planting my bed, I passed out completely.

Breaking At What Seems   Kyla M. Wassil

ELEVEN

Hearing my ringtone pierce through the air

had me scurrying to retrieve my phone from the kitchen counter. It was Chief Mortkin calling me in to assist with a horrific crime scene. It took me less than ten minutes to get dressed and run out the door.

When I arrived on scene, Max was standing over a slouched body lying in a pool of blood. A nearby witness paced back and forth in the distance, only raising his eyebrows once his gaze met mine.

"Kevin, come check this out."

I knelt down beside Max as his gloved hand turned the victim's face in our direction. My heart jolted as I jumped back.

"W—what the fuck?"

"Kevin, what's the matter with ya?"

"Nothing, I mean he just looks familiar."

I swallowed hard as my eyes remained fixated on the man who I saw in my dream the night before. How can that even be possible? I know I didn't murder this guy and I certainly don't remember ever knowing him.

Chief Mortkin overheard my comment as he neared my position.

"What did you mean exactly by our victim looking familiar?"

"I uh- shit, Chief...I'm not entirely sure."

The sudden urge to vomit occurred as I hunched over dry heaving against the brick wall. The witness from before came walking up with his eyes locked on mine.

"You would believe this man were to be as you say "familiar" since I saw you in the area late last night."

My eyes enlarged as they switched from him to Chief, then back again.

"What the hell do you mean you "saw" him? You're sure that you saw Sergeant Strode in this remote area at one point, last night?"

"Chief, I doubt I was over here. I..."

Chief Mortkin shushed me while allowing the witness to continue speaking. I became unnervingly unpredictable at this point while my superior allowed a stranger to openly convict me of a crime I have no memory of, in which contained the impossibility of even happening by my hand.

"Goddamn it, Chief! He's obviously full of shit! I wouldn't have done this." **I exasperated.**

"All though you claimed the victim looked familiar. Kevin, from a professional state of mind, I advise you to prepare an alibi rather than circumvent the issue, itself." **Max replied puzzled.**

"So what? Now I am being accused? I'm a fucking suspect? Christ, listen to yourself, Max! I...am...incapable of doing something such as this!" **I became hysteric.**

"You need to calm down. You are bringing a lot of unnecessary attention to yourself. Just take my advice and think about it. I'd hate to see anything happen to you."

Both Chief and Max looked worrisome for my sake as they glanced at one another, mentally deciding on what procedure to follow.

"Look, Kevin is a police officer. He sees the same people I'm quite sure in often cases. It's probably just a coincidence. Kevin would never do something to this extremity, Chief."

Chief Mortkin stood in indefinite silence while stroking his chin. I began panting as other standbys neared the scene. I couldn't breathe as I gripped at my tie trying to inhale.

"For the time being, Kevin, I want you to go about your day and finish your shift. I am taking this guy in for further questioning. We will have our time when you come into the station later, tonight. Understood?"

"Yes, Chief." **I puffed out.**

Fleeing the scene before any unnecessary eyes gained a look; I jumped into a taxi to pick up my patrol car at the precinct. Driving around aimlessly for a few hours gave me too much time in trying to figure out what I was doing out so late last night. The only person who would have any key facts in regards of my whereabouts would be Mandy.

"713...come in."

"713 responding, go head."

"We have a 10-56A. The victim called in himself. We traced the call from 170 Avenue A."

"10-4. I'm headed that way now!"

Slamming on my gas pedal, I flicked on my lights speeding to the scene. The apartment building was run down and there were a lot of stragglers hanging about outside. A lady from the fifth floor was yelling from her window, trying to gain my attention.

"This man across the hall keeps yelling to everyone that he has a loaded shotgun and wants to take his own life!"

"Okay, ma'am I need you to calm down. I am on my way up there now. Remain inside your home."

I busted through the entrance, feeling my heart accelerate with each step that passed beneath my feet. Making it to the fifth floor, the lady who was this man's neighbor poked her head out of her doorway.

"Is he in here?" **I whispered.**

She nodded as I drew my pistol, giving his door a knock. *"NYPD, I need you to open up!"*

Shuffling came from the other side, but no one opened the door.

"I am going to ask once more before I enter with force. I need you to open the door so we can talk. I don't want you to hurt yourself. I am here to help you. So, please open up!"

"You can't fucking help me! No one can! God himself doesn't lend mercy when my name is spoken. I am a joke!"

"Sir, that is not true. Whoever led you to believe so is wrong! Please open up so we can discuss this calmly."

"Calmly..." **He laughed.**

I leaned in to listen when the cock of a shotgun had me busting through his front door without a second thought. Pointing my gun to his chest, the man stood in sweat pants and a white tee shirt with yellow stains imbedded into the fibers. My breath was uneven as the pistol shook in my hands while staring at the double barrels pressed into the bottom of his jaw.

"Sir...Please put the gun down. There is no need to take your own life. What will that solve?"

"More than you can possibly imagine."

"Try explaining some."

"What good will it do Officer Strode?" **He leaned close enough to read my nametag.**

"Please, call me Kevin."

The man gripped the shotgun in his palms, glancing at a nearby open window behind him. Taking a deep inhale, he looked me dead in the eyes. *"My wife left me and took our son with her. Why? Because that selfish bitch claims nothing I did was ever good enough. It is my fault that we lived in a piss poor place such as this.*

The fact I failed to be a good man and provide everything she ever wanted. She always called me a lousy father and a pathetic husband that I started believing it. Well you know what? Fuck her!"

"When did she leave?"

"Three days ago…" **His eyes veered over his shoulder to glance at the window once more.**

I took a few cautious steps forward, placing my gun back into its holster—hoping to ease the tension. *"You haven't heard from her since? Have you at least tried contacting her?"*

"How can I when she took the car, my wallet, and both phones?"

"You should be proud that you at least have a home to call your own." **I fought to make light of the subject.** *"Why didn't you call this in any sooner? We could have made a report for kidnapping."*

"This fucking place? Please. I'm nothing but worthless scum a homeless man wouldn't bother scraping from the bottom of his shoe. I didn't think to report it because she has made threats like this before. I'm not going to drag the authorities into my personal business"

"That's not true… besides, we are here to help you. No matter what." **I side smirked.**

"What the fuck do you know, Kevin? You're a damn cop, you have a great life."

"Ha, I wish I could agree. It isn't all it seems, my friend."

Taking a few steps back, the man became closer and closer to the open window throughout our conversation. Taking a sudden look at me, then back at the window again gave me an unsettling feeling inside my gut.

"I hope the bitch is happy and gets all that she wants."

"Please," **I extended a worried hand, watching the tips of my fingers shake.** *"It doesn't have to end like this. Just hand over the gun and we can solve everything."*

"Save it, you know just as much as I do concerning her whereabouts. If you ever happen see her," **He released an unsteady exhale.** *"Tell my son that I am sorry and that I tried."* **I then followed his eyes to an old family portrait hanging in solitude on the wall.**

"Do you really want your son to go the rest of his life without a father? Who is this fair to, really?"

"He has the world's best mother, he will be completely fine." **The man chuckled, instantly fulling speed towards the window before I could stop him. In slow motion, I watched him do a 180 degree turn, shoving the barrel deep into his mouth.**

"Wait...please stop!" **I screamed.** *"This isn't the way!"*

Just like that, the man pulled the trigger sending brain matter flying as his body smashed through the window, descending to the pavement below. I heard neighbors screaming in terror as I reached the blood stained window. My stomach turned just looking down at his broken body.

Catching my breath, I ran a hand through my hair as hot tears escaped my eyes. *"Oh my...God."* **Falling to the floor below, I grabbed a hold of my radio informing dispatch of my 10-56.** *"Please send medical and investigators to the scene as soon as possible."*

Time seemed to lag on until Max ran through the front door, crashing down beside me. I pulled him into me, crying harder than I ever had while on scene. I have never lost someone in person on the job and I knew this would take its toll on me.

Max escorted me back outside, directing another officer to drive me back to the precinct. I rocked back and forth in the front seat as if the younger boy inside me found a way to surface. I sat petrified, waiting for Chief Mortkin in his office while he finished a phone conversation. Once the officer informed him of my incident, he quickly hung up the phone coming directly to meet me.

"Are you all right, Kevin? I know that was traumatizing but I want you to know we will get through this. I am going to have to ask you to fill out a report but first, I need you to answer some questions."

"Is this about the guy in the alley way?" **My eyes narrowed.**

Chief pressed his lips together scratching at his forehead. *"Just follow me to the interrogation room, it's quieter there."*

I shoved away from the desk with a huff, dragging my feet the entire way. Entering the cold room, I caught him signaling the guy behind the one way mirror.

"Have a seat, Kevin. I'll return shortly. Would you like some coffee?"

"Sure." **I replied blandly.**

My gaze sharpened on my reflection in the mirror, hoping the other person could feel my wrath on the opposing side. My stare remained stone until Chief Mortkin reentered the room with Max following close behind.

Slapping a pen and pad onto the metal table, Max gave a sympathetic side smirk. I reached my hand out accepting the Styrofoam cup as steam sat stratus atop the brown liquid.

"Kevin, in a case such as this we have to treat you just like we do the average Joe off the streets. You may contact a lawyer if you wish."

My head quirked to the side as my eyes glared at Chief Mortkin. *"Are you guys seriously about to victimize me because of something that guy said?"*

"Kevin, we brought him in for questioning earlier and the information he provided wasn't that of a fabricated

lie. A polygraph test was even provided. Either this man cheated the system or he in fact did believe he saw you."

"I want Mandy here. She's the one who can be more specific about my activities regarding last night." **I replied smugly.**

Max bit his tongue with a sigh as his hands laced against his forehead.

"We don't want to make this harder than it has to be, Kevin. It's part of our job as you know. Just answer our questions honestly and there should be nothing to worry about."

"I'll answer your goddamn questions, but you had better contact Mandy to get her side as well."

Max motioned for Chief to take care of that while he remained with me.

"Kevin, do you not remember anything from last night? Did you happen to have any alcohol beverages that might have clouded your memory?"

"No. I was completely sober. Mandy was the only one who drank anything last night—and that was before I got home."

"Then tell me everything you do remember from the moment you arrived at your apartment."

I released a rugged breath as I sat trying to gather my thoughts in chronological order.

"Be as specific as possible, please." **He tilted the pad of paper to begin noting down.**

"I came home. I know I was in a rather disturbed mood at that time. But Mandy quickly changed that by surprising me half-dressed on my couch."

Max's attention was quickly drawn at the thought of Mandy's body—far beyond what he's seen in person as his pen stroke became heavier.

"What uh… happened next?" **He cleared his throat nervously.**

"We fornicated…" **I arched an eyebrow.**

"That's it?"

"Max, I am not going to sit here and give you the graphic details to allure your mind and that of the pervert behind the fucking glass. Yes, we had sex for about four hours before falling asleep. Next thing I remember was waking after having a freaky ass dream that had that guy from the alley in it."

"F—four hours did you say? Wow," **His brows rose.** *"That's impressive. Anyway, what next?"*

"Thank you." **I smiled absentmindedly.** *"After I awoke from coughing a lot, I went to the restroom to rinse my mouth out so I didn't throw up. Mandy entered soon after and we took a shower at around five this morning. That's it."* **I planted my hands atop the metal table.** *"That's all I remember."*

"*Are you aware that anything you tell me can and will be your testimony? Lying as you know is prohibited by law and you will face a hefty charge for. Kevin, you are placing your career into severe jeopardy here.*" **Max lowered his tone.**

"*What in the actual fuck, Max? Yes, I know how the law works! Christ! If I said I didn't fucking do it, then I didn't! I wouldn't tell misleading facts just to fabricate a believable alibi when plausible answers were clearly required and provided. That is all the information to the best of my knowledge that I can provide for you. Why are you doing this? Do you believe I am guilty?*" **I searched his eyes with inner rage.** "*Because from the look in your eyes—it's really beginning to worry me.*"

"*No, Kevin. Of course not! I don't believe you to be guilty or even capable of something this heinous. I just have to follow protocol. I don't want to sit here and fucking do this shit just as much as you don't want to sit there across from me.*" **Max released his pen with a loud clink.** "*Evidence and DNA are the keys to locking down a suspect and closing a case after solving it. I am sorry to have to put you through this. Maybe you were just at the wrong place at the wrong time?*"

Interrupting our conversation, Chief Mortkin opened the door informing Max that Mandy was on her way. "*Send her in when she arrives. I am almost finished with Kevin.*"

"*Max, you've known me for years.*" **I regained his attention.** "*I wouldn't do this.*"

"I know, but you having some sort of premonition of this guy kind of raises a red flag. Besides, let's face it. You haven't exactly been yourself lately, have you?"

I tapped my fingertips against the table's surface clenching my jaw. "You're right. Let me just fucking tell you that I have felt indifferent. Why don't you picture going from being completely okay around strangers to suddenly wanting to harm the nearest person in the worst way you can think of. See if you don't begin to lose your fucking mind, Max." **I scowled.**

"Kevin, a statement like that can be enough to detain you." **His forced whisper hissed, causing me to twitch.**

A tap on the door broke our attention as my eyes looked in the location of my exit. Mandy poked her head through sending me straight to my feet.

"Baby, hey oh my God—are you okay?" **I grabbed her face for a kiss.**

"What the hell is going on?"

"I just need to ask you a few questions, Mandy."

"Why, did something happen? Is Kevin in some sort of trouble?" **Mandy's voice was exceptionally demanding.**

"Let me ask the questions, please?"

"No, no you're going to fucking answer me! Why is he upset? He's been crying. Kevin, what happened?"

Max called in Chief to escort me out before Mandy started a brawl at the police station in my defense. I was to stay put while they questioned Mandy—alone.

Staring aimlessly into space, I watched Mandy walk past Chief's office with her arms folded. Alerting my anxiety, I became nervous.

Max filed right behind, looking at me through the window curling his finger.

"Well, what did she say?"

"She claims she remembers you randomly getting up in the middle of the night around 3:30am, not having returned for almost an hour. She didn't ask where you had gone, but found a pack of cigarettes on your night stand." **He glared.**

I furrowed my brows trying to remember. *"Maybe I went down to the store. But that doesn't mean I killed that guy along the way?"*

"I'm not saying you did. In fact, we are led to believe it had something to do with the guy who tried framing you in the first place. Although if we didn't have other suspects, Mandy's information could cost you a lot,, Kevin."

"Then why am I a suspect?"

"How long have you been a cop, Kevin? Everyone is a damn suspect! The truth is, we are all worried about you and needed a reason to put you on a temporary paid leave."

"Suspension?" **I seethed.** *"For what?"*

Max faced the window, motioning for someone to enter the room. Chief came walking in with a pitiful expression.

"Kevin, we feel it's best you take several days off to seek medical treatment. Whether you are suffering PTSD, we need to be exact considering you are currently unfit for proper duty. We can't allow rumors to fly in a city like this. It will eat you alive and you know it."

"Ha, so now I'm a fucking lunatic? You choose to place one of your best officer's on paid suspension due to the fear of having the precinct's name tarnished on my behalf? How fucking cowardly..." **I crossed my arms, flexing my jaw muscles.**

"No, that's not what we're saying. You're taking things out of context. There's a doctor I trust with my life that I once had to see years ago that I am referring you to. His name is Dr. Sunter. He's one of New York's finest Psychologists. Don't take such offense, a job like this can mess anyone up. I am not asking, I am demanding you see him. You need help, Kevin. That's a direct order."

I sat in a momentary silence knowing it was true. I did need help, but with what exactly? I know I wasn't insane though I felt my mind was entering a state of psychosis while I slept.

"Fine. I will see him like you insist."

"Good choice. We will keep a close surveillance on your home just in case something is to go wrong. In the meantime, I will be checking in with Dr. Sunter on the occasion of each visit. We will get you proper aid and you'll be back on the force before you know it."

I shamefully took the business card from Chief's hand, allowing him to escort me back outside.

"Kevin, I'm just a call away if you need me." **Max added.**

Mandy was seated in the waiting area staring out the front doors. With no questions asked, she took me by the arm, kissing my shoulder as we left the building.

I fidgeted with the seams of my pants due to frustration on the way home. I entered a nostomania panic as the elevator doors opened to my floor. Anxious to be home, I immediately dropped my heavy kit belt to the hardwood, struggling to unbutton my shirt as my fingers spasmodically reacted.

"Here, let me help you." **Mandy insisted.**

Getting to my fifth button, I halted her movement as her hands reached up to my unkempt face. Water sat in the corners of my eyes as they met hers. I broke down completely as my knees buckled, sending me straight to the floor. I hugged Mandy as she knelt with me, allowing me to weep.

"It's okay, baby, I'm right here."

Breaking At What Seems   Kyla M. Wassil

TWELVE

Early morning cast its bright rays across my face as I lied paralytic. The whistling wind rang in my ears, though I could not move. The sound of Savannah's voice had my eyes flutter open as my fist clutched the crystal grains within my palm.

Breaking At What Seems

Kyla M. Wassil

My heart jolted with excitement as I removed myself from the couch, slowly actuating towards the balcony. Salt lined the doorway, along with stains on the glass from dried water spots. I ran a hand down my grainy face as I took a long look around my living area.

I noticed salt lining my front door, which drew my eyes towards the vile of Holy water sitting adjacent to a bag of salt that centered the floor. I continued walking out into the sunlight, breathing in the city air. Traffic below merely resembled rabid wolves restrained from free motion as they longed to pursue their destination.

Imagine something so small such as a fucking traffic light halting you from going and doing what you desired most. As I sit a perfect example of a disgruntled hostage being punished for something out of my control. Unable to roam the streets eager and adroit as my pride is crushed by the weight of destruction. For whatever is in my mind, I must have sought spiritual guidance as I dusted reflective fragments from my bare chest.

I took both rough hands through my overgrown hair, resting my fingers inside the indention of my scar for it hurt just by a gentle touch. My right eye twitched from the pain as I let out a subtle groan of disarray. I felt as though I was caged inside my own dystonia where I was forced to suffer an unwanted wanion that tore at my cortex. Stinging and burning while leaving me in a harmful destitution.

I have spent several days, upon countless hours trying to configure a means of my apprehension, yet I always end up in a dark hole—lost. I would start from the evening I was at my parent's, enjoying the simplicity of a ritual family dinner on Sunday. How I sat in wonder, staring at apparent photos of me in the scenes of my adolescence. None of it made any sense, that I couldn't remember some of the most important times of my life. But, I suddenly drew in memories of horrific lewd behavior I seemingly committed in past times. Being a young man, holding the nature of lascivious desires is common, but to unleash a dark steed with his coat shined in arrogance as his masculinity upholds improper stature would be considered quite troublesome.

    A rivalry sits within my head, only claiming victory day by day as I saw a stranger each time I looked in the mirror. I don't recognize myself, but the soft touch of my significant other seems to only disagree. Mandy sees the good in me; she sees who I really am, even beneath my facade of a kind masquerade.

    But I cannot come to terms with how she can love a man who is completely deserted in his own mind? When I touch her, my heart ignites fire throughout my body as I stand impassioned. Though, when she isn't around, I become this beast longing to devour the innocence around me.

    I breathe in, I breathe out; possibly waiting for life to consume me by swallowing me whole. Going twenty some odd years being content, to having your world tilt into a downward spiral really makes you question your belief beyond what is seen by the naked eye.

Breaking At What Seems
Kyla M. Wassil

I have counted minimal times I've found myself looking upward, thanking whatever great being above for the gift of life as well as the underserving things that have been granted to me. Though, my recent inflicted pain that has shackled my mentality only bounds me on my hands and knees, praying for a sign; praying for fucking assistance.

"If you were to think any harder, your skull would split into two."

My eyes flickered towards Savannah's balcony. I drew in a long breath of relief, taking in the sight of her pale face painted in dark makeup.

"I think if I were to think any further, I might just die from a brain aneurysm." **I smiled.**

"Why is it you're not at work?"

My eyes met the ground as disappointment punched me in the gut. *"I uh…I'm currently on suspension."*

"Ha, what the fuck did you do? Wrestle some poor old vagabond who innocently wandered the sleepless streets of Manhattan?"

"If it were only that simple." **I sighed.** *"I am on suspension because my alter ego has developed a disreputable state of mind and is slowly affecting me physically."*

Savannah's eyes were doe sized as her lips trembled. *"H—how do you mean, exactly? Like, when you say "alter ego" you mean…"*

"I don't know how to explain it, really. Most times, I am just fine and now I keep having these fucking nightmares where I am some sadistic parasite who's depraved enough to get his rocks off by torturing and killing innocent women. I just don't understand. Now my Chief thinks it'd be best I see a Psychologist."

Savannah stared blankly into me as she spoke. *"So, it's troubling you on the job? What do you look like in your dreams?"*

At first, I didn't know how to answer the question. Then I dug a little deeper. *"I don't know? I never see myself other than in first person view."*

"Have you noticed any specific details about yourself in which you can see? Maybe some physical aspects you don't carry in reality?"

Savannah unfolded her legs, coming to her feet. She stood against the railing never leaving my eyes. I have never seen her so intrigued since we have known one another. Wetting my lips, I tried to think more in depth but the deeper I thought—the more my scar began to ache.

I grimaced from the pain; pinching the bridge of my nose as a migraine nestled into my right temporal lobe. The distress only worsened and I clenched my jaw in the attempt to bear the discomfort.

"I—I can't be sure, Savannah. I'm sorry. Why does any of that matter, anyhow?"

Her mouth quirked as her expression remained perplexed. "I am just curious. Since the day we have met, you have given me this sudden hope for humanity. I can't really explain it, but I have always felt like there was a significant reason why you were brought to me. Maybe believing you were sent to my rescue, as cliché as that may sound."

"I'm not quite sure I'm following?" **I furrowed my brows.**

"Remember that day I came over and kissed you just to see if we saw the same thing and we did?"

"So what? I need you to be a bit more specific."

"I have to show you, Kevin."

I turned my head to look inside my apartment for other existence.

"She isn't there. I heard her leave earlier this morning."

"And she left me lying asleep, covered in salt? What the hell?"

"I feel as though I carry empowerment of requital in your favor." **Savannah smirked.**

"What's the catch to your humbleness?"

Running her tongue across her top lip, her gaze sharpened. *"Let me come over and I will show you."*

I swallowed hard, knowing I have missed her physical company. Hurrying inside, I walked around in sheer panic trying to figure out how to calm myself before facing her.

Several minutes had gone by absent a knock on my door. Becoming ill-minded, I cleaned up the sporadic mess about my hardwood before dressing for the day. It wasn't the fact I stood disappointed alongside my confusion. I just didn't allow it to bother me. Instead, I became peeved as I brought Gerry's bowl in front of Ferguson's.

Moments into a stare off, they both flared up in anguish. I became excited as they darted viciously at the glass, yearning to get to the other. The want of an epic outcome had me scoop up Ferguson, placing him within the personal proximity of Gerry's territory.

Immediately, they began attacking each other shredding scales as pink dye muddled the water. Gerry was overpowering as he unyieldingly struck the flesh of his opponent as they fought till death.

My eyes sat dark as my mind became dangerous while watching the aquatic battle, trying to contain my satisfaction. Soon enough, pieces of flesh floated freely about the water as the victor swam in survivor's tranquility.

Proud that Gerry had conquered, I brought myself down to a placid mind while cleaning his bowl. Seems we both shared the same want to destroy anyone within the region of a sovereign under the virtue of protection.

    Needing a release, I jumped up grabbing a hold of my pull-up bar. I yanked my weight into the air until my arms grew fatigued as sweat dripped down the recess of my back. Dropping to the floor, I strained through two hundred push-ups, longing for Savannah to appear beneath me. Wanting her nails to cut deep into my skin as the wickedness of my mind salvaged the oxygen it needed to burn essential life. I may pose a deadly threat, but damn did I love the way Savannah made me feel. Satanic and crude, instilling the bitter insipid that lied upon your tongue; I was accepting.

    Bored out of mind after hours of pacing throughout my home, I grabbed a bottle of liquor making my way out to the balcony for a mid-day smoke. Enjoying the burning of my lungs, I looked down seeing a patrol car from my unit strolling by. Curling my lip, I tossed back a scorching shot, flicking my cigarette down in its direction. By the fifth chug, my vision became blurry as my balance became unstable.

    Stumbling my way into the living room, I face planted the couch praying the fate of aspiration ceased.

    The cold hand pressed into my back made me jump out of my skin. I turned over, nearly elbowing Mandy in the jaw.

    "Jesus babe, you scared the hell outta me!"

"Apologies. I had to leave early for work yesterday considering I have this big article I am in charge of writing for next month's issue."

I reached my hand up rubbing the softness of her cheek, letting her blue eyes pierce through me. "No worries."

"By the way, what the hell happened to Ferguson?"

My eyes switched to the counter where Gerry swam around in silent triumph. My smirk suddenly fell as I forced down the lump in my throat. I didn't want to begin lying to Mandy, so I manned up admitting the result of my cruel nature.

"I became curious yesterday after you had gone. I wanted to see if they really did fight unto death and well…as you see, Gerry was the survivor."

Mandy's stare was blank, but her mouth remained agape as she watched Gerry looking back at her.

"Well, I don't even know how to even respond to that, Kevin? I wish you wouldn't have done that only because that's terrible. But, I must ask how did it make you feel?"

Her attention turned to me as her eyes cut through mine, awaiting a response. I wasn't sure why she cared to know, though what did I have to lose while explaining?

Breaking At What Seems

Kyla M. Wassil

"It might sound strange, but I—I thoroughly enjoyed it. As if they both resembled two gladiators in the arena, fighting for glory and survival. I would be in the Senate's chair, praying to the Gods that my titan conquered the riotous uproar of the savaged peasants who surrounded their presentation."

"How very detailed? So you're saying, you took exceeding pleasure watching two tiny creatures fight without a saving grace to control or stop it?"

I became uncomfortable as her eyes hardened. I felt like I was being pushed into a corner with no way out. Maybe I was wrong for torturing the damn fish, but so what? I knew what I was doing and I knew what I wanted so in exchange for a guilty pleasure, I commenced an unnecessary brawl. Did it make me a little more abnormal than others? Probably so; but in this case, I didn't think it would have caused so much harm towards Mandy's feelings.

"Mandy, I'm sorry? I didn't think it would have been such a big deal? Honestly, it felt almost uncontrollable in my defense."

"What do you mean "uncontrollable"?"

"I mean, I wanted to see the outcome because I did enjoy the violent rendition. I don't know how else to explain it."

"Well, save the rest for your doctor. Your appointment is in an hour. I suggest you get ready."

Our communication ended at that point. Mandy didn't dare speak further along the car ride to Dr. Sunter's office, either.

The travel was long as we jammed in traffic like sardines the entire way to the Upper East Side. Pulling into a carport of a very large building, a man stopped us at the security booth giving us a day pass to park. I ran my fingers through my hair, combing it over to pose somewhat presentable.

The office I dreaded sat on the 23rd floor and Mandy's heels disagreed with the stairwell. Pushing the button to the elevator, I watched my disfigured reflection part as the doors slid open. Mandy tapped 23 when another man yelled for us to wait on him. As the man dressed in business attire entered, my eyes darted on his every move as he returned a thankful smile toward Mandy.

I was leaned against the back of the cabin, gripping the metal hand rail. Hoping I could find the strength to contain myself as the man's eyes ran their way from Mandy's legs to her fucking chest. The smirk of interest that tugged at his mouth had my knuckles crack from the force of pressure.

"Do you work in this building, Ms.? I don't believe I have seen you around before." **He leered.**

My eyes flickered towards Mandy as she blushed in response. *"No, I am here with my boyfriend for his appointment."*

The clean cut man glanced over his shoulder, giving me a nod.

"That's too bad." **He smirked.**

Before I could release the railing in order to knock his wiseass out, Mandy immediately read my expression in the convex mirror taking my hand in hers. She pressed her lips together with an innocent nod as the doors opened to his floor.

"You two enjoy your afternoon. Here's my business card if you ever need a different change of scenery."

I reached out snatching it from his hand with a snarl only to see him put his hands up in respect of my territory. I looked down reading *Abram Brozek, MD. Cosmetic Surgery & Recovery Therapy.* **My skin boiled as he winked before the doors closed.**

"Thanks, jackass!" **I growled.**

"Kevin, what the hell?"

"What? He was gawking at you and I found it unpleasantly rude!"

Mandy laughed, giving my cheek a reassuring kiss. The doors opened to our destination lying straight ahead behind glass walls. I walked up to the check-in counter confirming my appointment as the receptionist behind the desk gave an overbearing smile, handing back new patient forms.

"Just fill these out and sign all highlighted areas. The doctor will be out to get you shortly."

Reading over the small print strained my eyes as the bright white paper shouted through the lettering. Signing my name a dozen times had me irritated by the time all was said and done.

For a long moment, I sat reading the paper while overhearing the receptionists babble on about their relationships while the other side of my hearing was drawn toward the home makeover episode that was broadcasting on their television. Mandy's attention was stuck on a New York Time's magazine, as she read over an article that seemed to be of competition by her under breath remarks.

"What seems to be so bothersome over there?"

"Nothing. Just this woman I work with who always tries to outdo me. In which, I sit in hysteria over the blatant fact that she is literally fucking her way to the top of our company. I have too much self-respect to display such vulgar discourtesy. Besides, I have a very sexy police officer who satisfies my every need." **She arched an eyebrow.**

Just as my eyes returned to the sentence where I left off, one of the receptionists called my name.

"Do you want me to go back with you?"

"Of course."

Following the woman into a bright room, she documented my weight and height before getting my blood pressure. Relaxing my arm, I could suddenly feel my pulse ticking inside my bicep.

"You are a little above average on your stolics, Mr. Strode. The machine reads 125 over 84 which isn't too bad, but you may be experiencing slight hypertension."

I rubbed the reddened area as she slipped off the monitor, allowing my pulse to dissipate back to normal function.

Escorting me to the main office where I sat in a chilled silence awaiting Dr. Sunter, pictures of the human brain and informative diagrams of psychology comforted the walls around me. His couch was cool, but comfortable as the warmth of Mandy's body heat extracted through her blazer; resting against my skin.

The door opened behind us as an older gentleman entered, wearing khaki slacks and a polo sweater.

I stood to my feet in order to properly greet the man. "Hello sir, I am Kevin Strode and this here is my mate, Mandy Culhart."

"Nice to meet the both of you. Please, have a seat and relax."

Going over my file, he read aloud a letter that was sent directly from my Chief. Both his and Max's input were the basis of the literal print.

"So far, I have gathered that you have been experiencing some issues at work. Your Chief has sent you to me due to the worrisome facts he's collected over your previous behavior while on duty. It starts with several weeks ago you had fallen asleep past your shift, to becoming overly aggressive while handling suspects. And I quote, "Pursuing unnecessary force while inflicting surmise towards inhabitants beyond own power is in violation of any person's rights." Which is also known as "cop brutality", is this correct?"

I sat in disbelief that my superior officer would write such a thing down about me; characterizing me as some untamed brute that was power hungry. To think Max might have had a hand in that literary opinion pissed me off even more.

"I guess if the paper claims such facts." **My jaw tightened.**

"I understand you would rather not be here if given the choice. Seeing as how your superior has referred you to me—it is, by law, appropriate to be abided. Understand?"

"Yes, I am aware of my consequences if I were to have not shown."

"Good. I want you to elaborate in your own words as to what you've been experiencing, lately."

"Where to begin? I um… I have been suffering drastic nightmares in which affect me at random times, which was clearly stated in that letter of reference. I cannot explain why or what they mean. All I know is I become angered and aggressive. Maybe even overly excessive where gratification is concerned." **I frowned.**

Dr. Sunter jotted down on his pad every so often as I spoke.

"Okay, can you tell me a little more about these aggressive tendencies?"

I looked over at Mandy as she waited for me to explain. I didn't want to so I let her give a grand example.

"I guess he wants me to explain, if I may?" **Mandy's voice crackled.**

"Please do."

"Uh, it was maybe the third time we've had sexual intercourse and he's usually very gentle. He suddenly became quite aggressive, choking me and handling me in the worst way. When I looked at him, it was almost as if I didn't recognize him. He stood so dark, his eyes were not his own and neither were his hands."

"So, Kevin became experimental during sex one evening and you not being used to it frightened you?"

"Yes, exactly."

His eyes switched to mine. "Kevin, how did you feel in that moment?"

"Like she said, I didn't appear to be myself. I get into these devious moods to where I want the aggression. I feed on negativity and want to be the worst person possible."

"Can you tell me how you act while on duty?"

Breaking At What Seems

Kyla M. Wassil

"I become overbearing, pushing the limitations of my power on those I am dealing with."

"I am going to put you on some medication to see how you do. I believe you may be suffering Post Traumatic Stress Disorder and maybe some stress anxiety. It is common for many officers around here to fall victim to PTSD under such pressure. Medication usually takes around three days to get into your system fully. I want to follow up with you on Thursday. I am prescribing Remeron, which is a mood stabilizer that acts like an antidepressant. It helps restore the natural balance of chemicals in your brain that throw you into sporadic feelings you can't seem to control. I do not advise taking your medication with alcohol substances."

I gave a side smirk, taking the prescription into my hand. It may have been a waived consultation, but I knew better than his chosen diagnosis. I understand the psychological disorder that potentially threatens anyone who is involved in my profession. I have seen plenty of traumatizing things, but to dream them and begin living them is beyond the bullshit of a stress disorder.

Mandy drove me straight to the nearest pharmacy to get my prescription filled. Standing in line, there were several people ahead of me. An elderly woman who was directly in front of me accidentally pressed the end of her cane into the tip of my toes, forcing me to let out a grunt of pain.

She was quick to turn around and look at me. *"I apologize, young man. Maybe you shouldn't stand so close next time."*

I flared my nostrils, motioning for her to move along. Mandy gripped my arm sympathizing with my irritation. My mind wandered along the medication that was displayed on either side of us. I felt like I had been standing there forever until the next available window called me over.

The technician gave me a two hour time frame for pick up. Mandy took the liberty in telling me not to worry about it, that she'd get them later on. Happy that I didn't have to waste time, I rounded the corner as some woman met me simultaneously running over my foot with her electric scooter.

Standing peeved, I lashed out knocking objects off the nearest shelving. *"Goddamn it, people! Watch where the fuck you're going!"*

"Sorry." **Mandy whispered, hauling me away.** *"Kevin, I doubt she meant to or the lady who hit your foot with her cane. You're just in distress and that's okay."*

"Easy for you to say, Mandy. You're not on suspension from your job. You are not under a constant surveillance while in the privacy of your own home. It's sickening. I feel like a caged animal with some pandemic disease." **I bit out.**

What surprised me was that no matter how upset I became, Mandy never once raised her voice back. She'd let me have my tantrum and continued on about her business. It didn't make sense to me; then again hardly anything seemed to, lately.

I lied on my couch attempting to watch the

television, unknowingly dozing off. I didn't like the idea of Mandy leaving me alone for the night and the absence of her existence kept me from sleeping in my own bed. The screen flickered across my eyelids as the sound of static muffled in my ears until the room fell silent.

Breaking At What Seems   Kyla M. Wassil

THIRTEEN

Mandy's warm hand pressed into my chest, waking me. For a long moment, I just stared at her while she stroked my face. I lost track of time, not knowing how long I had been asleep for. Being a cop, I am always to be on alert and my trust in people is very limited.

I granted Mandy sanction to my home weeks ago, thinking maybe she's a potential mate. I knew my mother and father would be pleased to finally meet her and the waiting had been long enough.

"Hey you, how'd you sleep?"

"Fine, I guess? My back is sore from being in one position all night." **I sat up stretching.**

"Well, I brought you your medication. I want you to take it now so you can begin to feel better."

I ran my hands through my hair, overlooking the pill bottle. The side effects were none in which I cared to endure. *"I need to get a haircut, but before I do that I want to ask you something."*

"Ask away, Sergeant." **Mandy smiled.**

"How do you feel about going over to my parent's for dinner, tonight?"

Mandy's eyes sparkled while she searched for words to speak. Coming to a mental agreement, her gaze lightened as she took my hand up to her face, kissing my fingertips. *"I'd love to!"*

"Great! Well first things first, I need to clean up the disaster on my head and then we can head on over."

"While you get your hair done, I will run home and get dressed. Do I need to wear anything specific?"

Breaking At What Seems   Kyla M. Wassil

    I lay back against the couch cushion shaking my head. Mandy's grin widened as she tapped the end of my nose before giving me a kiss goodbye. She has a high class style, in which I wasn't too worried about her choice of a first impression.

    I shaved up my face, before putting on a nice pair of black slacks and a charcoal grey button down. Rested on the edge of my bed, I dialed my mother's number informing her of the special occasion. Of course, she was overjoyed as her high pitched commotion rang in my ear. Ending our conversation, I sat in silence staring into the floor when the sound of clanking against the wall drew my attention.

    I stood to my feet, walking towards the head of my bed to listen further. I wasn't sure what Savannah was up to, but the sound of dragging nails lured my interest. I tilted my head to the side, waiting for more when light panting transpired through the wall. I felt my heartbeat pick up as I placed my hands firmly against the barrier only to have a mental flash in my brain.

    I could see Savannah pinned up against the wall with some stranger ramming into her. Though the man wasn't a stranger in the slightest…I stood appalled seeing an identical scar in his head. Savannah's eyes remained still, piercing through me like knives as her breath drew in raggedly.

    I felt my own lungs deflate as a sharp pain jabbed me in the right side of my head. A loud bang had my body push away as I ran into my bathroom in search for cold water. Splashing it several times onto my face, I looked at myself then at my scar that appeared reddened. Sore to the touch, I frantically switched my hands downward to fix my tie.

Pulling it as tight as a noose, I left it there until my teeth clenched from resisting such ample force. The foulness of my mood left me silent as I rode down to Vinni's barber shop. He, of course, was the bitter taste in anyone's mouth even after placing the sweetest candy to your pallet.

"Well, look who decided to rise from the dead. Where the hell have you been? Your hair looks terrible and your damn father has been wondering about you!"

"Yeah, yeah. Cut the small talk, Vinni. I have an important date today, so just shut ya trap and do your job."

"Someone is rather offset today? What's the big date, anyway?"

I smiled before I could even respond. *"I, uh… am taking someone to meet my parent's today."*

"About time you got yourself a dame! Christ, I was starting to believe you wore tights on your days off."

"You're such a bastard, ya know that?" **I laughed.**

I sat there tuning out Vinni's World War II banter while he cleaned me up. As his shears rounded the right side of my head, I felt the tenderness lurk beneath the cool metal. Ignoring the sudden nerve disagreement only to spare a dull explanation where Vinni was concerned, I smiled increasingly to hide my discomfort.

Spinning me around to view my fresh fade, my scar seemed to protrude more than usual.

"I swear that damn hack mark gets me every time. Anything else I can do for ya?"

"No, that'll be all. Thank you, sir."

"Bring that lady by sometime so this old man can have some visual entertainment."

Waving him off, I left a tip on the counter before heading out the door. Jumping into the taxi I paid to wait, my anxiousness to see Mandy tugged at my insides.

As the doors of the elevator opened to my floor, an eerie silence rose in the air. My footsteps seemed to thud along the way to my front door. A faint silhouette appeared buoyant in the middle of the hallway, causing uproar of my awareness. My nerves ticked as I slowly looked behind me wondering if any other witnesses were around. But there wasn't; it was just me.

As my head turned back, the shadowed figure transformed into Savannah. The walls vibrated boisterously and the lights flickered as if anguish dominated the scene. I put my hands up shielding myself while Savannah came running at me full speed, until crashing through my entire body like a freight train.

I spun around, nearly falling as a clamorous screech perforated my eardrums. Leaving them to ring, I fell into the wall trying to regain my balance. The annoyance of heels clacking from behind brought my eyes towards the elevator.

There came the belle of my heart, completely baffling me as the beauty I drew in had my knees weak. Though my ruggedness seemed sheik, Mandy's appearance was far beyond anything I could describe. My eyes ran up the smooth slit clean up to her hip as the lighting shined against her flesh. Her chest showed only enough to get me excited, leaving my heart explosive as she neared me.

"Are you all right? What are you doing out here?"

"I was just getting back and became instantly star struck when you came walking up." **I grinned.**

"I appreciate your fancy, good sir. Are you ready then?"

I glanced back at Savannah's doorway with a hard swallow. *"Yeah..."*

Pulling Mandy in by the waist, I placed a kiss on her neck followed by another to her forehead. The ride over to my parent's was quiet. My chest felt tight, and I couldn't fathom what it was that happened to me, even so much as an explanation for what I saw.

For the first time since I've moved in, I actually felt a little fearful of the surroundings I called home.

Opening the door with eyes wider than Venus, my mother squealed with excitement pulling Mandy

and I into her embrace. Her gaze softened, realizing the sincerity of happiness marked upon my cheeks.

"Oh my, Kevin she is absolutely gorgeous! Lukas, hurry and come see your son and his marvelous arm candy!" **My mother winked.**

No sooner did my father's curiosity have him peering out the front door for a peek. Waiving us inside, he gently pulled Mandy in, kissing her on both cheeks. Before we could eat, my mother threw the twenty-one questions our way. It wasn't often that I brought home a potential mate, so I let my mother have her moment.

While at the dinner table, all that kept my mind held up was seeing Savannah in the hallway. Even the powerful force I endured by placing my hands against the wall had my thoughts in a torturous bind. Was it something I was internally jealous of? Or was it actually something that took place, in which my feelings were beginning to evade from a deeper source that I developed the ability to physically witness them?

Noticing my tense posture, I felt Mandy's grip squeeze tighter as my fingers twitched. Chills raised the tiny hairs that blanketed the back of my neck as if someone was breathing so closely, they wanted me to feel it. The light symphony of a familiar voice vibrated across my brain, leaving my head to fall back as I drew in a deep inhale.

"Kevin, are you all right, son?" **My father grew concerned.**

I let out a subtle laugh, nodding my head. I was too lost in the feeling that was presently electrifying my entire nervous system.

"Perhaps you should go adjust yourself in the bathroom?" **Mandy whispered, glancing down at the front of my pants.**

I cleared my throat, quickly excusing myself to seek a more sequestered location. In the deteriorating strength from faintness, feeling domination shred my internal ego had my knees weak.

To regain control, I took ahold of the porcelain pedestal before me, glancing at the stranger in the mirror staring back at me. I could not entertain my perverse thoughts by falling victim to my sudden wayward impulse. But the discernable pleasure I craved heated my flesh, cracking at my esophagus for release.

Splashing cold water onto my face, I took a moment to regain self-control. Raising my eyes to reach my reflection, Savannah appeared ghostlike behind my shoulder. I shrieked, turning around in a fearful haste to evaluate, but nothing revealed itself to me. In a stiff moment of foreboding preying upon me had me stuck in place.

"Goddamn it, Savannah... if you're in here, I advise you to come out...now!" **I whispered, holding an unwavering gaze on the shower curtain.**

Staring harder, a slight breeze shook the fabric as my heart began to thud aggressively beneath my

chest. A hollow voice escaped through the air as I stood feeble.

"Come closer..."

The loss of breath crashed in my ear as fright dug into the core of my spine. Why would Savannah want to play games? *How*...**did she know how to play ones such as these?**

"What the fuck are you doing? I don't want to do this! I don't like..."

"Like what? Not being in control of your own emotions? Having no physical strength to bound them? Does it make you feel incompetent, Kevin? Perhaps... emasculated?"

"Stop it..." **I growled.**

"Take what you want, like you've always done. On this day, shall you have me against my own will...as your depraved thoughts and grotesque methods commence."

"I said fucking stop! Fuck you, ya fucking bitch! You are the one making me feel this way. You think you have some entitlement because ya had me first, huh? What the hell is it that you seek?"

"I did have you first! A very, very long time ago..." **The voice hissed.**

Startling me, I heard Mandy trying to enter from the other side of the door.

"Kevin, let me in. Are you okay in there?"

"Yes, I'm fine." **My voice crackled.**

Opening the door, Mandy fell into me leaving her cheeks to blush in my embrace.

"Who on earth were you just speaking to?"

"No one…myself, I guess?"

Turning her back to me, Mandy pulled out a tube of deep red lipstick applying another layer.

"You know, if it were a personal phone call, you can just say so?"

Ignoring her bombast, my eyes fell to her slim waist wrapped in silver silk, luring my hands to grip each hip. Mandy gasped as the air fell in a deadly silence. A chill crept up my scalp, pricking my final nerve. Holding a great sinew of fascination, I could care less about the prevention of my actions. Facing Mandy towards me, I ferociously hiked her dress up; wedging myself in between her legs.

"Let me have you…" **I groaned.**

"Are you crazy? In your parent's house, Kevin? Absolutely not!"

I dodged her concern, pressing my lips into her neck. Her shallow breath braised my ear as I drew my jaw back, firmly sinking my teeth in. Mandy's nails

retracted into the back of my head, falling into submission.

"*Fuck, Kevin... yes, yes you can have me!*" **She gasped.**

Undoing my pants, I no sooner entered Mandy as her legs clenched around me. Too busy being held in my own thoughts, Savannah kept flashing through my mind. Interrupted and confused, I pushed harder and harder until objects rattled from the sink, falling onto the tile floor. Mandy yanked at my tie, holding me closer…as if she held me with sympathy.

"*That's right, Kevin…find me… I know you feel me.*" **Savannah's voice echoed in my head.**

I twitched from right to left trying to shake the thoughts away. Unable to open my eyes, I envisioned following Savannah down a dimmed hallway. Watching her lure me in with a playful temptress smile and sex appeal had my veins contracting. Infectious as the poison directly from the fangs of a Black Widow, Savannah drew me in with one touch as we fell onto a cement floor.

"*Kevin, open your eyes baby. You're starting to freak me out!*" **Mandy cried.**

My vision landed onto the bathroom's light as Mandy's eyes remained fixed. Her bottom jaw trembled as she struggled to find words to express.

"*What's the matter?*" **My eyes rolled forward.**

"Kevin, your pupils were just pulsating. As if you were turning into someone or something else. It frightened me! Do you think you are already reacting negatively to your medication?"

I focused on zipping my pants to avoid the question. *"I don't know. I don't believe that's even possible?"*

"We should probably get you home. You're pale and clammy, your parent's will definitely notice something's wrong. I'm worried about you." **She frowned.**

I slowly nodded as we left the bathroom; reentering the kitchen to my parents sitting with blushed expressions. I furrowed my brows as my mother's hands shook in her attempt to take a drink.

"I think I'm going to go home. Ma, I'm deeply sorry. I think I may be coming down with something."

"Ha, oh yes! Get the both of yous home, especially if that shit is contagious." **My father laughed.**

I felt my face burn with embarrassment as my Mother's marred in disappointment. Looking down at my untucked shirt only intensified my shame while walking to the car. Mandy pressed her lips together, keeping her expression gentle as she always did in times like this.

I immediately kicked my shoes off as I entered my front door. Mandy's heavy steps thudded behind me

as she whipped me around, fighting to unbutton my shirt.

"Mandy…"

"Shh…who said we were finished?" **She groped my chest.**

Mandy pressed her index finger to my lips, walking me backwards to my bedroom. I smiled between our kisses, allowing her to lay me down this time instead. I needed to be brought back down, though it was impossible carrying the amount of infatuation I had towards Mandy. She needed to feel a sense of power, herself. Never taking a second guess, was the best decision I've ever made absent consideration. Willing to step down from your throne of absolute narcissism, allowing her to gain a sense of womanhood is where the essence of love comes to existence.

When I was just a teen, I was always a man of my own; a lone wolf having to learn survival through his trials and error. I would be the target of my peer's self-loathing while drowning in my own humiliation. It wasn't the object to release hatred and cleanse my negative energy on a bully. It was the thought of how it was going to feel the moment I witnessed their final breath.
On a hot summer night, I endured being dragged against my will to some drug persuasive bonfire. One in which we hashed shit out the old fashioned way, while drinking homemade smash. A guy who went to my school

Breaking At What Seems

Kyla M. Wassil

blasted his new-age techno through two giant subwoofers in the bed of his truck, controlling the mood. Kids were lighting torches and throwing around glow sticks while becoming mentally impaired. I lost my cousin throughout the night, becoming paranoid with my surroundings. Having several types of illegal substances shoved in my face continuously, I gave in to my annoyance by taking an unknown pill. The girl who placed it inside my mouth began laughing uncontrollably. It made me angry, as I downed a cup of an unknown mixed beverage.

Moments after losing my balance and coherence, I cowered inside trying to find a place of solitude. In the midst of seeking the nearest escape, a girl dancing carefree moved about in my peripheral. I watched her sway back and forth as her identity remained masked by black hair. A girl from my English class yelled my name, breaking my attention. She stood near a truck with murky aluminum that casted a clouded version of my reflection in which drew me in its location.

I dipped down to look at myself in the rearview mirror seeing a younger me… the actual man I stood to be, presently. But why? How could this be? For the first time after many times I've questioned my own morals, and come to find out it has been me the entire time.

I am the one to dream of such violence and rogue, shamelessly believing there was something wrong with me. Looking back, I watched the black haired girl run straight for the woods, far away from me.

Breaking At What Seems

Kyla M. Wassil

"Ugh, Jesus Christ!" **I sat up in the cold sweats, trying to catch my breath.** *"I know it's her...oh my God! I know...I know... I know now, damnit!"* **I began shaking.**

Mandy sat forward freaking out as I repeated myself over and over in terror.

"Kevin, what the hell? Wake up! You're having a nightmare. Baby, please open your eyes!"

I convulsed as her fingernails tickled against my chest, feeling her warm lips meet mine several times. Chills waved through my body as I drew in an exaggerated breath, coming back to consciousness. Dropping Mandy's hands, I slipped out of bed making my way to the balcony. The midnight air was dense and stale as I flew into the city's darkness.

"Savannah! What the hell are you doing to me? I know it's you, don't you dare try to run from this! All you do is fucking run from me, but I've caught your ass now!"

Savannah walked to the corner of the railing, beneath the moonlight. Her overwhelmed eyes glowed in the shadows as she came into view.

"Oh please, you've caught nothing. I allow you to see the things you do! What makes you think I am to blame?"

"Because, you wouldn't ask that if you had no notion as to what I am talking about. Stop messing with me! Tell me what it is that you want, and I'll do my best to help

you. I can't handle this shit any longer, it's exhausting me."

"Do you not hear yourself, Kevin?" **She laughed.** *"What I want I cannot have, no matter the measure or strenuous voyage it may take."*

"I know one thing... I know that you fucking want me. Because if you didn't you wouldn't place yourself into my sexual thoughts and desires. I don't know what the hell you've done to me, but I feel what you do...I see things only one could if they stood in the very same room as you. I feel your weakness, and desperation to have me near."

Savannah didn't look away as her eyes sparkled with honesty. *"You may think you "know" certain things, but you don't know everything..."*

"Maybe, because you won't allow me to?"

"I will change your life, Kevin. Do you not understand the power I can give you with the information I possess? You have to want it bad enough... you have to believe in it to reach that great extent!"

"How would it change my life?"

Savannah's stare became acute as she glanced behind me. *"We can't continue this now. She's coming, and she's angry..."* **She sighed, stepping back into the shadows.**

I turned to see Mandy in the living room, nearing me in a hurry.

"Okay, who in the hell were you talking to just now? Kevin, don't you dare tell me it was no one. Christ, if that were true, I can't even have you sleep safely inside your own home if you sleepwalk, too!"

"I'll be fine. I am just trying to straighten my mind. Maybe you're assumption was correct, with it being my medication."

Mandy pulled me inside, locking the door behind us. *"Then I don't want you taking it anymore. Not until you see your doctor, again. I thought they were supposed to help with your bad dreams?"*

"They are a substance to control my emotions, it's a fucking antidepressant."

"Just come back to bed. I am calling him first thing in the morning. This needs to stop before you…uh." **She stopped herself.** *"Don't look at me in that way, Kevin. You know what I am trying to say."*

Climbing back into bed, Mandy pulled me into her chest holding me tightly. The light sensation she created across my scar instantly put me to rest. My life could be at risk if I continued these late night self-interventions.

Breaking At What Seems   Kyla M. Wassil

FOURTEEN

Staring blankly into my coffee mug, I overheard Mandy engaging a quarrel conversation in the living room. Not wanting to remain prisoner on my bed, I kept my steps lightweight down the hall.

I could see the stress in Mandy's expression as she torqued her arm violently while she spoke. I didn't want to interrupt so to fill the void I sprinkled food into Gerry's bowl. The sun beaming through the window cast a reflection on the glass, presenting a dark figure behind me. I jumped out of my skin, spilling hot coffee in my lap only to see that nothing was there.

"I'm not going to call back? What don't you people understand? He needs to see Dr. Sunter, now! It's a damn emergency!" **Feeling defeated, Mandy ended the call.**

"Is everything all right?"

"I could ask you the same as you sit in smoldering hot coffee. Kevin..." **She sighed.** *"I tried getting you in today, but apparently they are booked until your appointment tomorrow. Can you make it until then?"*

I grabbed Mandy's hand as she used a kitchen towel to dry my wounded skin. Bringing it to my face, I gave a warm kiss to her fingers. I knew she was extremely worried, but I had to deal with my inner vex the best way possible.

"I just wish I had the answers to all the questions we have... I find it quite troubling that this is in neither of our expertise."

"Babe, I'm going to be fine. I've made it through much worse."

"How you find this humorous is beyond me. Kevin, this is your life, your career we are talking about! Have some compassion."

Breaking At What Seems

Kyla M. Wassil

    I sat there listening without interruption. I've never had a mate who cared so much and maybe I didn't know how to handle it otherwise. Mandy already held a great significance to me and I would hate it if something were to ever destroy what I felt, much more; take it all away.

    "I have to go to work. I am taking you in first thing in the morning. I don't give a mad fuck about what those receptionist broads have to say about it. Are you going to be fine, alone?"

    "Yes, aren't I always?"

    "Let's not forget who threw salt around and smashed their coffee table… have a good day, Kevin."

    I moseyed off to my bedroom to grab my hidden pack of Marlboro's, placing one in between my lips. The smell of fresh tobacco kept me pleasantly calm as I stood by, engaged in thought. I thought maybe if I kept it in my mouth long enough, I wouldn't feel the need to smoke it.
    Opening the top drawer of my nightstand, a shiny chromed Magnum glistened beneath the lighting. Always keeping it for safety precautions, taking a slug to the head might have seemed like a more appropriate solution to my problems.
    The sparkle of selifan hanging on my closet door concealed the navy fibers my body missed so dearly. Mandy left a small sticky note advising me to uphold a smile, and that it would be returned to proper purpose in no time. Discouragement was clutching at my last

fiber of hope and even though she was right; I still couldn't come to grips with reality.

Feeling a breeze across my neck had me on my feet, longing to inhale the city. I made my way out onto the balcony, watching the slow movement of early action down below. Several cars had passed before the slow, sketchy patrol car came creeping by.

What the hell was I thinking? I'm not a prisoner, nor was I wearing a fucking low jack. Disregarding the fact they had the right to follow me, I dressed in my running gear flying out the door. Running was something I yearned for more so than breathing. Not only are you breathing more excessively than normal, but your lungs and heart are working in sync to strengthen not just your body, but your mind as well.

How can we ever truly love and enjoy something, if we never stop to understand the work it actually takes for negotiable improvement? If passion ceased to exist rather in the finer arts or the typical originality of a hammer in hand; we'd never value its beauty or power to entice and inspire. When carrying a younger mind, it would seem we were invincible; able to do all things that are great. Through age we shed the credulous, developing an understanding of just how cruel the world and human race really is.

In the meantime, we cling onto these 'famous quotes' from inspiring icons and the words of an idol that shackled to our likings, creating a common interest. Why is it that we can memorize and forever live by a cluster of words, but fail to reason when we, ourselves, underestimate our own mentality to regain a wise mind and reassurance? For the human mind is an adventurous place, it isn't always on the safest route.

    I ran beneath the silver sky, feeling condensation sheet my skin until salt dripped from my top lip. Lost in the whimsical symphony of emphatic lyrics, I stopped in my tracks after spotting Mandy running on the other side of the park. I slowed my pace, observing her movement when a burst of jealousy kicked me in the gut.

    A young, fit male approached her with a long hug. Thinking Mandy should have been at work, I didn't quite understand why she would go through the trouble of lying to me. The friendly shove to his chest turned into him flirtatiously pulling her in by the waist. My breathing picked up as my nerves pierced my stomach like barbed wire. I couldn't bear it any longer so I took off sprinting in the opposite direction. I didn't bother taking a cab home: I just ran—the entire way. If I was going to break down emotionally, I needed to be in the comfort of my own shelter.

    At first, I was upset above all else. I paced back and forth in my kitchen while running a thousand scenarios through my head until it made me physically ill. Impossible to keep my tears at bay, I became angry. Slamming my weight against the refrigerator, to punching walls and aggressively grunting and screaming went on for several minutes. If this woman was going to be the first to break my heart, I was going to be ready for it; but I wasn't.

    The first time I have ever felt pain in my heart was on the night Max got shot, nearly dying in my arms.

From that moment on, I wore an iron shield of armor. Knowing what it felt like to almost lose a close companion made me fear what an actual heartbreak involving crucial emotions felt like.

    A detrimental storm was brewing in my mind, and for the first time in weeks, I knew it was really me who was angered; not my alter personality. Kevin Strode was pissed off and for the sake of any angels above, I begged for forgiveness on my misguided soul.

    Limited on furniture to pose as my worst enemy, I turned to a bottle of whiskey that rested in the freezer. Blowing a strong gust across my nose hairs, I downed several shots of chatoyant amber as it tore through my stomach tissue. A mind altering escape was the only road I wanted to walk down, though I've done it several hundred times before.

    Lying against the hardwood in a dark living room, I felt an overbearing presence surrounding me. Influencing my neurotransmitter, all dopamine was paralyzed as my hellacious inner entity placed us both in everlasting phosphorescence.

*   Standing by a loading dock, I watched the shore suck my feet into the sand as the tide rolled in. Khaki jeans barely folded above my ankles as a dampened white button down leeched to my torso. The fading sun cast a contrast across my chest, covered in a faint field of dark hairs. I ran a hand through my wet hair, slicking it back like some high-classed aristocrat. My eyes danced atop the ocean's surface as it illuminated through my pupils,*

electrifying my heart.

Mandy stood several feet away, holding up a pair of binoculars to watch the evening fleet of feathers disperse before the horizon. Feeling my eyes, she faced me returning the gesture with a peculiar smile. Dancing innocently, I mentally devoured her emitted charisma with the substitution of personal fatal designs. Kicking warm salt water in my direction seemed playful to her, but in that moment it disfigured reality with my deepest desire; and that was being covered in crimson as she begged for me to stop.

Barefoot and carefree, Mandy waltzed around the living room moving to her own beat. Restless and impatient, I had to have her body against mine. Standing before the fireplace, I cautiously walked up behind her. I mean, what the hell was I about to endeavor? Was I willing to execute my inner fantasies while wearing an unremorseful smile?

My jaw ticked as I drew in the sight of a temptress as alive as the universe itself. I am a lucky fellow to have the beauty of nature at its finest standing before me. I took ahold of her arm, facing her towards me. Eyes amplified enough to electrocute the neurons to my heart; stopping it completely. I had to take control, she belonged to me and I was certain to remind her of that. The bastard who held perverse intentions behind a fraudulent grin put deception in her actions and I, being a cop, could tell directly offhand. I refused to give her the power to break a heart she had no control over its vitality in the first place.

Appeasement tugged at the corners of her mouth as she looped her arms around my neck. The heat of the fire irritated my bare flesh, but my purpose kept me still. Leaning in to kiss me, I snatched her by the jaw with dominance. Her posture fell apprehensive as her hands reacted—digging her nails into my chest. Trying to escape my grasp, I yanked her in by the small of her back; keeping her within my control.

Becoming excited, I pressed myself against her pelvis as her fingers uncurled across my pecs. Growing by the second, I drenched myself in boastful pride as Mandy's behavior suddenly became risqué. Pulling her face beside mine, I asked who her little friend was; warning her of the brutal consequences if she dared to lie. Though she always had a way of manipulating me in my weaker moments, she had no existing evidence against me this time. Convicting me as the 'bad guy' and me allowing her to play the victim wasn't going to work any longer.

I've had my fair share of the media's freewill offering of explicit content. But it never compared to the physical aspects of realistic gratification to satisfy my needs. Mandy lured me to our bedroom, never parting her lips from mine. Feeling defeat creeping inches away from victory, I flung her onto the mattress. My dignity stood superior and it meant more to me than how she would feel about the outcome of this.

Desperately undoing her shorts, the back of my hand struck her face as she instantly stopped moving. This was going to go my way and she was going to fucking deal with it.

I used my shirt to tie one wrist to the bedpost before ripping hers off to restrain the other. I took a forceful grip at the band of her shorts, yanking them completely off. She sighed as I hovered over her, undoing my jeans. I felt my hardened flesh meet the dampness of Mandy's, quivering beneath me as the warmth of my breath tickled her chest.

I pressed my hips down harder, feeling her legs wrap around my waist. Never entering, I reached for the hunter's knife decorating the top of my nightstand. Pressing it to her throat, allowing the blade to rest momentarily, only brought on a greater fear in her eyes. *"If I were to cut your throat, your escape would be granted too easily. This is merely a simple warning."*

"Kevin, what the hell are you doing on the floor?"

I felt Mandy's stiletto tap against my ribcage as I instantly woke up. Having a major hangover migraine, I sat up to view her more clearly. Drinking last night must have given me a damn nightmare as close to life as they come.

"Sorry, I have no fucking idea why I'm in here. Just like I didn't know you went "running" instead of going to work this morning." **I glared.**

Mandy's expression was worried but she played it off by scorning me back. *"So now you have your little "watchdogs" spying on my every move because you can't do it yourself at the moment?"*

I stood aghast, unwilling to take part in her game of reverse psychology. *"Ooh...don't you dare try to talk your way out of this one."*

"This one? When the fuck was the "first time", Kevin? Jesus Christ..."

"I saw you with him, Mandy!" **I interrupted.** *"I went for a run thinking I needed a different setting. When I entered my second mile, I glanced across the park and there you were...with some other guy. Why? Who the fuck is he?"*

Mandy stood her ground, fucking with me even harder. *"How about, "who the fuck" is this little neighbor of yours that you always sneak away to have late night conversations with? The convenience of you being on suspension is no excuse! How do I know you didn't have a thing with her before meeting me or if you still do?"*

"Whoa... whoa!" **I waved my hands.** *"Why the fuck are you turning this on me?"*

"Because you haven't seen the way you've been acting, Kevin! I always find you somewhere supposedly talking amongst yourself. Which, I highly doubt. If you're playing games, it needs to stop! This isn't some high school emotional rollercoaster. It's real and mature and should be nothing but honest."

Seeing Mandy's eyes crystalize, I couldn't find the right words to say. Our first argument and it was over dishonesty, or just my insecurity?

"I—I do have a neighbor. That's all she is, Mandy. I swear to you."

"I've looked into your eyes, Kevin, when we are making love. You look either absent, or seeing someone else besides me." **Mandy broke down.**

I swallowed the knot lodged in my throat as I choked back my own tears and frustration. If Mandy has been suspicious of Savannah for quite some time, why the hell did she wait until now to mention it?

I walked into the kitchen taking a violent swig, slamming the bottle onto the counter. Pulling a knife from its holder, I ran my fingertips down the blade with a sardonic smile. Mandy arched an eyebrow, holding an unwavering gaze in the distance.

"You want to know an interesting fact about knives? They cut…as deep as the handler allows. That is what you're doing to me! Of course this isn't a "teen" relationship, you're just the first person I've let get to me in this way. Don't you see that I love you?"

Mandy's eyes relaxed with sympathy as I fell to my knees. Drawing my head into her chest, her grasp never loosened.

"I love you, too, Kevin… with everything in me. That guy you saw is the CEO of my company. He was asking how my latest article was coming along. That's it."

"Why haven't you told me you've been writing an important piece? I would have understood."

"Because…it isn't finished yet." **Her eyes veered from mine.**

The wheels in my head began to turn when Mandy looked away with a face painted in falsification.

"Just be honest with me then…no matter what."

I tipped her chin to meet my eyes, pressing a solid kiss to her forehead. I may have been in the wrong for taking out my work related anger on Mandy, but I will always carry what I saw in the back of my mind.

That night, I lied in bed like an insomniac, counting the seconds I could withstand blinking while staring blankly into the ceiling fan. Mandy lied on my chest the entire night until cracking her head into my jaw as our alarm sounded. Waking with no sleep had me obscenely cranky, though I didn't take it out on anyone who didn't deserve it. Knowing I had to make the trip to do some psychotherapy to control Dr. Jekyll and Mr. Hyde had me brooding for most of the morning.

Dr. Sunter was patiently rested in the comfort of his expensive leather chair as Mandy and I entered. He presented a welcoming smile as he jumped straight into our session.

"I deeply apologize for being unable to see you yesterday, Kevin. I want to know what it was exactly that you experienced last night."

Mandy raised an eyebrow as the tension rose between her tightly pressed lips.

"I keep having these dreams…only they don't appear to be just dreams. More like memories forming this devilish nightmare."

Dr. Sunter's eye flickered towards Mandy as her wide eyed expression held the validation of truth.

"You are free to elaborate, if you'd like."

My grip tightened around Mandy's hand as I released a pessimistic sigh.

"They're memories of murders…distinctive detail only either seeing it or living it could create such profound imagery. It's too vivid and explicit."

"And they are affecting your daily life, such as work?"

His eyes of ignorant disbelief strangled the bottomless pit layered with boiling ire. I was quite sure he had heard of more outlandish subjects in his career before now.

"Not only my work, but at home it affects my behavior and consumes me at the most sporadic increments of time."

"In other words, you're experiencing rapid mood changes in which dramatically affect your daily routines and/or activities?"

"Yes, but I feel you're not quite grasping my meaning, doctor."

"Look, Dr. Sunter, imagine being used to the normal behavior of your loved one… then it suddenly begins to deteriorate at a fast pace. One minute you are greeted with familiar eyes and the next, you're staring into the eyes of the purest evil you'd ever find even in the depths of your own nightmares." **Mandy interjected.**

Fascination raised Dr. Sunter's eyebrows as he ferociously scribbled on his notepad. "What else are these real life "nightmares" causing in your life?"

I became angry as I stood to my feet, violently ranting. Like venom to my chest, I had to drain it out before my heart exploded. "You think you know every goddamn thing because you present a fucking Ivy League certificate? I could care less! When I tell you I haven't felt like myself lately, then that's exactly what I mean!"

Timid emotion pulsated beneath the surface of his skin as his shallow breathing quickened.

"I never expressed that I didn't believe or understand you, Kevin. You're jumping to conclusions. I apologize if my reaction posed a misleading response. It appears evident that you might have symptoms of bipolar disorder."

"How is that? Neither one of my parents have it."

"You could be the first string. DNA morphs as generations pass. Being forced to endure dramatic *incidents that your career has faced you with could have sprouted the hair of your disorder. It's quite common with patients who carry a history of PTSD or traumatic memories leading to such. Anything can occur in life that conflicts with the mind, throwing your brain into dysfunction. I want to try you on a small dosage of Lithium."*

"I am not depressed!" **I snarled.**

"It's to prevent you from entering Bipolar Depression. It's a safe control substance, unless you suggest something else?"

"Bipolar causes shifts in moods and ability to function. It doesn't justify why I have obtained unseen memories, while devouring the ones I carry from my childhood era. It does not cause my identity to seem unfamiliar and pick up habits of another personality."

Dr. Sunter's eye froze as he entered a deep thought. His bottom lip twitched as a conclusion formed on his face. I was nervous to hear what his verdict on the matter was. Then again, I wanted to figure it out and take care of it before it fully matured.

"You're correct, it doesn't."

"If this helps, I've witnessed Kevin talking to himself." **Her stare was sharp.** *"Even though he claims it has been his neighbor. Though I'm quite sure your neighbor didn't follow us to your parent's the other night."*

"Kevin has been found engaging in a conversation while no one is around. He also tends to act differently, claiming all actions are out of his control. Well, sounds like you may be Schizophrenic and Seroquel is going to be your new friend."

"Schizophrenic? Do you realize what that means? It fucking means I can't be a cop anymore! It also means I lose not only my gun and badge, but also my purpose for breathing, ya bastard!" **I began crying**. "Don't you…don't you dare tell me that, you son of a bitch! I am not crazy."

"I need you to calm down, Kevin. I am prescribing you this medication for now. I have to write it in your diagnosis statement, if I lie I can lose my license."

"Oh fuck you! Let's throw empathy for the white coat that fears a slap on his wrist. My ass will be ostracized from the law enforcement. You might as well just publically castrate me for the entire state of New York to watch."

Dr. Sunter didn't break under the pressure I was clouding the room with. He saw through my smoke and bundled turmoil that itched to free itself. The swift rip of his prescription pad was like a glass shattering in a silent room. Seroquel was scribbled into the faint blue sheet of paper.

"I'll be sure to inform your chief that you need an extension on your leave. I need to be exact on what exactly is going on with you, Kevin. Please don't feel like I am *against you. I truly want to be of aid, I just have to get more facts that can make an accurate diagnosis."*

I cut my eyes, grabbing Mandy's hand to leave. As we entered the elevator, I became aggressively angry, mentally exiling my temper with an obscene outburst. I could feel my face heat up as my veins pulsated throughout my entire body.

Mandy folded her arms into her chest, remaining reticent in the far corner of the elevator cab. My fists crushed against the hazy metal reflection of the chrome walls that surrounded me until blood busted through my knuckles.

A seemingly so mysophobia was conjuring within my internal wants to rid of these pretentious feelings and behavior. In my twenty-five years of life, how is it that out of nowhere I lose myself, my religion, my desires, only to become this detriment animal that is hazardous to his own being.

I could sit alone, in a vacant room simply thinking to myself and yet the demon discovers a way out, laughing as he tortures the life around me. It wasn't the fact of being possessed; it's the initial truth that whatever was in me had complete control over me. I am one of Manhattan's finest police officers, yet I can't even maintain a civil restraint on my own actions. I would give whatever it took to not damage my life and soil the precinct that I represented.

The elevator came to a sudden stop as the doors opened only to reveal that smug bastard who held an eminent eye for Mandy. He entered with a reacquainting smile as his charm flooded the oxygen, making it impossible to breathe. His eyes met the bloodied indentations that marked the walls as a cynical smile tugged at the corners of his self-righteous persona. The darkness I radiated longed for the prick to come off with something slick, but instead he redirected his interest towards Mandy. *Of course.*

"Fancy seeing you again." **His exhale was exaggerated.**

I was positive that the gleam of his pearly whites flattered Mandy as she stood meek to the recent event that occurred. Without closing in the space between her and I, she entertained the conversation. Whether she was stepping beyond enemy lines, she had no idea what storm was brewing within my chest as her body language read sensuality.

"I could say the same. How have you been, Doctor Brozek?"

"Please, call me Abram. I have seen better days. But seeing a smile as bright as yours around the office each day would be an easy cure." **He winked.**

My jaw clenched so hard I heard the pop echo inside my skull. My face was pinched so tightly with disgust I dared for this display to continue.

"I appreciate the offer, but I am currently occupied at New York's magazine company. I just self-indulge in unbelievable events to a high degree."

"Is that why you hang around this guy?" **He nodded towards me.**

Right then I completely lost it. *"What the fuck did you just say? What is that supposed to even mean?"*

"It means exactly how it sounded. It's apparent you come to this building to seek some type of medical treatment, do you not?"

"That's none of your business!"

"I was just stating the obvious." **He casually shrugged.**

"Just like you state the obvious when you practically drool at the chops when around my girlfriend?"

"Look, I can't help that I appreciate the beauty of things." **He grinned with confidence.**

"That explains why you masquerade the true identity of "beauty" by using silicone and collagen to create your version of what a perfected design regarding a woman's body should look like, right? Only to camouflage a deeper, self-conscious, and apparent infliction you help the innocent "professionally" disguise. Lucky you, to get paid an overabundance to falsify one's appearance in the hopes to alter their mind on what the public eye perceives as natural pulchritude. Yet, you stand so arrogantly misled in believing you have the slightest idea as to what I am going through. Funny how I didn't need a fucking Ph.D. to revise your problem." **I followed up with a smile.**

Abram twitched his nostrils as he stood barren from his supposed sheik protection. Seems as if the man has never been put in his place before, and I surprised myself by not pounding my fist into his face. That was a lawsuit I didn't want to endure, because then I would have let the man carry an underserving victory by default.

The doors opened to his floor, leaving him to step out without another word. Mandy was quick to pull me in by the face, crashing her soft lips into mine. Mediating my conflicting nerves, I exhaled relaxing my posture beneath her touch as she sighed into my mouth.

Breaking At What Seems   Kyla M. Wassil

FIFTEEN

Three days had passed and I have been locked in a medicated state of mind as I remained isolated within the walls of my apartment. Eyes glazed over only to ignore each muffled incoming call that displayed my mother's name. Several voicemails, countless text messages, yet I refused to respond. I felt no need to burden my parents with such disturbing animosity. I wanted to astray from the possible bold headlines of what the volatile uneducated bureaucracy would spat about, only to slander my name and that of the precinct. Manhattan's NYPD didn't deserve such uncharacterized harassment, especially inflicted by one of their own.

    I stumbled my way into the kitchen to feed Gerry before turning towards the freezer. A silent serenade shared with fermented mash and Seroquel seemed to be the perfect concoction to subside the eagerness of my negativity.

    As I pulled the door open, cool fog rolled against my face causing me to suddenly shiver. I reached my hand in taking ahold of an unopened bottle of *Willet Bourbon,* twisting off its cap to inhale a fiery scent. The aroma sent a tingling sensation through the hairs of my nostrils, possibly singeing them down to the follicle.

    Pulling the bottle to my parched lips, I allowed the smooth amber to stream onto my pallet as it scorched my throat. The weather outside was shadowed by an overcast of grey cumulous obstructions that painted the sky. A masculine aver erupted my confidence only leading me to make an irrational decision. I slid the RX bottle across the counter top, squeezing it within my palm.

    Rolling two 100mg pills into my hand, I took a moment to reassess my intentions, though I knew what I was doing. Unstable they may believe me to be, but I knew better. I wouldn't allow this perpetual deceptive city to devour my integrity and morals until I took my last breath.

Giving myself time to execute the affects, I lingered onto my balcony as light droplets came crashing down from above. It felt cool against my skin as I lounged out beneath the forgiving atmosphere. Slowly falling into a daze, my body became limp as my eyes were forced to shut.

Staring down at a crinkled piece of paper inscribed with a fatal repertoire, I knew I was chasing the devil himself. I've waited for what seemed just short of a lifetime for this very moment. I've watched my victim since we were both seven years of age. A platonic obsession with a die-cast perfected stature, she stood a few feet away dancing to her own beat. Smoke from the bonfire assaulted my lungs as I stood at a dangerous proximity, letting the heat clothe my body. Intensifying my desire to wreck her world, the wickedness lurked upon my shoulder as I welcomed it with a devious smile.

For hours, I watched her intoxicate herself as her clan of adversity became unaware of their surroundings. Like a hunter, I shall patiently wait for the right time to intervene. My chest as hollow as the menacing voice in my mind, I kept a vindicated shield of armor that upheld a remarkable amount of time.

Watching her disappear into the shadows, I was quick to follow her movement. Standing in the shadows, I studied her actions as she became frantic, unaware of what was awaiting her. Stepping into the lighting, her eyes met the illumination of mine. "You scared me! I *have no idea where I'm at."* She admitted.

I took another step closer as she stumbled against the barn. Nearly losing her balance, I gripped her arm as she mistook my gesture. I spoke no words, leaving an eerie curiosity to linger in the air around us. My hand ran down the bare flesh of her thigh as I tremored inside.

Pulling me in, she kissed my neck tightening her grip in my hair as I clasped my hand around her throat. The wheezing gasp escaping her mouth caused her to react more aggressively. "I want you for myself." I whispered. "Gerry the juggernaut wants human affection?" She slurred with a giggle. I became ill tempered as I slammed her against the barn, watching fear rise in her eyes. Now she understood my meaning—stupid bitch. Thinking I wanted a pity fuck, she underestimated me.

Cupping her mouth, I dragged her around the back of the barn out of the eyes of any witnesses. Trying to undress me, I grabbed both wrists, walking her further into the woods. Stopping in a spot visible by the moonlight, I flicked open my switchblade mesmerized by its glistening blade. "What are you doing?" She asked fearfully. "Getting what I've waited too long to claim." "Gerould, if you want sex, just say so."

I chuckled to myself as she proclaimed to be naïve. "That isn't what I'm after," "What is it that you want, then?" Her voice crackled. My eyes darted at the moon then back at her. "The warmth of your blood…all over me."

The sound of her breath forcefully escaping her mouth moved her feet to take off. I was quick to snatch her up by the back of the hair, slamming her down into the dirt. She tried screaming, but I held the blade to her throat warning her to keep quiet. "If this is some sick game of yours, consider me disqualified."

I heard her friends calling for her in the distance. She longed to run, but my firm grip kept her by my side. I didn't come this far to back down now. The hole I dug for her was just a few feet away, I had to make it quick before I was caught. I was damned to have let that fucking happen!

Tying her hands with her own belt, she began crying only after realizing I was serious. I felt no sympathy for her as she strutted through the halls at school, acting promiscuous like she owned the damn place. It wasn't a lesson I was going to teach her; in fact it was a reality check. To show her that no one is better than the other.

Unbuckling my jeans, I stood flaccid momentarily. She begged me to stop but I didn't give a shit. This bitch didn't care about anyone else around her, but this time it was me who got the attention and gratification I yearned for.

Dropping her onto her knees, my member began hardening before her. The thought of killing her aroused me all the more. Pressing the blade into her neck, I took a quick slice as blood poured all over me. Its warmth comforted me and I ferociously pleased myself with the lubrication from her blood. I ejaculated so hard, it was unbelievable. That moment I knew this is what I wanted to do until I was to ever get caught. Not being able to scream as she bled out, I shoved her body over into the hole, burying her as dirt filled her lungs. I only kept her there until everyone left the bonfire.

Once in the clear, I undug her remains tossing her into the fire to destroy all evidence. My first will always be of my fondest memories, no matter how sick and depraved it was described.

I stood by sipping on a beer, watching embers flake into the air. The teeth I pried from her mouth rolled around in my other palm and a large smile overtook my face. Another one down and won't be found.

Feeling myself nearly choke on what seemed to be rain was a mistake. I opened my eyes, convulsing as foam developed in my mouth. Uncontrollably vomiting until I entered aspiration, I could hear a faint voice from Savannah's balcony.

"How fucking foolish and selfish of you, Kevin. I stand merely disappointed."

I tried to find my way as I gagged for air. In my sheer luck, I felt Mandy take me up from the ground screaming in panic for me to breathe. Losing light around me, I felt her hands press into my chest. For a split second, I looked up to see Mandy's movement completely freeze, as if she saw something that had frightened her.

"What is it?" **I asked faintly.**

"I thought I saw someone over there."

Her face as pale as the dead, she pulled my up by the arms hauling me off into my living room. Filled with hurt and anger, Mandy planted her hands against the sink as she broke down into a harsh sob. Meanwhile, I rested on the couch trying to calm my heartbeat.

"Why the fuck would you do that, Kevin? Why would you try to harm yourself like that? Are you that unhappy with your life?"

"Unhappy? I am being mentally tormented every fucking day! I hate how I feel, if it isn't enough when I look into the mirror unable to recognize myself. How would you feel? Now I see a doctor who is trying to dope me up because that seems to solve everything!"

"I need you to lose whatever unwanted terrorist you have within that is provoking this perilous behavior! Kevin, when I saw you lying out there, it wasn't the site of you choking that frightened me, it was the well apparent realism of watching you dying! Do you have any idea how scary that was for me or would have been for anyone else? Christ, if I had come in any later I would have lost you forever. I want to help you. I do not blame you for a damn thing. It's out of your control and that is what scares me more than anything." **Mandy sniveled.**

I had no other explanation or words of comfort, just watching her cry from a tragic experience I impended on her was unjustly. I was thankful she hadn't considered me insane, and walked out on me period. Pulling herself together, Mandy took out her phone, dialing a number.

"What are you doing?"

"Relax, I'm calling Dr. Sunter. Your medication is doing all but helping you!"

Forcing me to get cleaned up, Mandy wore a plagued smile masked with the substitution of adverse solicitousness. I stood in a daze as the elevator ascended in a rattled disorder. Dr. Sunter rushed us in no sooner than Mandy could finish a complete knock on the door.

Motioning for us to sit down, he read over my medical file. Gazing into my glazed eyes as the tiny vessels constricted, Mandy ran a warm hand down my pale cheek to ease my rapid heartbeat.

"From what Mandy had explained to me earlier on the telephone, I want to try something with you. I want to place your mind in a hypnosis state to look deeper into your memory."

"What is that gonna help, exactly?"

"First, tell me if you're experiencing memory loss."

"I am. But don't you go telling me I have fucking amnesia." **I snarled.**

"Kevin, please let the man help you!"

"Okay, fine. Yes, I have had trouble remembering things from my childhood. Almost as if I am gaining memories from someone else's past. They seemed to have *reversed in time, starting from older memories to back when I or…they were a teen."*

"When you say they, you're referring to whom?"

"I couldn't tell you…well, wait." **I paused.** *"My latest dream I had some poor girl I killed called me Gerry or Gerould. Something like that. But I know no one by that name."*

"Kill? You're harming people in your dreams to that drastic effect?"

My eyes glared as I mentally retrained the urge to punch his lights out for his dumbfounded expression.

"Yes, I kill people in my dreams. Only they are too real to be a damn figment of my imagination. I'm a damn police officer of the NYPD, why on earth would I long to harm anyone like that?"

"What of that large scar on the right side of your head. What is that from?"

I wetted my lips, taking in a large inhale. *"I had an abscess that required emergency medical treatment."*

"In your brain…they did surgery on an abscess? How old were you when this took place?"

"Seven…"

"That drastic decision had to be due to an infection, correct?"

"Yeah," **I chuckled.** *"How'd you come to that conclusion?"*

Dr. Sunter's brows rose as he neared me in a fastidious fashion, causing me to strain while swallowing.

"I'm going to relax your mind into a meditative state to draw out whatever may be bothering you inside. I will have complete control over how you react, as I ask you questions, I am only seeking a truth beyond your own mental comprehension. It causes the mind to absentmindedly respond only as you fall into my trust and safety."

"Is this going to hurt him?" **Mandy's voice shook.**

"No, I can snap him out of it at any given time. Kevin, rest your thoughts and allow me to take control of your mind. You will not be forced to do anything you do not want to during this session, so we are all clear." **He placed his hands securely on either side of my head.**

I closed my eyes hesitantly, as I swallowed the nails that scratched down my throat. I took several deep breaths as Dr. Sunter placed me into hypnosis. I saw myself as an innocent child running through a wheat field beneath the incandescence of purity. Elaborating on calm details of what I saw, I entered a deeper state of mind. All sound faded around me, as I allowed Dr. Sunter's voice to carry me through.

My body sank into the couch and my legs felt heavy as if they were made of lead.

"With each word I utter, you are falling faster into sleep until I bring you back. Kevin, you see yourself in a safe environment, as if you're floating on a cloud impossible to fall and fail. What do you see?"

"Myself, only I look different."

"It's been years since you've recognized your growing stature. How do you appear now, Kevin?"

I felt a sharp pain split down the center of my skull as my body twitched in response. Held in Dr. Sunter's hands, my jaw clenched against his warm palms, as my eyes flickered in disagreement, rolling to the back of my head. I felt whatever or whoever he was looking for come to surface, deciding to present itself here and now.

My voice scratched and growled as I fought to overpower the uprising of something rather dangerous. Breaking at the surface of what seemed impossible, I merely lost myself as a devilish creature sat comfortably in my vacant skin.

"Oh my God! Why is he convulsing like that? You said this wouldn't hurt him!"

"Quiet! Mandy please, I have no explanation as to what his mind is doing right now."

"Kevin! Baby, please can you hear me?" **Mandy cried.**

Pressing his fingers firmly into either side of my head only caused further disruption, as Dr. Sunter

lowered his tone. He knew exactly what was happening, although he didn't want to place fear in Mandy.

"You can't save one who lacks the heartbeat and oxygen that makes the bitch pose to be lively." **I laughed sardonically.** *"Though my soul is far from gone."*

"What in the hell did he just say?"

"Mandy, leave the room now! Please? I need to be alone with him!"

"No! I refuse to leave him in this demonic state of mind! What have you done to Kevin?"

"Just go!" **Dr. Sunter demanded.**

Hearing the door slam violently, I sat in a momentary silence. No movement, no verbal expression, just as still as a devastated neighborhood after a hurricane. The concerned sigh of Dr. Sunter's agitation lingered in my ears as he leaned in closer.

"All right, you bastard. Come out of there, whoever you are!"

My dark eyes fluttered open, digging a hole into his mind as my face remained stone.

"You dare to save someone who has long departed? She is gone, it's best you leave all alone."

"Who are you referring to? If this isn't Kevin, tell me who you are…" **Dr. Sunter wasn't curious, he was afraid…afraid of what exactly he was dealing with.**

My stare intensified as my pupils dilated, allowing all light to enter into my brain. I began to laugh only watching obscure threat stretch across Dr. Sunter's expression.

"I'm quite sure you're well aware...doctor."

The door flew open behind us as Mandy stormed back in demanding answers. I felt faint as I went limp, falling over onto the couch cushion.

"Kevin...Kevin open your eyes. You're in a safe place, everything is okay now. Can you hear me?"

My eyes met a beam of light from a small flashlight that was being shined. I gave a nod as Dr. Sunter assisted me to sit up. Becoming fully alert and aware of my surroundings, I searched around for Mandy.

Dr. Sunter placed a gentle hand upon my thigh asking if I was all right.

"What happened? Where's Mandy?" **I panicked.**

"Calm yourself, she's outside waiting for you. She is concerned, but I assured her that you were going to be just fine. Do you remember anything from our hypnosis session?"

I sat jogging my memory, but drew a blank. *"I vaguely remember seeing myself when I was younger, after that I don't what happened. Why?"*

"*Interesting.*" **He scratched his chin.** "*Honestly, I've never seen anything like this before. Since we are in complete privacy, anything you tell me stays between us. I need some solid answers to find any for you, Kevin. What exactly has been going on with you, from beginning to now?*"

"*I truly have no idea where to even begin. When I moved into my new apartment, I began to have the strangest nightmares, thinking it was due to being in an unfamiliar environment as I tried to adjust. Then I met my neighbor Savannah Rayn, and she's witnessed me having these sporadic mood swings. When Mandy came around at first, things seemed to be placid in her presence. Then my nightmares gained vehemence to where I began to fear my surroundings. I even sought spiritual guidance from my priest, Father Delatonni.*"

"*So did you have any type of relation with Savannah beyond "friendly neighbors"?*"

"*I mean, at first yes. I developed strong feelings for her, but she claimed we could never be together. I figured it was because she was seeing this man that I'd catch creeping into her apartment at the most random of times. I'll admit it pissed me off. Jealous as I may have seemed, I met Mandy one afternoon on a ritual park run down at Tompkins Square.*"

"*Have you relayed these crucial figments to anyone else?*"

"*My best friend and partner, Maxwell Harty.*"

"What did he think of them?"

"He just thought they were strange. I mean, what else was he supposed to believe?"

"Did your behavior begin to take a rapid course of change the more these dreams occurred?"

"Yes, tremendously! I began smoking for an unknown reason, but I know I'd do it in my dreams. I began drinking carelessly, and became brasher towards felons during my hours of duty. So… they placed me on temporary sick leave, which is why I'm here." I sighed.

Scribbling dramatically on his notepad, I could see something unraveling in his eyes as he attempted to piece my facts together. For once, he seemed sincere about my issue instead of standing in disbelief.

I relaxed my shoulders, sagging back into the couch as he continued asking me questions.

"What was the ending result of you and Savannah?"

"Well, at first we saw each other frequently. If she ever were to stay over, she'd be gone by morning's light. It frustrated me how she'd disappear like that all the time, leaving me to believe she was hiding something. That's when she expressed that we couldn't have anything "real" as she described. So I let it go, and pursued things further with Mandy. Savannah acted a bit jealous of her the last few times I've spoken to her. But, I haven't seen her around much lately. I've been too busy dealing with this shit."

"How did you feel while around Savannah as opposed to Mandy?"

"I mean, I felt pretty good, maybe even a little negligent and aggressive where my actions and thoughts were concerned. I know this may sound crazy, but one time Savannah came over wanting to "try" something, so she kissed me and somehow we both ended up sharing the same imagery and it freaked us out."

"What happened afterwards?"

"She left..." **My eyes veered off staring into a bookshelf.**

"Which is something you claim Savannah does quite often?"

"Yes. Since Mandy has taken over my life, I haven't seen much of her since."

"Well, I advise you to go home and get some rest. I will be in touch with you as soon as I can gain some definitive answers."

"You honestly entrust my mentality beyond the point of sending me back home? I don't even feel safe there, anymore."

"When you were still passed out, I took the time to explain your condition to Mandy and how to take care of you. I won't be prescribing you any medication this time."

"Why is that?" **I arched a brow.**

Dr. Sunter drew in an indisputable breath as his eyes reached mine. *"Because you don't need any…"*

I ran a hand through my hair as I stood to my feet; Mandy was by the door patiently waiting. I could see the horror concealed deep in her eyes as her mouth corked into a sympathetic smile.

Breaking At What Seems

Kyla M. Wassil

SIXTEEN

Seventeen hours and counting, I lied paralytic on my balcony watching the stars in the sky fade into the illuminating sunrise. I timed myself on how long I could stare into the sun before my eyes began to sting, drowning into my tear doused sockets. A pack of Marlboro Red's later, my lungs sat in a debris filled carcass, sending microscopic fragments of ash into the air with each harsh cough I passed.

    Bloodshot sclera's rested within the comforting dark circles overlooking the sweat secreted map of flesh lying out on the lounge chair. I could hear the friction of an opening glass door to my rear, as a contrasted figure stood in my peripheral.

    My eyes landed on a petite stature, baring the skin of a Berith prowling to possess my emotions. Heels clacked against the cement, cracking echoes into the air as she came into view. Lavender silk shielded her personal regions the crude beast in me longed to skin with his serpent tongue.

    Silently throwing a leg to the other side of the chair, she slowly lowered to straddle me. The sharpness of her nails glided up beneath my shirt, raising it over my head. Her eyes never straying away from mine with a gentle index finger that ran down my face, stopping against my lips.

    My jaw clenched as my nerves wrenched throughout my entire body. Refusing to drop my bottom jaw, Mandy struck her left hand like lightening, grasping my throat with a discomforting squeeze. Narrowing my dark eyes, I opened my mouth while gripping her hips, pressing my thumbs deep into the muscle. Rolling her body to the sensation, Mandy extracted her finger placing it against dampened fabric.

    Growing rigid beneath her, she suddenly stood up sliding her bottoms off. Magnetizing her hands to the band of my NYPD inscribed sweatpants, Mandy tugged them downward inch by inch until fully revealing my length. Reaching to my naval, the head of my erection laid salacious, ready to indulge in the warmth of Mandy's moist tissue.

Raising her hips, Mandy shoved me in with one swift thrust. Letting out an aroused groan, my jaw fell open with shock as she slammed into me. Pulling her body down against me, she tightened her grip in my hair as I pried into her relentlessly. Imbedding her nails into my chest, I sprung forward hoisting Mandy onto my waist.

Taking three very risky steps, I cautiously made my way to the balcony's corner. Trusting me with her life, Mandy's back floated dangerously over the edge, posing as the dramatic shadow over the traffic below.

Securing my hold, Mandy did the same around my neck. Watching the persistent city movement, I felt the panic of anxiety creep into my gut as my mind portrayed our spirits to appear Raven like.

Drawing my head near, Mandy whispered into my ear. *"Don't you quit on me out of fear, baby—just hold me."*

I dropped my head back allowing Mandy to slam into me aggressively. I watched her expression change as she looked over at Savannah's balcony; her eyes engulfing black. Smiling sardonically, a subtle boastful laugh escaped her lips as she released a loud sigh into the air. Her thalassic eyes locked onto mine as her muscles pulsated against me, falling into a deep climax.

A pleasurable eruption pierced my gut, extricating my orgasm, leaving me to feel convincingly fervent. Not seeking pause, Mandy motioned for me to lay her down onto the lounge chair, pulling me down on top.

Locking her legs around me, I found the strength to reframe from becoming flaccid until she was beyond satisfied. Making our way into the house, things finally ceased after a long, intimate shower.

My pelvis was tender from all the exertion it endured well over the past two hours. Weakened to the core, Mandy lay powerless beside me as I stroked the soft flesh of her arm. A strong presence lurked out of sight, disturbing my need to fall asleep. Something so close I could feel its breath raising the hairs on the back of my neck.

Rolling over onto my back, I kept the sheets draped lowly across my hips, running my fingertips against the tightness of my chest. I could feel my rapid heartbeat thudding beneath as a thin layer of sweat coated my skin. I wasn't asleep; then again I wasn't fully alert, either. A slight breeze drifted across my torso, hardening my muscles as they ached with chills. My eyes only dared opening once the warmth of the sun's rays stretched across my face.

Strutting my immodest being into the living room, I stood naked in the doorway of the balcony feeling the contaminated air blow through me. The white transparent drapes waved in sync with one another as the fabric tickled against me. Held captive in my home for the past three days hadn't prevailed as horrible as I'd imagined. Fragile, warm hands wrapped underneath my arms, as soft breasts cupped against my back. I overlapped the tiny delicacies, pressing them firmly against my chest.

"I would hope by which the pride you're standing in is the result of all acquitted negative energy you've held for so long, authorizing me to assist their release."

I could hear the smile in Mandy's voice as I turned to face her. Sapphire eyes darted at mine like glass marbles, witnessing her devious expression.

My cheeks pulled up into a devilish grin. *"I couldn't imagine it being from anything else."* My voice lowered.

"Your phone has a missed call. I figured you'd like to be aware of that."

Furrowing my brows, I headed to my bedroom to retrieve my phone. Max was the one who called, leaving a perturbed voicemail stating that he had some things he needed to share with me. Without any hesitation, I had him come over straight away.

Mandy stood in the kitchen pouring shots of whiskey while I let Max in.

"Hey! Come on in." I smiled.

Looking at Max dressed to perfection in his uniform placed a bitter taste in my mouth, as my eyes landed on a file box he clutched beneath his arm.

"Kevin, you might want to sit down for this..."

"Okay...what is in the box, Max?"

Breaking At What Seems — Kyla M. Wassil

Mandy rounded the counter handing me a shot before sitting down. Holding the shot glass inches away from my mouth, I motioned for him to begin. He refused until the whiskey disappeared.

Licking the residue from my lips, I became anxious as Max peeled off the lid. Pictures of missing girls came into view; I swallowed hard seeing that famous look of worry rest on Max's face.

"Take a look at these articles."

"Why do I need to do this?"

"Just take a weary look, Kevin. I'm curious about this particular case."

Knowing it was against our code of conduct to bring police work home unless authorized, especially to an officer on "mental leave", I knew it had to be something serious.

Browsing through, I glanced over horrifying articles of these victims murders. My heart froze once I came across a profile photo of Savannah. With trembling hands, I held out my glass for Mandy to refill. Taking the paperclip from the stacks corner, papers stated her date of disappearance to the day the precinct decided the case had gone cold. 1996 was the year of the paper leaving the irrevocable, very undeniable truth before me. I could feel the color drain from my face as I choked the whiskey down.

"Kevin, do you recognize that girl?"

My hyperventilating stopped me from giving a clear response as I spastically jumped up to grab the bottle of whiskey from the kitchen counter. Completely traumatized, I forced several gulps down without a hiatus.

Drinking too much to handle in less than thirty seconds, my body torqued towards the sink leaving me to violently wretch until my knees buckled. Both Mandy and Max ran to my rescue, walking me back to the couch. I sat in disgust, not wanting to look any further, but Max insisted.

"Why are you having me do this, Max? God…this is impossible. It has to be! There's no fucking way…"

"No way that what, Kevin? Answer me. I need an answer to who she is!"

"Is this some kind of sick prank? Why would you guys do this?"

"Kevin, honey I don't believe Max or anyone who has any type of empathy would intentionally hurt you. Even to fabricate a death of an innocent person." **Mandy rubbed the top of my hand.**

"First off, answer me this. Why are you poking around in cold case files?"

Max dropped his head with a sigh. *"Chief Mortkin assigned me to do so. Will you just fucking answer my question? Who the hell is she? What do you know about her?"*

"I—I can't just answer without sounding completely insane. That girl is my fucking neighbor, I've seen her on multiple occasions and I've spoken to her…I've even fu…" **I paused.**

Mandy's eyes enlarged as she quickly looked at me waiting for me to finish my sentence. *"You're saying you've had relations with some girl who has been missing for nearly twenty years?"* **She sat astounded.**

"No, it isn't like that… well at least not what it would seem like. Christ, this isn't easy to neither explain nor come to terms with its reality!" **I exasperated.**

"Max, has Kevin been seeing…a ghost perhaps? I mean how do we even know she's still alive? You guys would have to have known about her existence."

"Listen, all I know is Chief explained that he and a few other officers took her suspected killer out that same year. Not having found any evidence, Savannah had seemingly disappeared without a trace. If no further physical evidence is to surface within a certain time frame, the case goes cold."

"A fucking poltergeist has been communicating with me all this time? How did her name even get back to you guys?"

"Dr. Sunter had a long meeting with us, explaining how it rang a bell once her name passed your lips. He claimed he had taught a college seminar for a psychology course Savannah had been taking her junior year at Columbia University. He remembered the city being in *grave danger when a serial killer was on the rise at that time. He was known to stalk the girls on campus and a cluster of a specific type began disappearing. Most victims were recovered, but the killer failed to leave traces of DNA. It took our unit almost fifteen years to finally catch the bastard."*

"How was he executed?"

"Gunshot wound to the chest. Chief admitted the man looked to be pulling a weapon from his waistband and to protect him and his partner, he shot and killed the man on spot." **Max explained.**

"Then why is this "trapped soul" targeting to torment me?"

"Hell if I know, Kevin? You and I both believe in Catechism and know not to question the unknown, or what is not seen by the eye means to never provoke the uninvited into our world."

I was angry and confused, lost and overwhelmed as I tried to piece together the impossible. *"Max, you don't believe me to be crazy, do you?"*

"I believe there is someone trying to reach out to you for help. For whatever reason, if it is Savannah, there's a greater justification as to why she is targeting you. There's something powerful you seem to possess that has attracted her presence and want for you."

The truth behind his words shattered me like glass. Savannah was the only one who could answer the questions I had and demanded to know.

"This is a lot to comprehend. I don't want Chief thinking I need to give up my gun and badge, Max." **Hot tears formed in my eyes.** *"I am an auxiliary officer for the Goddamn NYPD, Max! I will not be forced to retire on a mental note just to satisfy the fork tongue of our public press, entertaining the cowardly unknowledgeable media! Maybe I am just a little more intuitive with my spiritual side, but that doesn't tarnish my purpose."*

"Kevin, I'm not suggesting that in the slightest. I don't believe you to be demented. I just feel we should keep this low key to detour away from the hawk's eye of Manhattan. I'll probably come back over if I happen to find anything else."

Standing to our feet, I placed my hands on my hips with a sincere smile. *"It really has been good to see you again, Max. I needed to before I lost my sanity."*

"I will do whatever I can to help you. If it is you she seeks, maybe you should pay a respectable visit on the voyage to your unanswered questions."

I sat for hours alone in my apartment long after Max and Mandy had left for work. I needed the time to reassess myself, organizing the questions I had in store. After one too many dry martini's down at the Rue B, I walked myself home with a stagger.

Having the place all to myself gave an unstable certainty to pursue Savannah, though I knew I had to; especially for my own sake.

Stepping out onto the balcony, I immediately saw Savannah leaned over her balcony smoking a cigarette.

"I was beginning to wonder if you'd ever face your new found fear in confronting me. I can sense the curious vibes all the way over here."

"Why didn't you tell me?" **I gripped the railing.**

"Tell you what, Kevin? That I wasn't your neighbor, but in fact a lost wanderer who seeks peace of mind? I highly doubt anyone would take that lightly."

I shook my head. *"How is it possible that I only see you, that when I've touched you… it was very real? I've felt your lips against mine, I've felt you inside and out to the point of ejaculation. Try explaining that!"*

Savannah rolled her eyes dramatically. *"Kevin, the eyes see what the heart wants to feel. I had you so drawn in that I could control your emotions in order to relax your thoughts. The only way I could achieve that was by mentally arousing you. In your mind you'd envision us having sex as it felt realistically pleasurable."*

"Stop it!" **I replied disgusted.** *"You literally mentally fucked me for what reason, Savannah? What the fuck are you looking for?"*

"How do you know I was "looking" for something?" **She snapped back.**

"Because the day you came over and kissed me, it wasn't practical magical or some coincidence that we both saw the same thing. As if it were on a damn movie projector."

"Like I told you, there was just something about you. I knew from the beginning that you had something I needed inside, but I had to pry it out of you."

"By befriending me? Savannah, each time you come around I'd feel uneasy, disgruntled and aggressive. I only saw things…"

"Yes, when I wanted you to. I needed certain memories of yours, but ever since you created a spiritual barrier around your home, I cannot cross it. I became frustrated, getting back at you in my own ways. If I couldn't be within your touch, I couldn't get inside your head."

"What memories do you speak of?"

"I can't be the one to tell you that. Your psychologist is the one who knows about that scar on your head. Ask him and you shall find your desired answers. I'll be here once you find out."

"Wait! I need to know now! I'm tired of being left in the dark!"

"You wouldn't have been if you were to believe sooner." **Savannah's voice faded.**

Mandy stood so close to me in the elevator, static formed between our clothing as an electric impulse shocked my hand once it touched the metal doors. Dr. Sunter had my file lying open on his desk with his fingers laced above.

"I'm quite sure you have a plethora of questions. But I must have a clear conscience going into this." **He released a rugged breath.** *"Savannah…have you really seen her?"*

"Yes. More than you'd believe." **My tone deepened.**

"Incredible! What I'm about to educate you about is your medical history, along with some historic events to help you understand just how remarkable you are. I searched your files to find the mention of your brain surgery. I am hoping you are prepared to have belief in what I'm going to say."

"I'm listening." **I narrowed my eyes.**

"I contacted the very surgeon who operated on you years ago. He explained having to make a very critical decision in regards of your life. He had to replace your entire right temporal lobe because the viral infection destroyed too much tissue. Almost out of ideas, he contacted the morgue telling them to transport brain tissue from the most readily available body that had no signs of damage. The interesting part is that it was tissue from a

man named Gerould Kirby. He was the serial killer all of New York feared, that I'm sure Max introduced you to."

The room started to blur and spin out as a rush of hot flashes waved through my entire body. *"I have half of a fucking serial killer's brain...inside my fucking head?"*

"As plausible as it seems, somehow after the brain matter fused with the rest of your tissue, your hippocampus neurons fused with those existing inside Gerould's tissue. Having done that, it began to take over your right hemisphere, attacking your memory. Sounds opposite of inevitable, but scientific facts are hard to ostracize."

"So, that's why Savannah needed to get inside my mind? Because, I have his memory and he was the one who kidnapped and murdered her."

"Max explained how her body was never found, right?"

As my mind entered a state of shock, my jaw fell agape as I finally grasped Savannah's actual intentions. *"He said the case had gone cold."*

"Then there's your answer. She may be sticking around a familiar place because she's a lost soul. I'm not just a doctor, I'm a type of anatomical scientist, so explaining this isn't simple to stomach. I don't believe in anything unproven. Though, I believe you hold a dangerous relic and will advise caution if you wish to further understand it beyond my professional explanation."

Breaking At What Seems
Kyla M. Wassil

I knew there had to have been more to the story than that. I just needed to hear it from Savannah.

"I'm going to excuse myself for today. There's still unfinished business I need to tend to before I can move further with this. I know you long to know just as much as I do. Like you said, you don't believe in what obtains no valued "proof". I don't need to give my Chief a reason to make false accusations on my behalf. I'm not only willing to conquer the truth, I'm destined to."

Dr. Sunter said nothing further as I took my leave; anxious to get home. I watched the sun dip behind the buildings, playing peek-a-boo as its luminance seared my eyes. Sagged into the taxi's backseat, I looked out the window as life passed by in slow motion, witnessing ordinary people doing ordinary things. Maybe it wasn't a curse that had been put on me; maybe it was a gift from some deranged oracle to test me beyond my means.

I rested on my couch within a silent household, lost in the abyss of my own thoughts. Tipping the frosted bottle, my eyes reached a clear view through the bottom of the glass. Polishing off the last fourth of bourbon, I sat with numbed lips overlapping a bitter pallet. I could feel her waiting for me; I just had to come up with a plan that would get us both the help we needed.

Stretching my legs out, I noticed a new coffee table placed before me. Lost in a complete daze, I didn't understand how I could have missed that damn thing. Mandy must have picked another one up that suited her liking, matching the plainness of my apartment. A stack of papers peeked out from a vanilla colored folder that lied alluring on the edge. Plunking the emptied bottle onto the pellucid surface below, the glass on glass collision cracked an echo throughout the hollow air. Left in plain sight, I pulled the folder towards me out of curiosity. Mandy's handwriting was inscribed on its cover.

"When tranquility meets mayhem." **I read aloud to myself.**

I opened it, briefly overlooking random notes she had written down for that huge article she had been working on. Nothing seemed to be out of the norm until I read across some etched out notes regarding events from my life. Mandy had been keeping tabs on my mental behavior in secrecy. I wasn't sure if I felt either betrayed or completely skinned and exposed, leaving me in discomforting shambles. I knew Mandy's intentions were innocuous, but I felt I'd be more accepting if she would have brought it to my attention beforehand. Even though I'd be presented as a '*John Doe*' character living what seemed like a psychedelic life based on fiction, it wasn't the case. Fiction is a denoted label to fascinate cordial minds consumed by intellect diversion. No matter the amount of reviews or ratings Mandy may gain from this so called '*literary masterpiece*' she was commencing, I will always be held captive in a frenetic state of mind. Not caring to dive any further, I flipped it closed sliding it out of reach.

My eyes veered towards the door to the balcony as I drew in a daring inhale. Making my way outside, Savannah was perched on the edge reading that same old book I saw her with months ago. Appearing restless, I knew she could sense my solicitous vibes as she turned her head in my direction.
Leaning against the railing, I mirrored her welcoming smile as we began talking in a familiar tone.

"So, I take it you finally found what you've been wondering this entire time?"

"Not everything, I still have a dozen questions that I need to know the answers."

Closing her book, Savannah slid to the ground giving me her undivided attention. *"Enlighten me, Kevin. I've longed to fulfill the wonders circling that intricate mind of yours."* **Her gaze sharpened.**

"I need to know for the sake of my own sanity that I'm not mentally impaired…"

"Kevin, what you're looking at is very real. Like I had explained earlier, I've convinced your mind to believe what you wanted to and what I needed you to. Therefore, you could physically touch me and feel for someone your mind was too naïve to believe otherwise. Sounds crude, I know."

"Since this isn't some cruel prank of yours, what exactly do you need me for?"

"It's quite simple..." **A devilish smile twitched at the corners of her mouth.** *"I need you to let me in so you can help me find my body. I can't be free until my soul is satisfied with the truth. My life was taken not by choice, but by the hands of a greedy, depraved monster who bared no morals or remorse for the things he'd done."*

"You just so happen to know I conceal these memories? What if I can't remember?"

Savannah threw her head back with a disagreeing chuckle. *"Of course you can, Kevin. You're my killer..."*

Her words combusted through my entire body, rattling each nerve as my right eye twitched. I couldn't fathom the fact I had a derange lunatic implanted into my brain, that he was actually a part of me all of this time and I was never aware of it.

"When did you come to terms with knowing he was in me?"

"Being a ghost, I have certain abilities but longing to be marked as an angel, I have to abide by strict limitations that I know I've recently manipulated to get what I need."

"That day in the park...it wasn't something I had thought I saw. It was actually you standing there between the trees, wasn't it? Y—you followed me?"

"Kevin, I have been with you everywhere. I just didn't allow you to see me unless I wanted to be seen by

you. I possess that power, and the only way I can validate that is if you believed in me. Which you did, I told you that you'd have to really want to understand… in which you do. Hence the very reason we are here in this moment."

I drew in a rugged breath, dragging my hands down my unshaven face trying to process each detail. *"You put me through hell you know? To the point I thought I was losing my mind."*

"I know…" **She sighed.** *"I watched you stagger out here the night you overdosed. I was beyond upset with you. I knew if you had died that night, I'd be lost forever. All though I am envious of Mandy, I am grateful that she saved you."*

"I stand grateful myself." **I crinkled my nose before licking my lips.** *"Before your unexpected departure, what is it that you wanted to be in your lifetime?"*

"Something relative to your line of work. I wanted to be a Psychologist in Criminology, in which the time my life was taken, I was studying just that at Columbia University."

"I'm sorry you could never fulfill your dreams, Savannah." **I felt my heart sink in my chest.**

"No need to apologize for something that was out of our control. I've dwelled too long and have spent many years a drifter. I'm ready for my deserved freedom. I'm tired, Kevin. I want to rest peacefully."

I ran a hand through my hair dragging it down the back of my neck. *"If we are to do this, how exactly is it to be done?"*

"Well, first you have to grant me passage through the holy barrier you've shielded your home with. The only one powerful enough to do so is your priest. I would then have to place your mind in the state of relaxation I can control in order for you to let me in. You know exactly what I'm referring to." **Savannah's eyes narrowed.**

"Through sexual desire. I can talk Father Delatonni into coming over to assist me spiritually. I bet he'll get a kick out of witnessing such a thing." **I chuckled.**

"I must warn you, it can be painful and uncomfortable. If you are planning to have an audience, I suggest you be very precise on what will be taking place. To some it will be confusing, but to others it may seem as if they are spellbound."

"I can explain only to those who are closest to me that understand what's been happening. Tell me, that day in the hall when you bum rushed completely through me, why did you do it?"

Savannah's eyes lowered in dismay. *"I was angry with you... even though it is something out of our control. I was upset over the fact that I can't have you like I desire to. I may be a lost soul, but your energy towards me made me grasp some sort of liveliness. I became addicted and knew if I didn't stop, I'd wreck you for good."*

"Is that why you pushed me to be with Mandy?"

"I wanted...no, I needed to see you happy, mentally and physically. Knowing I could never provide those specific emotions even though you may have assumed they were real, they never could be in existence. Kevin, you're the most humble human being I've ever encountered in the last eighteen years. I'd hate to push you away on a bad note leaving you to wonder the rest of your lifespan. You deserve clarity and honesty."

"If things were different..."

"Shh...don't say it. Because if we lived in a perfect world, I'd be twice your age." **Savannah laughed.** "Though, I'd still find a way to make you mine."

My cheeks drew back into a large smile, feeling my heart warm to her sense of humor. *"As crazy as this journey has been, I am glad it was me who was chosen."*

"Don't get too excited, our "journey" has merely begun." **Savannah winked.**

"Did you have to fuck with me at the dinner table while at my parent's? Christ, Savannah you freaked the shit out of me in the bathroom."

"What can I say? I feed on the predilection of having my way with you."

I shook my head, smiling as I pulled myself away to make some personal calls. Jumping into what seemed highly unlikely; I didn't know where to even begin when it came to explaining what I needed help with. Father Delatonni was more than willing to help

considering he specialized in the subject, but Dr. Sunter was wearier of the offer.

    I left the option openly available for him to come, while Max on the other hand had been busy commencing a plot of his own. He formed a small forensics search team to help us find Savannah's remains. Knowing the risk he was taking, Max has never failed to be there for me when I've needed him most. I've never needed him as badly as I did now, and he knew it. It was my time to persuade the committee into believing I deserved to continue my career in law enforcement. The only way to do that was to have a major breakthrough and this was that opportunity. For it called to me in the high frequency of further possibilities in the future.

Breaking At What Seems   Kyla M. Wassil

SEVENTEEN

Mandy lay up next to me on the couch with her legs thrown over my lap, focused on writing while I tried building up the courage to explain the impractical. Today was the day that would forever change my life, maybe even those who were to be involved as well. The words I yearned to express sat in conjunction inside my mouth as the urge to simply speak jabbed at my tongue. Staring into my coffee mug wasn't going to solve the matter nor stabilize the tension. Either way, I felt I was in a steel constructed bind impossible to ever escape.

"Why didn't you feel the need to tell me about your uh... article you're writing?" **I said dryly.**

Mandy furrowed her brows as I grew annoyed by the second. *"I—I guess it didn't cross my mind to have to?"*

"It never occurred to you in asking permission? Though I seem like an open ended interpretation, I still possess my right to object your attempt to publically shame me!"

"Kevin, it isn't like that in the slightest! I would never dream to ignominiously hurt you! I love you with every fiber in me, my personal interest and desire to write about you is nothing short of adorn in its purest."

My chest tightened as my hands lurched forward taking her in by the face. *"Then make love to me in your purest form."* **I groaned.**

Mandy's folder dropped to the floor as she crashed her mouth into mine, climbing onto my lap. Tearing her hands through my hair, I slide my hands underneath her shirt firmly cupping her breasts. Moaning into my mouth, I pressed my hips further into her causing her deplore to exceed in sound. Pressing her

forehead to mine, Mandy's eyes struck through me like daggers.

"Take me to your bedroom…" **She whispered.**

I took an extensive amount of pleasure in taking the time to remind myself of how real this was while tangled up in the warmth of Mandy's flesh. I needed a physical relaxation before daring to bombard my mind with such a critical request.

…Later

My eyes shot open to the sound of my ringtone going off. I looked over to retrieve my phone seeing Dr. Sunter's personal number on the screen. Before I could even say hello, he started to speak.

"I've taken some time to think long and hard about getting involved, and even though it's going against all that I believe in, I can't turn a blind eye away from a patient I care for. I'm agreeing to help aid you through this as far as my profession will allow. I'm just going to be there to supervise incase anything out of the norm were to happen." **Dr. Sunter then laughed at his own unintentional pun.** *"I just want you to be cautious with what you're choosing to entail in."* **He became silent.**

"I'm as ready as anyone can be and I understand the consequences at hand. I just figured asking for you to

partake would give you a different perspective on life, itself."

"I'll be arriving at your apartment building around six." **He released an ascertained sigh before hanging up.**

Mandy turned over asking me why Dr. Sunter felt the need to come over, and by the look on her face she didn't seem too keen on hearing what information my eyes withheld.

"Do you believe in paranormal existence?"

"Why?" **She drew her brows together.**

"Because, what we are about to encounter might change your mind if you claim to not." **I went on explaining.**

Mandy seemed all the more intrigued to be a part of the event after knowing she had validation to back her story up. I wanted her to gain the position she longed for, Mandy didn't want to skim by writing basic shit about small occurrences or articles for sports issues. She also knew that with me doing this, I was going to hit a milestone in my career that would change Manhattan's history for good. Any strayed mind shall be put at ease after uncovering the truth behind a man once notorious for years of slaughter and torture. The only way to find my other half…was to retrace my own historical steps.

A tap on the door had my heart thrash beneath my chest as I hopped up to answer it. Father Delatonni stood somber beside Max, waiting for the events to occur. A hesitant smile twitched at the corners of my mouth as I motioned for them to enter. While Father Delatonni began preparing for a spiritual passage, Mandy answered another knock that soon followed.

Max appeared relaxed in civilian attire as he scoped out my bedroom. *"So, is this where the legitimate "magic" is to take place?"* **He laughed.**

"Pretty much where it always does."

"How is this going to work exactly?" **Max shoved his hands deep into his jean pockets.**

I shrugged in return. *"Father Delatonni is going to summon a higher power, asking permission for the Holy Ghost to grant Savannah serene passage to cross my spiritual barrier."*

"You actually blessed your own home?"

"Wouldn't you?" **I shot back.**

"If Savannah's spirit isn't apparent to cause disorderly harm, then why is she to be judged?"

"Has Catechism taught you nothing? Just like in any other death case scenario, our soul waits inside the purgatory where God will determine Savannah's further voyage to Heaven's acceptance. Consider this her test to

God to prove she is worthy of entrance after being cleansed of her venial sins."

"Sins?"

"She's been a deserter from God since the day of her passing. I would be too if my conscience refused peace and sacrament, while my soul wandered the earth searching for the nearest clue."

"Wow, she's literally a trapped soul. You're saying that in order for her to move on from this world, she first has to know what happened to her the day she disappeared and the only way she can do that is through…you?"

A conformable smile stretched across my face as I clutched Max's shoulder. *"I am the one who carries the memory and truth she has sought for eighteen years. Even though my alter personality and the sins it conceals are punishable by Hell, I still have a chance to clear my soul from detriment by freeing Savannah's soul, guiding her back to God."*

"Holy fucking shit… you're a damn soul saver? That's like the coolest shit I've ever heard! Generally, you'd only hear about this in a book or movie." **Max replied briskly.**

Father Delatonni came walking down the hallway chanting a request through prayer as he drew an air crucifix with incense repeatedly. Mandy walked closely behind with her arm hooked to Dr. Sunter's, whispering back and forth to one another. Nervously unbuttoning my Mets jersey, chills

danced a layer across the flesh of my chest as the sound of my name tickled my ears. I knew Savannah was itching to cross through and get to me; I honestly couldn't wait to feel the power surging throughout my body.

Climbing into bed, everyone stood before me, surveilling my every move. The much needed deep inhale I longed for expanded my throat, pausing my lungs.

A subtle glow was slowly nearing from the hallway. My chest stiffened as Savannah came into view wearing an ivory Flora gown, with skin illuminating perfected porcelain. She wasn't the grudged out independent lioness I was used to seeing, she was more undefiled; causing my arousal to erupt from her vibrancy. I knew Father Delatonni saw her as the muscles in his hand reacted, dropping the burning incense to the floor. Catching his reaction, Max became anxious as his breathing accelerated into panting.

"I—I want to see her…how can I see her? I mean, will I?" **Max stammered.**

"*Just believe, Max. You have to really want to.*" **My words seemed hollow.**

Savannah's smile caused me to shudder as she climbed on top in a prowling manner. The chill of her hands pressed into my chest provoked my member to rigidly ossify.

"*Kevin, make me real…*" **She whispered.**

A masculine groan escaped my mouth as I pulled her firmly against me. Crashing her ethereal lips against mine placed my mind into tranquility. Paralytic and feeble, I lay beneath her feeling her skin warm as I penetrated into the vision my mind created.

Pain surged through my gut, pricking agitation into my twitching nerves. The scar on my head burned with excruciating force, causing me to groan and whine with mercy.

"It hurts, make it stop! Please..." **My words faded.**

"Breathe me in and taste my thoughts, Kevin. You can find me... come on, baby."

Savannah's soft voice guided me into a meditative state of mind, forcing me to slam into her harder. The energy she placed upon me was tearing through my soul as she clutched the electrons of my episodic memory. The further I let Savannah in, the more my body endured physical suffering.

"Is this really happening right now?" **Max spazzed.**

"Why is it hurting him? Don't you allow this... "thing" to hurt him!" **Mandy warned.**

Soon all sound had faded around me as I fell into what seemed like a simple daydream...though it was far from just that.

Breaking At What Seems

Kyla M. Wassil

Falling a thousand feet into nothing but darkness had my heart pounding through my chest. I could still feel Savannah's grasp on my face, reassuring that she was still with me. A hard landing felt like a boulder had crashed on top of me, knocking the breath from my lungs.

My eyes opened, inviting the tree tops into my view. I was in the middle of the woods, wandering about for my destination. Savannah appeared between the trees just ahead; swaying around alluringly. Walking in her direction, an ominous presence cast a larger shadow over me, quickly reminding me of how defenseless I really was.

"Come on, Kevin. He's this way…" Savannah motioned for me to follow her deeper into the wilderness.

The vague contrast grew in brightness as my steps halted behind a red barn. It was familiar to me, so I continued to walk closer. "Hey you fucking faggot! Where the fuck have you been? I need to drive into town to go to the library." I looked to see my perverted ass cousins standing with their arms folded. Refusing to move, the bastard threatened to beat the shit out of me if I paused much longer. Jetting after them, my surroundings began to flash forward at rapid speed fast enough to make my head spin. "Kevin, you're almost there!" Savannah became excited. Approaching a library, I hesitantly walked inside. At first I glanced around for a librarian when I stopped on Savannah reading at a nearby table.

A large gust of wind burst through my body, setting me in the timeline as I now stood in first person. I knew I was tapped into the veins of Gerould's memories as my hands appeared to not be of my own. I had a scar from a knife wound on my right hand between my thumb and index finger. Running my left thumb over it nestled a comforted memory of a fight almost lost. I was getting older; grey started to peek through my scalp, and my calloused hands were growing weak from the things I've forced them to do.

I pulled my hat down lower to hide my identity, the public media has spread too much about the things I've done, already. They even sent their rabid law enforcement after me once my profile sketch was leaked into the wrong hands. I just had to have one more, even if I died trying, I wouldn't stop unless I became physically incapable of continuing. I looked over at Savannah more nervous than I ever have at another female. She wasn't the usual type I preferred, she was definitely something different. Pale complexion and hair black as night, with excessive eyeliner. She was dressed in leather with fishnets disappearing down inside her combat boots. Acknowledging my intense gaze without moving her eyes away from a Psychology textbook, she gave a smile.

"Do you need to borrow this book, too?" She asked with sarcasm.

"No. I'm not fascinated with what it's about. I'm intrigued with who is reading about it." My tone lowered.

She quickly looked at me with a daring expression. "Are you a professor here at the college?"

I pressed my lips together failing to respond. Returning her attention back towards her book, she sighed. "I'm Savannah."

My sheepish smile forced my eyes to narrow. "Gerry." I replied standing to my feet.

I could feel her eyes follow my leave but I didn't halt my movement. I've seen Savannah plenty of times around the campus; it was my favorite hunting site. Savannah was a loner much like myself, each time I've seen her she was either reading a book or fucking around with terra cards. I've just never been this close to her since the first day I laid eyes on her. Hearing the door fling open behind me caused my steps to instinctively quicken.

"Hey, Gerry, wait up!"

I gave a rather large smile before turning my head around. Savannah came running up next to me clutching her textbooks into her chest.

"I think I've seen you around campus before. It's okay, you don't have to be embarrassed. A lot of people your age still seek a higher education. I bet you've reached your Master's degree already." She giggled.

I didn't know how to take her comment, but I knew it irritated me. "What's that supposed to mean?" I snarled.

"Well, it means I just thought since you failed to answer my previous question, I assumed the obvious.

You're not a teacher, you're a student." Savannah apologized.

"Why do you choose to follow me?" I stopped.

"I wasn't trying to invade, just simply make conversation. If you like admiring me around campus from afar, I figured there must be a more extensive desire you held in confinement."

I continued to walk towards my truck becoming more and more agitated when I realized she was persistent. "Are you interested in older men or something?" I stopped abruptly.

"You don't look "that" much older. I'd say mid-thirties?"

"Very nice observation, but I don't think your interests amount to my years of experience."

"Don't assume that you're too much for me just because I'm younger."

I placed my hands on my hips returning Savannah's harsh gaze. "You're willing to go home with someone you'd just met?" My eyes narrowed.

"Personally became acquainted with, yes. Physically meeting you by the eye, no."

I smiled at her sarcasm, opening my passenger side door. "Well, let's see just how inviting you really are."

I drove in a contemplative silence listening to Savannah sing along with the radio. If this woman wasn't all but incredulous, she was carelessly naïve to my inner belligerence.

Pulling up to that same red barn, I escorted Savannah inside. Setting her books down onto my makeshift kitchen table, Savannah took a long look around. I wasn't too worried seeing as how I had nothing revealing that might pose a harmful threat. Taking my hat off, Savannah turned to watch me advance in sliding my jacket off. Raising an eyebrow, a smirk tugged at her left cheek.

"Take this off as well..." She plucked at my tee shirt.

I was hesitant, but something about her caused me to feel submissive for the first time, ever. My nervous hands trembled like my body was caffeine deprived as my muscles twitched and tightened. Savannah ran her hands up the curves of my biceps, trickling her nails down my chest and abdomen.

"Well, the sight of that changes things. I want you to press your chiseled body against mine and fuck me like the stranger you claim to be."

Cupping her face, I pulled her in pressing my forehead to hers. "Oh sweetie...I'm going to do more than just that." I replied inauspiciously.

Hoisting her up onto my waist, I slammed her down onto the mattress as she tore off her clothes; sating my lust. I fell onto her filling the space between her legs as she grabbed my hips, pushing me in further.

"See how tempting I am and how easy it was for me to lure you by using your wants against you?" Her nails dug deeper, searing the flesh on my back.

I suddenly became enraged at the thought of Savannah conquering the task to make me feel emasculated. No one has ever been able to control my feelings and this bitch somehow crashed through the floodgates. Infuriated beyond reaching a level of tolerance, I grabbed the knife I hid between my mattresses, holding it above her face. A satisfied giggle fell from Savannah's mouth.

"Too bad I won't be alive to tell them who you are…" She smiled.

"You…you know who I am?" I became panicked.

"Majoring in Criminal Psychology has it perks."

Immediately backing off of her, I yanked up my jeans throwing my jacket on to shield my bare torso. I knew I couldn't let her go and expose my true identity but I continued to motion towards the door advising her to leave. She redressed herself in bewilderment, pulling her books snuggly into her chest. I was stuck in a moment where I actually considered letting her go, maybe it'd give me a reason to leave and start over somewhere new. Then the reminder of a police profile sketch floating around New York's media brought me to an undeniable verdict.

Breaking At What Seems — Kyla M. Wassil

Just as Savannah reached to open the door, I abruptly approached her while taking my right palm to the back of her head, smashing her face through the glass window. Still alive but faintly in a daze, I watched blood trickle down her face as reflective shards pierced the skin of her angelic face. My anguish rumbled in the pit of my gut as I slammed her head once more against the wooden frame. Her books dropped to the floor with a crashing echo as I pulled her into me by the hair. Dragging her through the kitchen, I threw the table and chairs out of my way frantically digging inside my utensil drawer. My eager hand landed upon the handle of a large cutting knife, throwing me into a whim to slaughter Savannah to pieces. Slicing her throat until the blade reached the rigidness of her esophagus; I sawed straight through, severing her head completely. No matter how badly I desired her all this time, I was damned to let any bitch control me like that. The lesson was well deserved, and the pain in her eyes as she had fallen victim to my blade was but a glorious victor.

After exhausting myself in a maniacal outburst, I stood in a room spattered with blood as I appeared drenched in crimson from head to toe. I felt my eyes burn with each blink as I overlooked the mess I'd made. With the absence of remorse or empathy, the puddle of blood I stood in was a reminder of how to regain my purpose, leaving me to smile boastfully.

Hours later, I sat in the bed of my truck monitoring the fire that burned most of the evidence. Fresh blisters still stung my palms from digging a hole beneath the barn. Knowing she was probably my last, I wanted to keep her close to remind myself to never become so dangerously vulnerable again. A sinister smile played on my lips as I savored the whisky residue inside my mouth.

The next day, I casually drove into town trying to forget about the night before when a police car was parked outside of my destination. It was a liquor store I favored amongst any other in the area. Trying to remain inconspicuous, I ended up catching their attention a second too late. Realizing who I was, they yelled for me to stop but I instead took off running in the opposite direction. Cornering me down an alleyway, a policeman tasered me to the ground before I could get away. I attempted to rise to my feet after kicking the officer in his gut when his partner ran up shooting me right in the chest. Barely clipping my heart, I lied on my back bleeding out as my breathing lessened with each inhale. I witnessed the murky rejoice filling their eyes with security as the world faded to black. Sgt. Mortkin was the last sight my eyes enclosed on as the glimpse of his name plate flickered beneath the streetlight.

"Jesus Christ!" **I twitched coming back to consciousness.** *"Savannah, I know where you are! But my God, what happened to you…I—I just can't even grasp the reality of it right now."* **I cried.**

"Kevin, go find me…" **Her voice evanesced.**

I sat forward seeing everyone's frightened expressions. It was as if they just witnessed my

resurrection after an execution. Mandy ran to my side running her fingers through my sweaty hair, checking me over. Savannah had disappeared long before I could fully awaken. Looking at Max as he took a step forward to approach me, I reached my hand out.

"Max, I know where to find Savannah's remains. They are located in a remote area up around Morningside."

"I'll contact my forensics search team straight away!" Max informed while sprinting out of the room.

"Wait! I can't let you put your career at risk for me, Max."

"And I can't allow you to go alone commencing police work illegally, either." He yelled back.

Father Delatonni and Dr. Sunter checked on my status before leaving.

"In all my years of practicing medicine, searching and studying until my eyes dried, I have never witnessed something so incredible such as this. Kevin, you are gifted in many ways. The force would be ignorant to not allow you back." Dr. Sunter smiled. "I'll be in touch, and watching the news of course. Good luck to you, Kevin."

"Also, see you back in the lord's house soon I hope, my son." Father Delatonni added.

Leading them to the front door, Mandy made sure they both had left safely. Now I had to wait for

Breaking At What Seems — Kyla M. Wassil

Max's call in order to take the trip to the last place I ever saw myself going. Back to where it all began.

Breaking At What Seems   Kyla M. Wassil

EIGHTEEN

Running a razor over my unkempt face, Mandy appeared in the mirror behind me. Placing her head against my back, she proceeded to wrap her arms around my torso. Drying my skin, I splashed a hint of Brute onto my fresh face feeling it sting inside my pores. Turning to face Mandy, her eyes were filled with excessive worry. I cupped her face as her eyes lowered to my chest, running her fingers along the chain my police badge clung to. I drew my brows together seeing a tear rolling down her cheek.

"Mandy, look at me. What's wrong?"

Her eyes reached mine as her nose reddened in the lighting. "Nothing is wrong, I just can't express the pride I hold for you. You truly are an amazing man, Kevin."

"I appreciate that, I have to do this for more reasons than I want to explain."

"I understand that. Watching you the other night was unlike anything I've ever seen. You were so focused, so captivated by…her and I just…"

"Mandy… I am yours, I was always meant to be so. Savannah had that strong connectivity due to the circumstances. Don't feel impotent in accordance with someone who can no longer stand where you do. My heart is yours, and shall forever be as long as you claim it."

Mandy released a subtle laugh of reassurance, holding a sincere gaze into my eyes. "I love you, Kevin. I don't believe there has been a moment since we met that my interest wasn't empowered by you.

"I love you, also. Please, don't allow your worries and fears regarding me hector your mind, deviating them from what's honest and evident."

Mandy sniveled, attempting to maintain her composure. *"Go out there and show this God forsaken city who you were meant to be. That being the most illustrious officer Manhattan is privileged to have on the force. I need a greatly overrated, not to mention powerfully exaggerated ending to your story."* **She winked.**

Max awaited me outside in a large blacked out van. The side door slid open and I took a deep breath, yanking the flaps of my NYPD jacket with determination. Max's inviting smile guided me in as familiar faces came into view.

"Officer Gibbs?"

"Yeah, I figured he'd be a good asset to the team. I also asked Dr. Jane Ramsone who is the head of our forensics department, along with Dr. Nishi Hemaka, our DNA specialist, and our outstanding Forensics Anthropologist, Dr. Diane Ravous to assist."

"I can't believe you actually pulled this off."

"This is a huge break in all of our careers." **Diane smiled.**

"You're unafraid of losing your medical license?"

"Sergeant Strode, doctors are notorious thrill seekers. We live to push the limits in finding a cure or answers to questions no one is brave enough to discover." **Dr. Hemaka added.**

"Touché. Max, I know some of the scenery I saw is located around Henry Hudson Parkway."

"Up towards Harlem?"

I nodded while watching the scenery change outside the window. The luscious greenery thickened with darkness the closer we reached our destination. My skin burned as my heart accelerated with anxiousness.

"We're close." **I panted.**

Max continued traveling down Riverside Drive making my nerves explode in a diabolic frenzy. Coming up to a side road, I informed Max to take an immediate left. Several seconds had passed until a pale red barn revealed itself further down. I clasped my hand firmly onto Max's shoulder, mentally preparing myself for what was about to happen. Its location was in a secluded area, yet obviously plain in sight for any curious lurkers.

"Is this it?" **Max asked.**

I tapped his shoulder hinting to park so I could get out. Nearly tripping out of the door from ducking too lowly, I stood before the torture chamber my mind recollected in my dreams as it came to life.

Slowly approaching the grotesque structure placed me in an unyielding despondence. Reaching my hand out to grasp a simple touch, Max warned me to take caution. As my flesh unified with the flaking red paint, a static shock surged through my body as clips of

various victims flashed in my mind. Stinging my scar beyond excruciating vengeful infliction, my muscles stiffened as my eyes rolled to the back of my head. I could hear Max repetitively calling my name as I seized out.

Falling to my back, tears stung my eyes as I struggled to breath. Max and the others extended an arm to help me stand to my feet. I needed to continue on about my reasoning before my thoughts became pyrophoric, leading to dangerous behavior.

"Come on, let's go inside." **I suggested.**

Grabbing gloves and medical examiner kits, everyone followed me towards the entrance. Coming up to the door with the window missing caused bile to creep up my throat as I bit the tip of my tongue in revulsion.

Reaching my hand out to grab the handle, I paused hesitantly. I didn't want to see Savannah's final moments again, so I instead rounded the barn until finding the front doors.

Dust debris blew into the air from the disturbing friction. The barn opened to a dimmed space with random pieces of furniture decorating the gloomed provision. Fidgeting for my flashlight, I slowly made my way towards the back. Though the barn was vacant, I could still feel the presence of a thousand eyes glaring into my soul. Anything I laid a hand upon sent horrific emotions through my mind as I continuously remembered each one of *my* victim's murders.

A window cast low lighting into the kitchen area.

To help our vision, I strutted up to it smashing it with my flashlight. Everyone began looking for evidence with their instruments while I glanced around with sheer disgust.

Officer Gibbs tripped over the corner of the mattress, accidentally falling on top. Shining his flashlight downward, he immediately jumped off losing his breath. Knowing I had to visually see the room from Gerould's point of view, I approached the bed apprehensively.

Easing my way down, my breath became shallow feeling chills wave across my flesh. Staring into what was left of Savannah's murder scene, I closed my eyes to watch it one last time. Sweat formed on my face, trickling down my spine as my hands became cold and clammy against the adhering fabric.

Savannah's painful shrills pierced my brain, causing me to cry in agony for her sake. Grabbing at my nape, I pointed my flashlight towards the area in which Gerould dismembered her. Max motioned for everyone to begin a further search only in that direct spot.

Opening my eyes, I watched Dr. Hemaka use a UV LED lamp illuminating countless quantities of blood spatter.

"Dear Jesus, this is unbelievable!" **Dr. Hemaka stammered.**

"Hard to believe Savannah would ever play the card of credulity. She knew what she was doing by taking

the risks after knowing their consequences. Bold and brave, she stood fearless in the shadow of stupidity."

I walked up to the window I recently shattered, leaning my back up against it surveilling everyone's movement. Allowing my mind a mental break another ache cracked through my skull, bringing me to my knees. My hands planted against a mosaic rug sending a rush of heat up my arms. Finding the corner of the rug, I yanked it back to discolored pieces of wood that looked to be out of the ordinary.

"Guys...over here."

"What did you find, Kevin?" **Max dropped down beside me.**

I yanked the pocket knife from his belt, wedging the blade between the cracks to pry it open. Diane shone her light over the area while struggling to slide on a pair of latex gloves. Loose dirt appeared underneath; I proceeded to begin digging when Diane quickly grabbed my wrist, halting my movement.

"Don't! There's a special technique required so you do not tamper with DNA on the remains." **She informed.**

"Apologies. I'll let the professionals get started, then." **I backed away.**

Crouched down, my knees began to go numb as my hips weakened from excessive pressure. The whitening of a mandible poked its way through the dirt

as Diane brushed away particles of filth. I took a hand to my mouth wanting to retch until my stomach itself came up.

"Christ, I—I don't know if I can do this right now." **I felt faint.**

"Kevin, calm yourself. We still don't know whose bones these are and who they might belong to. Only proper lab testing will determine the results." **Dr. Ramsone reassured.**

Though her words were enlightening, I still knew the possibility of those results. I was certain in which area Gerould chose to hide Savannah, but for the sake of my career, I needed the validation of scientific proof.

We must have sat for hours, pulling up bone by bone until there wasn't a fragment left to be found. Diane placed each one in individual forensic bags, medically labeling them in shorthand. As the day stretched on, I became more and more anxious to get the hell out of there.

"If this was the area in which Savannah's body was buried, then we have nothing else left to find." **Diane claimed.**

"Kevin, can you be certain that there are no other possible victims lying about somewhere in the area?" **Officer Gibbs asked curiously.**

"Not as far as my memory goes. This is the only place in which she lies unaccompanied. I'm ready to go!

I...he wanted her close...the others he would burn or bury elsewhere that I cannot specifically detect."

"I'll take you back home after I drop them off to pick up their cars down at the forensics lab."

Taking up all of our tools and belongings, we filed back out to the van, driving in mollified reticence. Saying farewell to the most amazing team I've ever worked with, I hopped into the passenger's seat staring back at Max. He gently placed a firm grip on my leg, sharpening his gaze.

"Don't worry, Kevin. I'm quite sure the bones we recovered today are hers. Just remain patient while they figure this shit out."

Entering my home, I could have face planted the hardwood from fatigued exhaustion. Instead, I stood still, dropping my jacket to the floor as a faint silhouette came from the darkness of the hallway. Mandy's bright eyes locked on mine as she strode towards me, longing for affection. Looping her arms around my shoulders, a dulcet tone left her lips streaming into my ears.

"I've missed you. I've also exceedingly fantasized about you while you were away."

Her gentle words tickled my ear as I wrapped my arms tightly around the petite body that yearned for satisfaction. Releasing her hold on me, I watched Mandy's bare feet enter the kitchen soon hearing the sound of rummaging through cabinets.

Creeping closer to see what she was doing

brought a smile to my face once my eyes landed on a bottle and two glasses. Accepting her invitation to indulge in alcohol, I didn't need liquid courage for what I was about to do.

Turning her to face me, I hoisted Mandy up onto the counter top as she brought a glass before me. Diving in for a kiss I needed so desperately, I crashed my mouth into hers. My pulse quickened, ticking beneath my skins surface as Mandy's legs tightened around me. Breathing harder into my mouth, Mandy reared back downing her glass. Always clothed in the warmth of a temptress' audacity, she stood bold to her purpose at any cost.

Pulling my glass to my lips, I lowered my bottom jaw allowing the Merlot to steadily flow into my mouth until the last drop. Meanwhile, Mandy held an unwavering gaze observing my every move.

"I've missed you more than words can explain." **I smiled.**

"Then don't express to me verbally, show me emotionally Kevin. I need to know I have all of you, that it's just you now."

I tipped her chin to reacquaint our eyes as my expression remained doused in sincerity. *"It is only me. I won't ever hurt you, I would never dream of..."*

"Shh…I honestly don't want to imagine anything you have been forced to see. Just know you will never have to suffer like that again as long as you're with me. I will do my absolute best to keep your mind from losing itself."

"Mandy, you're the only clarity that I need. You clutch my sanity, keeping my feet planted firmly on the ground. I apologize for ever allowing my mental discrepancy to make you feel worried or fearful. Just know I value your effortless, unconditional love you've provided along the way. I adorn each and every aspect you present and appreciate the utilized trust you've implemented in our relationship."

Suddenly my phone sounded from the bedroom, dissolving the moment. A frown fell upon my face as I excused myself to retrieve it. Max was on the other end carrying a voice compacted with solicitude causing me to be nothing less than attentive. I could see Mandy posted against the door frame in my peripheral, baring an inquisitive expression.

"Hello, Kevin? Hey, it's urgent! I have the golden paper in my hands as we speak. The Pathologist's forensics report came in if you're interested in listening?"

"Yeah, of course? Let's hear it!" **I replied anxiously.**

"For starters, our anthropologist, Dr. Ravous teamed up with Dr. Rahki to analyze the remains properly by law. DNA testing came back a positive match for the remains belonging to Savannah. So far, what I'm gathering is there were no apparent signs of forensic fauna left on her bones, stating over a decade's worth of time for decomposition. Her dental records matched those in which we found on site. Her skull showed a deep indentation, followed by various cracks suggesting blunt force trauma

wounds which were the cause of death. The doctor's claim Savannah had reached her untimely demise long before dismemberment. Tiny groves found in her humorous, radius, and ulna to both left and right arms all match the ones on her femur and tib/fib, again on both legs suggesting a violent force was made with a blade used to sever her limbs. Skull still had vertebrae C1-C3 attached, stating her throat had been cut until her head was completely decapitated. They found DNA fragments all over Gerould's barn but none in which appeared on Savannah's remains. Sad to say the bastard really did a number on her."

Listening to Max go on had my stomach in knots. I knew it would be disturbing to hear but I had no idea it would feel so real.

"They went back to investigate more?"

"They had to! There is so much more beyond just who and what we were looking for. Thanks to you and your friendly spirit, Chief decided to reopen the case and continue to recover anything else that pertains to Gerould's case. Savannah wasn't the only one who remained unfound around that time. Even though you claim no exact memory of the other victim's whereabouts, the case is too colossal to stop at just one recovered body."

"How'd you get him to do it without firing everyone who was involved?"

Max paused for a moment. "Well, because Chief Mortkin and his former partner were the ones who took

Gerould out that night outside the liquor store. According to Chief, they were on his ass for quite some time. Taking the rabid dog into custody wouldn't serve any purpose beyond giving the bastard undeserving justice with a fair trial. You know how these kinds of things work, Kevin.*

"I'm sure Chief and his partner used a "self-defense" tactic to get away with that one."

"Exactly, but to give you a more positive report, they are lifting your suspension and allowing you to come back to work as soon as everything is cleared. Dr. Sunter sent over your release exam, stating that there were no findings he collected that proved evidence against your mental health or in any case that you're unfit for proper duty. I figured you'd rather hear it from me."

The shock had my jaw drop. *"Max, I can't thank you enough for taking the time to consider helping me with this madness."*

"Hey, there once was a time that you had saved my life and if you hadn't, I wouldn't have made it as far as I have today. I'm just trying to return the favor in protecting what you love most, that being one of the best officers NYPD has ever seen. Take care, you should be hearing from Chief sometime soon in letting you know a definite return date for duty."

Mandy's warm touch caused my glossy eyes to meet her wondrous smile. *"Is everything all right?"*

I drew in an excessive inhale giving a nod. *"It was Max with the forensics report. The bones they found were in fact Savannah's."*

"That's an enormous relief. That's what you'd hoped for, right?"

"Yes, it is." **I sighed.**

Mandy's brows drew together in a speculate degree. *"Then why is my hero so distraught over the fact of regaining a peaceful mind?"*

"I guess it's just been an extensive amount to take in. Merely unbelievable I would have to say."

"Which is completely acceptable in your case, Kevin. I'd expect nonetheless."

"If God did one thing right, it was bringing you into my life." **I groaned into her mouth.**

I motioned for a refill before taking a waltz out onto the balcony. After becoming aware of everything that's been going on lately, it had now became a rare occasion that Mandy ever set foot out there. I honestly couldn't blame her; maybe she disclosed fear of witnessing the supernatural or disagreed with leaving herself openly susceptible to revet the inevitable. Either way, I appreciated the time and space Mandy gave me for when I needed a break, or the simplicity of silence in solitude to reassess my thoughts. I choked on my wine feeling it dribble down my chin as Savannah's voice broke through the air.

"I always knew you had the courage, even the golden heart of desire to make something right when it appeared to be opposite. You'd stop at nothing to solve any subject if you believed the prevailed evidence wasn't enough."

"Is this you thanking me?" **I wiped my chin with a chuckle.**

"Kevin, my hollow words will never be enough to state my appreciation. You did something most would shove off automatically because they are too naïve to dig a little deeper."

"Well for clarification, you gave me no choice."

"Even if the circumstances were different, I know you'd still do whatever in your power to help me. You're not like most living, you're humble and you sincerely care for the welfare of others. Even those who no longer exist." **Savannah winked.**

"Don't say that shit." **My eyes darted.**

"It's true? Tell me what NYPD officer would go to this extent and uncover the body of a girl whose been missing for nearly two decades? I'm the girl who will forever be branded as a historical horror story for Manhattan. You found me Kevin, you did that!"

"I didn't do it alone…"

"But you swayed the opinion and minds of those who would never care to believe otherwise. I just want you to be proud of your work."

"I am proud, Savannah. I just choose not to gloat on the topic of how painstaking this was for me. How detriment it could have been to my career without knowing the severity of your situation."

"Are you feeling regretful?"

"No! I'm just trying to adjust and accept reality for what it truly is. How I serve to protect the sick nature of deranged minds on a daily basis. I have admittedly seen horrific incidents that would traumatize anyone, but to actually feel it and see it play by play will change you for life. Of course, I'd never hold regret for doing what is just. I will always stand respectfully lament for the loss of others I couldn't save. Being a police officer, you have more responsibility than to just "serve and protect" your jurisdiction and the city, alone. To some, you are labeled a conniving jackass who wants to see others fail to abide by the law just to feel a sense of entitlement, much more... the taste of power. It isn't true, this is a passion that involves the integrity of a thousand men to one when practicing what it truly means to assist someone in need. People are not misfortunate, we are just human and we tend to make mistakes in order to learn the lessons life gives us. Although, some trials may seem more detriment and unfair as opposed to others, we all have a sole purpose while still able to breathe. I am like the gatekeeper who prevents those who attempt harm from distributing it publically wide. I love my job, don't get me wrong. I just hate seeing the extension of error instilled in the reckless behavior of others representing our generation and that of the future. I admit, we cannot control everything, but we can sure make one hell of an attempt to prevent it!"

"Imagine that, Kevin the almighty Sergeant is censuring his feelings. We are all born into this world innocent, ready to learn and explore. Some live, others dream of living. Lavish or niggardly, we all have the right to pursue limitless encounters of displayed opportunities. Some of us are born with a gift to specifically fulfill their purpose." **Savannah's eyes rose to meet mine.**

I swallowed hard as her gaze intensified. *"If it weren't for all of the horrible mishap in this world, then people like me would have no purpose. Maybe it was a blessing in disguise that this all happened, in fact it's what I want to believe. I can't take credit for a heroic rescue when it was you who saved me…"* **I paused.**

Savannah furrowed her brows with interest. *"How is it that I saved you, Kevin Strode?"*

An innocent smile plastered across my face. *"Because, you've opened my eyes to what it really means to love someone to the point you'd cross any body of water to get to the other side if it meant they were awaiting you. You've extended my beliefs when I thought something like this was impossible, it made me realize nothing really is, is it? You brought out the bold bravery I never knew I concealed deep within. I am the one who is to properly thank you, Savannah Rayn."*

Resting her arms in a folded manner atop the banister, Savannah wetted her lips before responding. *"Meet me outside your front door for a sec."*

I cocked my head to the side with wonder but Savannah wasn't letting up until I agreed. Making my way through my apartment, my heartbeat accelerated as I reached for the door's handle. As soon as Savannah came into view, I felt her suddenly fill my vacant arms. Hugging her was like withstanding the winds of a tsunami as they impaled straight through to my nervous system.

"What was that for?" **I barely caught my breath.**

Savannah stepped back to meet my eyes. *"My way of properly expressing overdue gratitude reserved for you."* **Placing her fingertips to my forehead, she puckered her lips making a kissy sound.**

"What are you doing?" **I chuckled.**

"I'm ensuring that any bad spirits stay far away from you. Sign of protection, I vow to keep you safe throughout the rest of your life."

"Like a guardian angel, huh?"

"I was forgiven and my job now is to be your spiritual safe haven. It's proof of my sacrament to the lord, himself."

"Sounds like you've been granted passage through the holy gates by receiving your wings." **I smiled warmly.**

"There is an extravagant alternate world beyond the stars that mother the city. Your unrelenting faith has proven such. Take care, Kevin Strode. It has been but a pleasure."

"Will I ever see you again?"

Placing a hand to my chest, Savannah smiled. *"In here you will. I will always be able to hear you and see you no matter where you are. This isn't goodbye, forever."*

I inhaled deeply as she turned to walk back towards her apartment door. An illuminating light clothed her as she walked straight through as if it were open. Leaving me in solitude, I felt in my heart that that wouldn't be the last time I'd ever see her.

Breaking At What Seems   Kyla M. Wassil

NINETEEN

One week later

Trying to rinse the soap that was perpetually burning my eyes, my cell phone consistently rang from the top of my bed. I yelled for Mandy to answer it but could only hear light conversation. Entering the bathroom, Mandy drew back the curtain informing me that it was Max and that it sounded urgent. I quickly turned off the water, pulling a towel to my face.

"Christ Max, can a man not take a decent shower before you bark demands at him?" I joked.

"I wanted to inform you that despite the televised publicity regarding Savannah's case, Chief has considered holding a ceremony in celebratory honor of our success and hard work."

"Now how in the hell did you get away with this one, Maxwell Harty?"

I could hear his devious chuckle echo through the static reception. "Let's just say the media has their way of finagling things to entertain the public by altering fiction with factual events. Pretty much telling the people what they want to hear and leaving the more pressing matters to the officials. Thank that gorgeous mate of yours for me."

"When exactly is this "ceremony" set to take place?"

"Tomorrow at noon, down at the Landmark on the Park banquet hall. You'd better look spiffy in your dress uniform. I'll see you tomorrow."

I could see Mandy entering the bedroom in the distance, grabbing something from the nightstand.

"Hey babe, could you come here for a moment please?"

"Yeah, what's wrong?" **She asked, inserting her earrings.**

Securing the towel lowly around my waist, I pulled Mandy tightly into me placing a kiss on her neck. *"I've never expressed just how truly amazing I find you. I love you so much, and I thank you for whatever it is you've done for the sake of my sanity."*

"Kevin, what are you talking about?" **She tightened her grip, feeling me weep.**

"Max told me that article you wrote upheld the satisfaction of a great story and pleased the city."

"Well damn him for ruining that information. I wanted to be the first to tell you. I have been offered a higher position as their Social Strategy Editor. I have a copy of the article I wrote about you and it just so happened to be a huge break for my career!"

"That's magnificent! Mandy, I am so proud of you! I respect your work and the fact you kept it impersonal."

"Kevin, I will do whatever it takes at any cost to protecting the man I love with every fiber in me. Also, not to spoil your moment of achievement, Max already told me about the ceremony but confided in me to conceal the information until he told you, himself. I now wish I had asked him to return the favor where my article was concerned." **She laughed.**

"What is your idea of celebrating that good news? I will take you wherever your little heart desires."

Breaking At What Seems — Kyla M. Wassil

Mandy pressed her lips together with a hum. *"We have a shipload of exciting news to celebrate. I say let's leave the dinner and winery for tomorrow's event and just have a night together indoors?"*

"I couldn't agree more." **I groaned.**

The following day…

I stood in the mirror adjusting my uniform as jitters surged throughout my body. The clack of Mandy's heals informed me of her presence as she stuck a lent roller to my blazer. Turning to take in the sumptuous material that comforted silk skin had my jaw clenched tighter than a wrench. My eyes ran up the smooth shine of her legs as I mentally undressing her with a sharp gaze.

"Did your mother never teach you that it isn't polite to gawk at someone?"

"Oh baby, I do believe I've earned a "get out of jail free" card for just this one time."

"You look dapper. I've yet to see you in your dress attire, and might I say I'm ready to tear it from your rigid stature."

"Watch your words before we end up being late, little lady."

Mandy strutted forward, running her hands up my chest. *"Do you think they'd charge me for having their top officer show up late, after he willingly chose to revel in ecstatic intercourse?"* **She whispered.**

"I will arrest you myself, don't push your luck." **I tapped my index finger off the tip of her nose.**

Arriving at the banquet hall, I saw all of my superiors along with my fellow officers from the precinct dressed to the nines. Max and his fiancé greeted us with a large hug, escorting us inside. Chief Mortkin soon took the podium, silencing all conversation.

"I want to thank you all for attending today's ceremony. Your presence proves the honor of Manhattan's Midtown North 18th Precinct. I want to start off by expressing how much of a privilege it has been in working with each and every one of you. You're all but the finest officers New York has ever seen. Today, we pay a grand tribute to Investigator Maxwell Harty, as well as Sergeant Kevin Strode, for their extensive loyalty and limitless integrity excluding any hardship for the work they endure each and every day. I am humbled to be in the same room as these two great leaders." **He motioned for us both to join him on stage.**

The clamor from the audience's clapping made me all the more nervous. We stood on either side of Chief as he continued.

"Due to Sergeant Kevin Strode's outstanding performance and undying passion for the intense career he's chosen, the bureau has agreed to promote this fine young man to a well-deserved position of Lieutenant. I know I speak for everyone in this room when I say job well done. Your excellence and continuance to go above and beyond needed to be addressed. We thank you for remaining an important part of the precinct for it'd be unfortunate without your unrelenting dedication. We appreciate your great service and unconditional efforts you've put forth each day you come in for duty. When you wear your uniform, it isn't to be showy and prove an entitlement to raise power above the public. You resemble a trusted value of your city, executing the officer's creed in every decision you make. You represent the state of New York, you represent the people, and you represent yourself as a distinguished individual carrying the detailed duties of a police officer. You do not do it for glory or to be labeled a "hero". You all serve your city because you desire to and because you were destined to uphold a respectable image for this fine organization. With the confidence invested in me by the state of New York, I now present to you Lieutenant, Kevin Strode."

A standing ovation immediately followed once Chief concluded his speech. As he and Max placed on my newly shined butter bars, my eyes met the back of the auditorium to a familiar face. In between the doorway I saw Savannah smile and wave, congratulating me one last time. A sense of pride erupted in my soul as my eyes grew watery. I gave a nod of acknowledgement as I refused to blink; indulging in

Breaking At What Seems — Kyla M. Wassil

the final moment I was to ever catch sight of her again. A boasted smile was left imprinted in my brain as my eyes were forced to shut from drying out. In that instance, Savannah had come and gone, just like that. I still have yet to ever see her again. Days have long passed and sometimes I catch myself daydreaming about her smile and pale blue eyes driving into me like needles. I will always look to find her and I was quite certain I would never stop.

Breaking At What Seems   Kyla M. Wassil

Breaking At What Seems   Kyla M. Wassil

EPILOGUE

It had been two months since my promotion.

I've been granted more power but also a shit ton of paperwork to do each night while held captive behind a desk. I actually missed just riding around in my cop car for hours, looking for someone to break the law.
Coming home from a long night down at the precinct, Mandy awaited me at the apartment. Catching a

glimpse of the maintenance man I once envied, I abruptly approached him.

"Excuse me sir, may I take a look in there for a moment?"

The man stood confused. *"Might I ask what for?"*

"I am curious to see the renovation process. I'm with the NYPD, give me a break. I won't mess with anything. I just want to have a look."

The man chewed at his cheek, jingling his keys in deliberation. *"Make it quick. I don't need to lose my job because some nosey officer had to look at God knows what."*

I returned the gesture with a smug look while he opened the door. At first, I was hesitant to enter, but the existing presence lured me inside. I turned to see the maintenance man surveilling me.

"I'll be but a moment. Please?" **I requested privacy.**

"Close the door behind ya when you're through doing whatever it is you're up to."

I walked further into the abyss of Savannah's empty apartment. Nothing but dust fragments and paint buckets comforted the room. I centered the living room shoving my hands deep into my pockets. Closing my eyes gently, I mentally summoned a lending ear from an old friend.

"Savannah..." **I exhaled.** *"You told me you would always hear me, I need you to know wherever you are that I miss you greatly. I've felt a sense of peace since you've gone, but I still feel you everywhere. Sometimes, I get upset because I strain so hard hoping to see you. Even if it were to be for a split second, I'd be content. There hasn't been a minute that's passed that you haven't consumed my curious wonder. I pray you're doing all right and finally feel the freedom you've long deserved."* **My attempt to keep my tears at bay soon failed me.**

Wind blew through a window left open to tone down the fumes of fresh paint. Opening my eyes, the gleam of silver rested in the sill drew my attention. Walking closer, the sight of the very necklace Savannah always wore came perfectly into view. I swiped it clean from the window, clutching it against my chest. Circulating all round me, I knew Savannah could hear me and that her response was sincere through the silence.

I lost control of my emotions, falling to my knees sobbing like a child. My face felt hot as a heavy flow of tears escaped my dark eyes. Fighting to regain control, I could feel someone standing over me. Raising my eyes to an extended arm, I almost lost my breath thinking it was Savannah, but instead it was Mandy wearing a sympathetic smirk as tears rolled down her cheeks. Helping me to my feet, Mandy allowed me to cry into her shoulder.

"I just want it to hurt less." **I sobbed.**

"Kevin, honey, it's okay. Please come home and let me ease your pain and cure that worrisome mind of yours."

Accepting her invitation, I followed Mandy back to my apartment, grabbing ahold of the handle behind me. A faint silhouette standing in the center of the room caught my attention as I halted momentarily. I couldn't unmask an exact identity but my heart knew who it might have been.

Smiling to myself, I gently closed the door along with that chapter of my life. I could genuinely say I was finally ready to move forward and except fate for what it was.

THE END

Breaking At What Seems   Kyla M. Wassil

In dedication to our local heroes—Officer T. McCullough, Officer M. Canales, K-9 Officer J. Meeks, K-9 Officer J. Wurst & Officer S. "Bones" Jones.

We appreciate your service in keeping our community safe.

~Thank you~

Breaking At What Seems   Kyla M. Wassil

Made in the USA
Charleston, SC
06 December 2016